Anne Moncure Crane Seemüller

Reginald Archer

A Novel

Anne Moncure Crane Seemüller

Reginald Archer
A Novel

ISBN/EAN: 9783337026257

Printed in Europe, USA, Canada, Australia, Japan

Cover: Foto ©Andreas Hilbeck / pixelio.de

More available books at **www.hansebooks.com**

REGINALD ARCHER.

A NOVEL.

BY

ANNE M. CRANE SEEMULLER,

AUTHOR OF "EMILY CHESTER" AND "OPPORTUNITY."

"The essence of greatness is the perception that virtue is enough."

BOSTON:

JAMES R. OSGOOD & COMPANY,

LATE TICKNOR & FIELDS, AND FIELDS, OSGOOD, & CO.

1871.

Boston:
Stereotyped and Printed by Rand, Avery, & Frye.

THIS STORY

IS AFFECTIONATELY DEDICATED

TO MY HUSBAND,

IN TOKEN OF THE HAPPY DAYS IN WHICH IT WAS WRITTEN.

REGINALD ARCHER.

<hr>

CHAPTER I.

" This little pig went to market;
This little pig staid at home;
This little pig got a piece of bread and butter;
This little pig got none;
This little pig cried, ' Wee, wee, wee ! I can't get
over the barn-stile ! ' "

IT is no exception to St. Paul's usual wisdom, that, on becoming a man, he "put away childish things;" for even such slight anachronisms as can be contained in threescore years and ten are generally neither prudent nor profitable.

But there is another aspect of the subject, which Christ glorified forever when he took little children in his arms and blessed them : and it seems, at times, that we would do well to take our own childhood in our arms, and let it bless us; going back to those innocent early days when we were both good and glad. It strikes one as almost a necessary part of Charles Lamb's tender heroism, that he remembered with such love and pity the child he had been; and, looked at in this light, it would appear better for us not to "put away childish things," but to cherish our spring-time recollections, whether of tenderness or of humor.

Among the latter may be placed "The Melodies of Mother Goose." Belonging properly to babyhood, the value of these rhymes has so increased to me with increasing years, that it might almost be said I

> "Only hold my treasures truly
> When it seems as if they passed away."

These little stories in verse are so full of meaning, that it is a ceaseless pleasure to study them and their applications. It was in thinking of the remarkable power of characterization displayed in the narrative which heads this chapter, that I was strongly reminded of the family whose varied fortunes these pages are to relate. The portrait of each member was so strikingly drawn, that the rhymes seemed an allegory to which the clew had just been found.

In structure, the two families did not differ. Each consisted of five individuals; and, curiously enough, the order in which the pigs are enumerated corresponded with the ages and characters of the young people. From the account, one would suppose the pig family to be "after the order of Melchisedec, without father or mother," — at least, no parents are mentioned ; and the Archers preserved the resemblance by being orphans. The pigs appeared to have retained their connection with each other, to have lived somewhat in the bonds of unity, in spite of their varied characters and pursuits. So with the Archers. They dwelt as long as possible under the same roof, and to the end were held together by the strong ties of family feeling and family pride, — sentiments which have power to override differences in belief, taste, and occupation. The most fitting introduction for each member of this household will be in connection with his or her porcine representative. Let us begin at the beginning.

"This little pig went to market."

Enter Tom Archer, the eldest of the family.

The merchant I take to be like the poet, — born, not made. American life, in which most boys are put into clerkships, as into mills, to be ground out a certain product, would seem to contradict this opinion ; but the statement, founded on statistics, that failure comes surely to more than three-fourths of those who go into business, tends in the other direction. True mercantile talent is as distinct, original, and characteristic as musical genius or the poetic faculty. Shrewd, clear insight into the facts of a case ; an

1 *

ability to have an opinion, and to hold it; above all, an instinct as to the probable result, — these stamp a merchant of Nature's own making. The mercantile eye may not range very widely; but it sees with amazing clearness within its own line of vision. One cannot take liberties with the multiplication-table with impunity; and it demands of its votaries, and, indeed, imparts to them, a degree of its own ex-actitude in their habits of thought. The supply of this special talent seems never to fail. Within a cer-tain number of men, some born prince of the count-ing-room is sure to appear: in each family, there is, almost invariably, a mercantile brother, — the little pig who goes to market.

Tom Archer went thither at a very early age, and found himself the right boy in the right place. He could win all the marbles in the school, and re-invest them in the spare cakes and apples of his compan-ions; while he drove a thriving trade in the barter of pencils and jack-knives. In those days, he was rich upon nothing a year, and, in time, accumulated a boyish fortune by bold speculation upon an original capital of five cents. Even in his childhood, being a born trader, he found his market everywhere, and went to it.

Growing up to man's estate, he was, without being handsome, eminently pleasant-looking, though neither romantic nor imposing in manner or appearance. Small in stature, but well-knit and active in frame, with that physical energy which keeps a man up to the mark, and never permits him to fall behindhand in any thing, he was a ceaseless mill-stone, which required endless grist. He was one of those beings who have a taste for hard work, and who rather enjoy drudgery as a safety-valve for their superfluous vigor. His eyes alone would have shown his temperament, apparently taking in at a glance that which ordinary optics would be moments in perceiving, — very bright, cheery gray eyes, that harmonized well with the crisp wave in his brown hair. The good, broad forehead told not only of strong perceptive faculties, but also of a width of thought which does not always belong to such characters as his. Evidently good-natured and good-humored, it was yet impossible to doubt the presence of a high, hot temper within; and, though kindly and serviceable to those about him, no one ever took liberties with him, or questioned for an instant that there would be a ready blow behind his word where the case required it. Those in his employ found him a strict, steady master, demanding of them what he required of himself, — a full day's work in every day; but they depended upon his justice, and, if the need were, upon his generosity, with an unshakable faith.

In the matter of his downright, ingrained honesty,
Tom Archer had greatly the advantage over a character in history which he otherwise strongly resem-
bled, — I mean that patriarchal prototype of traders,
Jacob. This biblical hero's mercantile talent, and
his ability to drive a bargain, are undeniable; in fact,
seem far more finely developed than his moral sense.
He went to market at every opportunity, carrying with
him all available goods, trading in every advantage
his position afforded him. His mother's love, and
lack of principle; his brother's reckless nature; his
father's blindness; his uncle's confidence; his own
cunning, and habit of quick observation; his industry,
perseverance, and capacity for ready lying, — each
and all he used as capital, drawing the highest divi-
dends from his investments. So innate was this spirit
in the man, that his very prayer and vow to God are
but a promise of *quid pro quo* to the Almighty. Perhaps in this his petitions were scarcely singular; for
most of us demand a direct answer to our supplica-
tions, and expect some specified equivalent in return
for our prayers. But it required the moral courage
of that early period to use such plain words to in-
form the Lord in exact terms of the amount of
food, clothing, and general assistance, for which his
allegiance could be obtained, as Jacob did when he
"vowed a vow," and " called the name of the place

Bethel." A man's religion is the keynote to his character; and I imagine few persons have ever spoken out their creeds so unreservedly and truthfully as did Jacob upon this occasion.

And yet it is of this cunning, unscrupulous, grasping trader, that the purest, sweetest love-story in the world's history stands recorded. It is not David, poet and singer of Israel, not Solomon, wisest of men, not Moses, prince, hero, and lawgiver, but it is Jacob, who loved one woman, and served for her fourteen years, which " were but as a single day for the love that he bore her;" whose tenderness and devotion increased down to old age; who cherished her children after her as he did nothing else in existence; and who, as his own end drew near, passed over the events of his life to talk of Rachel, and her death and burial. His love for her seems the one flower and bloom of his nature, gaining a strange beauty and strength from the very bareness of the remainder of his being. His faults were many; but recalling that rare example of faithful devotion, which still lives fair and lovely in the world's heart and recollection, verily women, at least, should judge him leniently and tenderly.

This exceptional nature was partially but strikingly reproduced in Tom Archer, the first of my pigs and of my heroes.

` " This little pig staid at home."

Maria Archer might best be described as the domestic virtues incarnate. Even when a pretty young
girl, she was evidently born to the career of a home-
life, and took to housekeeping as a duck takes to
water. Like heaven, order was her first law; and
she hunted down dust as a deadly enemy. Unlike
ordinary mortals, the house-cleaning period was to
her a season of pleasure rather than of pain, during
which she felt the inspiration of a true vocation.
Her administration over the family purse and the
family servants gave evidences of genius; while the
quality of the meals was to her truly a crown of
glory. No matter how many sisters she had possessed,
to Maria every man in the household would have
turned instinctively to have a button replaced, to inquire after his clean collars, or to complain if breakfast were delayed. There is always some such person
in every well-constituted domestic circle, — some one
who gives the real home-element to the fireside;
whom the male members are sure to love most, and
treat with least respect. Peculiarly unselfish and
affectionate, the small duties and sacrifices of every-
day life were her pleasure; for she possessed the
beautiful womanly trait of being happy just in so far
as she was needful to some one else. A reticent,

timid woman under all other circumstances, beneath her own roof-tree she was a power: there, and there only, she felt strong, capable, and confident in the discharge of her duty. Unhappy when on the wrong side of her front-door, she took care that such should seldom be the case: in fact, this little pig staid at home.

But she paid a price for so doing, which increased as years went on.

She looked so long, so faithfully and steadily, at persons and things around her, and at them alone, that her sight became microscopic. What she saw was undoubtedly there; but she perceived it far too accurately for her own comfort. She could not learn the sad truth which is daily forced upon us, that life is at best a compromise, and that we are obliged to accept persons as they are, and not as we trusted and hoped they might be. The woman's high, pure conscience made her judge all objects by an absolutely fixed standard: she could not receive the measures and rules of this world, and think things right because others so held them. Such persons are necessary to the world's continued existence; and even to approach such a woman is to let in a ray of heaven's own light upon our murky, earthly atmosphere. Her view of person or act was always that which righteous eyes are compelled to take;

but she made the woman-like mistake of sometimes expressing her opinion at inopportune moments. The self-control which larger experience would have given, the strength of nerve, and diversion of mind, which excitement and pleasure would have supplied, she missed by her form of life: in fact, it was both to her sorrow and her joy that this little pig staid at home.

"This little pig got a piece of bread and butter."

Two points in this small descriptive biography impress me as wonderfully true to life: first, that he neither strove after the object in question, nor worked for it, nor even paid for it, but simply "got" it; second, that it was "a piece of bread and butter," — the material advantages of existence, the satisfactions of time and sense. The line is Reginald Archer's memoir summed up in a single sentence.

If human beings are merely animals of a higher grade; if to eat, drink, and be merry, and to-morrow die, be the true philosophy of life, — then Reginald was the most successful person I have ever known. All that other men painfully achieve, he seemed to have thrust upon him. Every advantage that can be estimated by avoirdupois-weight, that can be set forth in figures, became his as by natural right. Never exerting himself to gain any thing, that which he desired drifted towards him as by a species of gravitation. Nature appeared to have striven to send into the world, for once, the perfection of animal creation, giving him every thing but a soul. He was as beautiful as an antique statue; and to look at him was to feel that ancient Greece should have been his country, and his proper period the days of Aspasia. He would have well suited those pleasure-loving pagans; for pagan he was himself. That magnificent form; that absolute freedom and grace of motion; that classic head and face, with the glittering bronze-brown hair waving off from the white forehead; those violet-blue eyes, that looked almost black from the darkness of their lashes, — to gaze at them was to fancy, that, had he indeed lived among those Greeks, they would have mistaken him for a wandering Apollo.

Reginald little regretted not being born in that far-off time and place. His only sorrow on the subject was, that his advent had not been delayed several centuries, when material life shall have attained greater smoothness than at present; and, for the same reason, his choice of a birthplace would undoubtedly have been Paris. But, true to his philosophy of "taking the best of now and here," he wasted little time in idle lamentings, and "gathered honey all the day from every opening flower," even though it sprang from the uncongenial soil of the United States of America.

He had that species of good spirits and apparent good nature which arises from wholesome blood and perfect digestion; but self-denial and self-sacrifice were things of which he had been born simply incapable. Amusement, excitement, and the varied forms of physical gratification, were essential to his existence; and he claimed them with less regard for the feelings and sentiments of others than ordinary mortals would display for insects under their feet. This joyous, *debonair* gentleman was as remorseless as a law of Nature. If what he did hurt you, " Ah, so much the worse for you!" he would think, with the sweetest smile in his violet eyes. Reginald only respected those who forced him to do so, and only spared those who did not spare him. He injured no one, unless to gain some personal advantage; disliking the sight of mental suffering as he did that of poverty or sickness. Of beauty or agreeability, no one could be a finer or a fitter judge; but the moral aspect of a case, with reference to his own action, never presented itself to his mind. In this, as in much else, he was scarcely an Anglo-Saxon; for it is an exceptional American or Englishman who can do wrong without some slight after-regret, without a consciousness of degradation in his own eyes. I fancy it is only Frenchmen who can sin with absolute serenity. I imagine that to the Gallic race is reserved the blessing of being born free from sufficient conscience to produce occasional discomfort.

But Reginald Archer was beyond his countrymen, and possessed this happy faculty to perfection. One recognized its presence at first sight, though disregarding it, as one generally does those curious forewarnings. To be introduced to him was to distrust him, despite the charm of his beauty and grace ; to know him a week or a month, be you man, woman, or child, was to lose the very remembrance of such a sensation in blind admiration ; to know him for years was to shrink from him with dread, as a beautiful monstrosity. Your first, faint foreknowledge that this exquisite animal was soulless and conscienceless grew then to certainty.

Still it must be confessed that he seemed to find his loss a gain ; for I have known few persons who received so large a piece of the bread and butter of life, or who so literally "got" it without toil, without money, and without price.

"This little pig got none."

The contrast between Arnold Archer and his brother Reginald was so strong, that it struck every one with whom they came in contact. Whatever one was, the other was not. In appearance, character, and career, they flatly contradicted each other. If one were a type of the lucky individual, surely the other was the representative of the unlucky man. A long, awkward, homely person, never knowing exactly what to do with his hands and feet; looking ten years older than his real age; shrinking from observation, and yet possessing a curious facility for being in the way, — he contrasted like shadow with his brother's sunshine. Always meaning for the best, and acting for the worst, he certainly was a trial to patience of ordinary proportions. A capacity for living in dreams, of deceiving himself as to facts, was his striking peculiarity, and was at once his bane and his blessing. He never saw person or object as they appeared to the rest of mankind. But I confess I do not feel justified in putting this among his misfortunes. Viewing ourselves and our fellow-beings as we are generally compelled to do, I doubt if any change, any escape from the truth, should not be regarded as an improvement; any loss of insight, as a blessed blindness. Arnold possessed, in reality, that treasure towards which Charles Lamb aspired, when, asked by Hazlitt and Coleridge which he preferred, "Man as he is, or man as he is to be," he replied, "Man as he is not." There are moments when this reply of the pleasant wit seems to me the bitterest cry which can go up from a human heart. Perhaps this ability to see, and see not, was the merciful compensation which Providence sent Arnold Archer for all that he lacked in life. Perhaps there are times when most of us would exchange it for all we possess; when we mourn over lost ignorance as bliss; when, having learned the value of even a fool's paradise, we close our eyes desperately, in the vain hope of shutting out that which we have seen but too clearly. Held in bondage by our own perceptive faculty, we grow to envy those who are capable of self-delusion, who are not compelled to see those they love just as they are.

To Arnold Archer, facts were by no means the stern tyrants they are to most persons. To him, characters and events were, so to speak, clay in the hands of the potter; and he moulded them to suit his own fancy, firmly believing in the creation of his imagination.

"Arnold's friends are legitimate objects of worship," Reginald would say with his usual smiling contempt for his brother; "for they are like nothing in heaven above, nor in the earth beneath, nor in the waters under the earth. He breaks none of the commandments in bowing down before them."

Arnold would have done his enemies, had he pos-

sessed any, equal injustice; would have regarded
them as fiends, delighting in congenial, demoniacal
society, and suitable for it alone.

Practically weak as was this character, it was essentially poetic. To him, all Nature was a delight, and
fed a divine inner thirst; to him, all beauty, whether
of person, thought, or act, made life lovely. He had
that apprehension of purity and nobleness which
gives the soul the freedom of heaven here and hereafter. Dim-sighted as regards this world, he had
that higher vision which sees far above and beyond
it; perceiving even here the reflected glory of the
world to come.

Arnold had been educated as a physician, and was
devoted to the study of his profession, although he
was totally unfit for its practice. Punctuality was to
him an impossible virtue; and he lacked in an equal
degree that capacity for energetic, steady work, which
is essential to success in any pursuit. He chiefly
exercised his skill upon a collection of invalided
animals, for which he built a species of hospital in
the back yard, where he would take infinite pains
in curing some sick kitten or lame dog, to grieve
over their base desertion of him as soon as they were
well. He was an enthusiastic naturalist; and his
greatest delight was to spend day after day in the
woods, from which he returned laden with ferns,

leaves, and not agreeable insects: this, of course, to his sister Maria's unspeakable disgust. She was very fond of him, and extremely patient with him upon every other subject; but upon the question of his leaving his treasures in every portion of the house, however inappropriate, she waged a warfare which knew no truce.

"Arnold, I cannot have horrible bugs crawling about my parlor and dining-room," she would solemnly protest. "Why, they will be walking into the very teacups soon! I can not and I will not allow it." And there really seemed some justice in her objection.

Undoubtedly he was an exasperating person with whom to live under the same roof. His idea of the dinner-hour worked upon a sliding scale, according to his appetite or occupation. China and glass ware slipped through his fingers as though to escape his awkward handling; and to watch his sister Maria, as she saw him wander aimlessly among the fine, fragile ornaments and objects in the drawing-room, placing and replacing them without apparent purpose, was to feel a sincere respect for the self-control which enabled her to restrain her impulse to take them away from him, and set him in the corner as a troublesome child.

Reginald's contempt for his brother was so profound, that it seldom reached speech; but he evidently regarded him with the dread one feels of a raw Irish servant permanently attached to the house. The two had no comprehension of each other, and kept apart as far as possible. But it was only another evidence of the strength and generosity of Tom's nature that Arnold was his favorite brother, whom he protected like a child. The elder man's natural impatience and quickness of temper disappeared when his brother became their proper object: he held his *protegé* responsible for nothing. Arnold's practical thinking and acting Tom took upon himself, and, in case of shortcoming, felt that the blame rested on him for not having foreseen the probability, and provided against it.

" Tom, you treat Arnold as though he were a sort of divine idiot," was Reginald's characteristic criticism. "I wish you would take me in hand, and provide for me in the same way. It would save me a great deal of trouble."

" Thank you, my dear boy," was Tom's cool rejoinder, though his quick, bright eyes darkened as he spoke; " but I think you are pretty well able to take care of yourself: at least, it won't be the divine element in your nature which will prevent you from doing so. Let Arnold alone: you have no more comprehension of him than you have of Sanscrit. But I wish, with all my heart, that either you or I were as good a man."

"Thank you back again," Reginald replied laughingly, with unruffled mood; "but I should wish my share of the desired good to be taken in common sense, if it would be the same to all parties." And the discussion ended at this point, as it always did.

Finding that Arnold would never succeed in the practice of medicine, and thus gain a livelihood, Tom had taken him into his counting-room, hoping by patience and drill to fit him for the duties of a clerk. But he had signally failed. What his acute mercantile mind underwent during the attempt, no one but himself knew. Misdirected letters, important messages forgotten, bank-business deranged, engagements unfulfilled, — all these accumulated, until the wonder was that insanity did not ensue in the head of the house. Tom grew nervous if the smallest duty were left to Arnold's care, and gradually diminished his occupations until his place was a sinecure. To keep Arnold out of the office, and to give him as little as possible to do when there, became the tacit understanding between the chief of the establishment and his clerks. Nothing pleased all parties better than for Arnold to go off on long fishing and naturalizing expeditions; as, let the press of business be what it might, it was easier to do his work than to take the chance of his mistakes, or to rectify them.

"Are you sure you can spare me?" he would ask, having his own ideas of making an honest return for the salary he received; and indeed, if his unsuccessful pains and trouble were calculated, he gave a just equivalent.

"Certainly, my dear fellow. Go and enjoy yourself as much as possible, and then come home and tell me all about it." And the elder brother would go cheerily back to his counting-room, and put his shoulder to the wheel with renewed vigor. Thus he supported Arnold, without undermining his uprightness, or allowing him to feel his dependence.

With nothing which most men hold as valuable, Arnold Archer was the happiest member of this family; and I am inclined to write him down as the most enviable little pig in my collection.

> "This little pig cried, 'Wee, wee, wee! I can't get over
> the barn-stile!'"

Reviewing the careers life opens, the conclusion is at all times inevitable, that there are few better methods of providing for one's self than that of joining what might be called "the grand army of the incompetents." It may be true that God helps those who help themselves; but it is certain that the world proceeds upon the opposite principle. Those fortunate individuals who can coolly and consistently act upon the theory that their fellow-beings owe them a living, certainly have strong grounds for the policy of their course. Considered mathematically, the case seems clear. If you work for yourself, you simply have the support of one person; whereas, if you emphasize with sufficient persistence your inability to assist yourself, your relations, friends, and even chance acquaintance, will gradually assume that responsibility, and you enlist an indefinite number of individuals into your service. The majority of men and women lack the nerve to allow a fellow-being to suffer the consequences of his own actions, or want of action; and the amount of sustenance is amazing which can be extracted from the most unwilling support by the simple process of leaning upon it, and refusing to move. In the mind of the person burdened, the first emotion is apt to be extreme irritation; but almost any one will succumb under steady, unremitting pressure. A quiet despair settles upon the most recalcitrant, when it is found that there are natures analogous to India-rubber, which recover instantly from any blow, leaving you exhausted from your exertion in dealing it. A certain flabbiness will defy the most vigorous effort to make it self-sustaining. If a person will not stand on his feet, to persist in holding him up is too expensive a process: it is cheaper, in time, strength, money, and temper, to make up one's mind to let him rest comfortably, and feed him as he lies. In fact, a certain incompetency may be regarded as better than a certain competency, and, conjoined to what might be called an infinite receptivity, is one of the finest investments in life.

The most curious circumstance of the case is, that such persons are almost always popular. It is true that we are apt to like those whom we serve better than those who serve us; and we become attached to individuals who are constantly claiming our aid and attention. They appeal at once to our higher and lower natures in calling upon our generosity and in soothing our vanity.

Of all persons I have known, Ellen Archer, in her small way, turned her helplessness to greatest account; her inability serving her more than ability avails others. Unequal to any fixed plan, she merely followed her instinct. But her success was like that of genius: in fact, she might be said to have a striking capacity for incapacity. A pretty, fair little woman, evidently not very strong in mind or body, even indifferent strangers naturally put out their hands to help her; while, as the youngest member of the family, her brothers and sister treated her as a child all her life. Had Ellen and Maria lived together for sixty years, the elder would have gone on darning her sister's stockings, and otherwise attending to her wardrobe, during the entire period.

Upon Maria fell the whole burden of the housekeeping, the ceaseless worry of meals and domestics: she had to be up betimes, and regulate all her movements by the family convenience. On the other hand, Ellen would descend when she pleased, to murmur if the order of the breakfast-table were not perfect, and to be mildly reproachful to Maria for the coldness of the coffee.

Then would follow the little scene which occurred periodically in that household.

"Why don't you come down in time if you want things in proper condition?" Maria would say, irritated by the injustice of the situation. "It is the least you can do; for you never help me in any thing. Why can't you take half the housekeeping off my hands? It is as much your duty as it is mine; and I can't see why you don't do it."

"Oh, for Heaven's sake, don't let Ellen have any thing to do with the housekeeping!" Tom would exclaim, laying down his newspaper in the energy of his horror at the thought. "I should never get my breakfast in time, nor have any thing fit to eat," — using the strongest argument with Maria, with whom Tom's comfort was a sacred thing. "Besides, she isn't strong enough for it;" which was not at all the case.

"I am very fond of my home," Reginald would smoothly remark, saying that which was true only so far as his home afforded him a place where he could do as he pleased, and have every thing he wished, without paying for it; "but I cannot consent to sacrifice my digestion upon the altar of family feeling. If Ellen is to keep this house, my only resource is a restaurant or a hotel."

"Maria, how can you suggest such a thing, when you know how delicate Ellen is, and how unequal she would be to the exertion?" even Arnold would join in.

Meantime, Ellen, not even put to the trouble of arguing her case, would sit like a pretty little martyr, who, when she was reviled, reviled not again, and, when the subject dropped, would enjoy a full meal of every thing that was best upon the table. There, after some faint further protest from Maria, the matter would rest; and there, indeed, she wished it to remain. The housekeeping was her pride and occupation; and it would have broken her heart to surrender it to other hands, though she did not wish it made difficult by irregularity in the household. But her grumble was to her, as to most of us, a precious privilege: it worked off the nervousness which comes from strain upon body or temper, and left her cool and comfortable. Perhaps she availed herself of the relief too often with regard to evils which experience might have taught her were too radical for her to remedy.

As far as Ellen was concerned, her sister had no real wish to put any additional duty upon her; for she fully participated in the family bondage towards that young person. But, when Maria was exasperated, she had a fashion of speaking out unwelcome truths, which she perceived at all times, but which her amiability generally held in abeyance, and always prevented her from acting upon. Ellen and Reginald kept her permanently provided with such material, though she judged and sentenced her brother for far darker deeds than those peccadilloes, those sins of omission, for which she blamed the poor little pig, who, by nature, could "not get over the barn-stile."

CHAPTER II.

IN which of the great cities of the Atlantic coast
the Archers resided, it is not necessary to state;
but it was one of the centres of American civilization
in which the national character is fully exhibited.

For several generations, the family had possessed
cultivation, position, and at least moderate wealth;
and it still maintained that *status*. The surroundings
of these young people had been those which environ
most young Americans of good connection : they had
been born into that comfortable, unromantic form of
existence which is too familiar to need description.
The surface of our democratic society is somewhat
level for purposes of literature, though beneath it
we may find fresher blood and deeper passions than
elsewhere. The Archers began life under the ordinary auspices. As children, they inhabited a handsome house in a fashionable neighborhood, were sent
to the finest schools, spent money freely, and had not
a want ungratified, scarcely a wish restrained. Then
and always, they were part of the best society in

their city; and to be first-class in one's own place is the practical limit of aristocracy, enabling, as it does, the American merchant to meet princes royal upon grounds of equality. In their veins ran both Cavalier and Puritan blood; and it was curious to watch the predominance of either race in each individual. The old problem of mental and moral inheritance appeared in this as in all cases, leaving it unsolved now and always.

Within these commonplace outward limits occurred the passionate emotions and tragic events of the story I am about to tell; within these bounds human nature found exercise for its highest and lowest instincts.

The mother of this family had died when most of her children were at school; and the father had soon followed her. Just before his decease, Mr. Archer had taken Tom into partnership; and, upon the parent's death, the business and the support of the family had naturally fallen to the son. Thus Tom began life with expenses which almost consumed an income that must have rendered him very wealthy in a few years, had it been allowed to accumulate. Each child had inherited a sum sufficient for educational purposes, and a small annual income. For further dependence, the men had their professions; and Tom was only too glad to provide a home for his sisters.

But Arnold's doctoring turned out a failure, and Reginald's law a farce; and then Tom found that the penalty of being able to do a thing is being allowed to do it. As he could afford to sustain the family, it became tacitly settled that he should bear the expenses of an establishment of which his brothers and sisters shared the full benefits. Tom considered this perfectly just, except, perhaps, in the case of Reginald. Some faint doubts occasionally arose in his mind as to the propriety of the strong, splendid gentleman deliberately living upon him; but, being as hospitable as an Arab or a Virginian, he would not have refused daily bread to a stranger, much less to one of his own blood.

But that which did exasperate him, and which he constantly resisted, was Reginald's cool way of levying contributions upon him in order to purchase luxuries which Tom would have considered entirely beyond his own purse. Reginald could always afford any thing, and scorned to regard the matter of price, though his brother was often compelled to do so. Yet such was Tom's family feeling, that he could not bring himself positively to deny the claims his brother made upon him. He knew that Reginald would manage, in some way, to extract a certain sum of money from him in a given time; and he made mental allowance for it, as he did for taxes

and household wants, in his estimate of the year's
expenses. But he tried to keep it within definite
limits by a contest over each demand.

· These small battles always occurred in Tom's
private counting-room; where, indeed, most of his
confidential talks with his brother took place.

After his late breakfast, Reginald would array
himself in gorgeous apparel, and take his morning
walk down town; generally making Tom's counting-
room his resting-place and turning-point. Here he
would lounge for a while, smoking his brother's best
cigars, reading his newspapers, occupying his easiest
arm-chair, and, if the other were at leisure, talking
to him by the hour of any thing which interested them both. Reginald liked nothing better than
to chat with Tom; chiefly because they invariably
differed, and because his elder brother always had
a strong opinion of him and his sentiments, and used
scant ceremony in expressing it. Overfed with
flattery, and sick of too ready submission, he relished
the conversation of a man who mentally defied him,
just as he enjoyed the pursuit · of a woman who
resisted him. Calmly confident of ultimate victory
over both, he thanked both for the momentary stimu-
lus and spice they added to his existence.

Coming in from the fresh morning air, radiant in
appearance, and faultless in dress, he would stand

with his back to the fire, and freely criticise all that was before him; often throwing down the gauntlet for the amusement of seeing how Tom would take it up.

"Good heavens, Tom! how can you wear such a coat?" he one day exclaimed as he scrutinized his brother, and discovered that the garment in question was of the style of the past season. "Why don't you buy yourself some new clothes?"

"Because I have to pay for yours," was on the tip of Tom's tongue as he glanced quickly up from the letter he was writing.

Tom Archer was a gentleman, and could not cast past favors in a man's face; but he looked at his brother for a full moment, sorely tempted to let him hear the truth. Kept comparatively poor by his bounty to this very man, that the other should assume a magnificent disdain, founded upon advantages purchased with his money, seemed beyond endurance. Tom had to cool slightly before he could trust himself to reply.

"My dear fellow," he said at last, speaking very deliberately, "in the matter of spending money, you have me at an extreme disadvantage. You see, I indulge in that most expensive of all luxuries, — I pay my debts. If a man can only make up his mind to dispense with this extravagance, there is scarcely any other he may not enjoy, he has so much spare change, so much spending-money left free. But, being hampered by such weakness, you must not expect me to compete with those fortunate beings who are entirely free from it. Strangely as the word may strike you, I have sometimes to economize."

" Ah, indeed ! — I am sorry to hear it," Reginald returned, with delightful superiority to any exhibition of emotion or temper on the part of his brother. " But to come back to the matter in question. When you do get a coat, I shall be most happy to choose it for you; for you know you have very little idea of what is becoming, and still less of what is fashionable. Good-morning !" And he bowed himself out with a grace and good humor wonderful to behold.

He wisely concluded that this was scarcely an appropriate time to ask for a loan, — Reginald always called them loans, as sounding better, — as he had intended doing; but, his needs — otherwise his tailor — being quite pressing, he came back to the charge on the following day.

Tom's mercantile instinct, and habit of reading men's faces, usually warned him when Reginald meant money; and he took a grim pleasure in watching the variety of ways in which his brother would lead up to the subject, in wondering how he would return to the attack each time he fell back defeated before Tom's entire want of comprehension.

" By heavens ! if he wants my money, he shall ask
for it openly," Tom thought, between amusement
and irritation. " He sha'n't think I am walking into
his traps blindfolded by his flattery. If I must be
squeezed like an orange, he shall not imagine I am
such a fool as not to know it."

But Reginald was an experienced tactician, and
understood his man perfectly. Letting his real purpose rest for the moment, he began the discussion of
some subject upon which he and Tom differed totally.
Dexterously exciting his brother, he forced him into
expressions which were as truthful as they were
bitter, but which he knew the other would regret
after he had used them. Then, when Tom was a
little exhausted by his own energy, and a little re-
morseful for his hard words, Reginald said casually,
as though it had just occurred to him, —

" By the way, Tom, if you can spare a hundred
and fifty dollars, I wish you would lend it to me."

" I haven't much money to spare, Reginald," the
other replied, drawing his breath rather wearily ; "but
I will see what I can do." And he turned towards
his check-book as he spoke.

An odd smile came into Reginald's eyes as he saw
how accurately he had calculated the instinctive generosity of Tom's nature, which made him never so
willing to oblige any one as when he imagined he
had been harsh towards him.

"What do you want the money for?" the elder man demanded, beginning a regular formula.

"To pay my tailor," returned the other promptly, well prepared for the catechism he was undergoing.

"Let me see the bill," Tom went on; and the other quickly produced the document.

"Well, I will give you a check, payable to the man's order." And the younger brother soon had the paper in his pocket.

"Tom," broke out Reginald, with apparent entire irrelevance, after he had been lounging about the office, talking upon general subjects, for half an hour, but always with the same odd smile half glimmering in his face, "doesn't the Bible say something about the children of this world being wiser in their generation than the children of light?"

"Yes," Tom answered slowly, reading his brother's meaning far more clearly in his face than the other imagined: "that is the commendation given to the unjust steward; but I don't think I should care to be an unjust steward,—a lying, thieving scoundrel,—even at that price."

"Perhaps not. But there is a good deal of truth in the remark; and, upon the whole, I strongly agree with the biblical verdict," Reginald replied.

"I don't," said Tom; "at least, I haven't thus far in life. But you must work out the problem before you can give the exact answer; and, when I have come to the end of my experience, I will let you know the result."

"And I'll do the same for you. When I have lived out my life, I will give you my testimony. But I don't think I shall change my opinion," Reginald added carelessly, as he gayly nodded, and went his way.

He little imagined the manner in which he would fulfil that promise; he little dreamed of the exactitude with which he would keep that pledge. To both men the very sun would have lost its light could they have foreseen the hour when those words would again be spoken between them.

For his close and invariable inquiry as to the application of his money, Tom had his own reasons, well understood on both sides. There were portions of Reginald's life, the mere thought of which raised Tom's righteous wrath and loathing disgust; rather than be made a party to which, he would have seen every cent he possessed at the bottom of the sea. In the early days, he had begun by sternly refusing to aid Reginald while he led such a life, hoping to keep him in order by keeping him poor. But he found his brother merely spent his own means on his luxuries, open and secret, and went in to debt for his necessities. Then came duns and disgraceful scenes from creditors, until Tom was whipped into paying what the other owed, merely to save the honor of the name and the family.

From that time he made up his mind to face the hard fact, that Reginald's existence was beyond his power of purification ; but he resolved to know the exact use of his money, and to keep his hands clean from even indirect participation in sin.

Reginald's one aim in life had been personal, physical gratification : he had not an aspiration which really deserved to rank higher than a desire for a good dinner. Even his love of art and elegance was a purely animal instinct ; was literally " the lust of the eye, and the pride of life." He had begun his social career by an intrigue with a great leader of fashion, a woman ten years his senior, whose somewhat over-ripe charms, and long experience in their dexterous use, still enabled her to attract most men, and to gratify her omnivorous appetite for admiration. Like himself, at once emotionless and passionate, of cold heart and hot blood, each afforded all that the other craved, without troublesome sentiment to mar or disturb their enjoyment. Strong in her social position, and shielded behind the fact that she had never come to open disgrace, though with scarcely a reputation to lose, she was the person of all his set whom Reginald's keen perception selected for his pleasure and his profit. As no real feeling had entered into their connection, its dissolution produced neither pain nor anger; and though soon tiring of each other, and passing on to further conquests, they always remained good-humored acquaintances, willingly giving each other a helping hand on occasion. Both natures were too bare of either conscience or fine feeling to experience shame or sorrow. As neither knew elevation, neither could be conscious of degradation: they shared the comfort and ease of other animals in partaking of their lack of any diviner part which would have rendered them capable of suffering for sin.

As Reginald began, so he went on. Without regular occupation, he sought in society his employment and his play. But when Dr. Watts gave utterance to that immortal sentence, that "Satan finds some mischief still for idle hands to do," he announced a fixed law, from which there is no deviation. It truly seems that men must choose between work and wickedness; and this man chose the latter alternative. Every woman was to him simply an object which could afford him more or less gratification; and to secure as large a degree as possible of such pleasure was the occupation of his time and thoughts.

"'Insatiate Archer! would not one suffice?'" exclaimed one of his companions, using Young's words, half in jest and half in earnest, when some action of Reginald's slightly shocked even him.

"No," returned the other quite frankly; "not if she were the Graces and the Muses combined in one person. No human being is worth loving beyond a certain length of time; and to me one pretty woman is as good as another, if she has taste enough to like me. On the other hand, I am of the opinion of the lover in the old song, 'If she be not fair to me, what care I how fair she be?' I know what stuff women are made of. I give thanks for what I get; but I am not fool enough to suppose that I have not had predecessors, and will not have successors. I know perfectly well that what a woman grants me she would concede to any one else in the same position; and I value her favors accordingly. 'When lovely woman stoops to folly,' it is generally as much to gratify herself as her lover. As to the rest of the fair sinners, I say of them, as St. Paul said of another class of persons, 'They are bought with a price,' and a very cheap one at that. I don't blame any of them: it is just what I should do in their places, and it suits me exactly; but I don't want to flatter myself, and I like to state things as I see them."

"Well, my dear boy," said the young man addressed, a little startled at the open avowal of an opinion upon which he acted daily, " your creed has at least the advantage of fairness and justice. You give women exactly the liberty you claim, and don't think wickedness any worse in them than in yourself."

" Certainly," answered Reginald. " My dear fellow, if there be a God, and a definite right and wrong existing in his mind and in our natures, — which I am not at all prepared to affirm or deny, being very slightly interested in the matter, — I am not such an idiot as to suppose that he will acknowledge any sex in sin; that he will look at the actor instead of the quality of the act. I have never supposed that the wrath of God, like the wrath of this world, is reserved for the feminine gender; or that, if there be a judgment-day, men and women will not stand together before him, to be judged by one fixed and equal standard. I hear myself called by rather hard names sometimes: but I am neither a coward nor a lunatic; and consequently I acknowledge, that, when I commit an act, I abdicate forever my right to criticise it in any one else. Not being of the ' whited-sepulchre ' kind, I don't make myself ridiculous by condemning a woman for enjoying herself as I have done," he coolly wound up.

" Reginald, do you believe in any thing? " broke out his companion.

" What do you mean by any thing ? — an hereafter and hell-fire ? I suppose that is what you think I ought to be considering. I believe in cause and effect, and a moral law of grayitation, — from which you can no more escape than you can get outside of your own skin, — which will take you just where you belong both here and hereafter. As to the next world, I know nothing about it. What I do know is, that in this world, at this moment, the weather is glorious, that " (taking out his watch, and looking at the time) " in three hours I shall have a capital appetite for a capital dinner, and that, in the mean time, I have an appointment with the handsomest woman who has come out this season," concluded this frank sensualist, looking so grandly beautiful, so overflowing with animal life and enjoyment, as he sauntered on through the sunshine, that his companion could only gaze at him with envy and admiration.

This comrade was that shadow which such men always possess ; that constant associate and assistant selected from the large following they are sure to draw after them. In these days, Leperello's place is generally supplied by some minor Don Juan, who is rather an apprentice to the trade than a hired servant. Knowing that such leaders and followers must both make wealthy marriages as a provision for their advancing years, the latter think their chances improved by the companionship, hoping to pick up some rich crumb which may fall from the master's table. As a general rule, their aim is entirely beyond them : they fail by hundreds where the one strong, successful nature gains its end, and by middle age wear away into a mental and material poverty, which would be pitiable if it were not contemptible.

Of this class was Reginald's *alter ego*, though still in his nine-days' puppyhood, not having opened his eyes to his natural fate. Reginald's utter inferior in pluck and acuteness, he was his superior in the possession of some small emotional nature ; and he could not follow his friend entirely in act, far less in assertion. Like all moral cowards, he was more shocked by a broad statement than a black fact, provided the first were made openly, and the latter kept conveniently in the shade. Lloyd Truxton, the individual in question, was, to human sight, good for no earthly purpose ; but there were times when Reginald was too much for his nerves, and he began to hesitate as to the road he was walking, to inquire doubtfully of his master whither he was leading.

" Reg," said the other at last, " do you believe in anybody's real goodness ? "

" Well, I don't know. That depends," was the answer, beginning rather indifferently. " You know what I think of women ; and as to men, when you have added the weak ones to the wicked ones, I hardly see that you can find room or material for another class. As far as my experience goes, I could catalogue people under those two great heads, if it were not for my brother Tom; he staggers me!" Reginald exclaimed, warming up, and growing interested in expressing his opinion. "Tom's the shrewdest, coolest, pluckiest fellow I have ever seen: there is no such thing as scare in him; and yet look at the life he leads! He is a regular Sir Galahad in a counting-room, yet able to hold his own against the strongest of those who tilt against him. Most people's goodness doesn't affect me very greatly: there is a little too much of 'the recompense of the reward about it.' It amuses me to see them intriguing for a high place in heaven, just as they work for an elevated situation here below; to watch them investing in prospective in the next world, just as they put out means to the best interest in this one: it entertains me to see how the cowards try to dodge the perdition they feel to be the natural consequence of the lives they lead."

"Well, really, Reginald, I can't say that I blame them very much. I don't suppose any of us want to go to the Devil if we can help it," Lloyd's fellow-feeling prompted him mildly to expostulate.

"I believe Tom would do what he thought right,

though he believed it would take him straight to hell!"
the other exclaimed so vehemently, that Lloyd looked
at him in astonishment. "His religion isn't 'other
worldliness,' as Leigh Hunt called it. He is like St.
Paul: he 'presses forward to the mark of the prize
of his high calling:" not the prize, but the mark, the
elevation, is what he strives after. When I attempt
to state the sum of life, I am obliged to put Tom
down as a certain quantity; and I confess he alters
my reckoning entirely. He's a queer fellow, — a
very queer fellow!"

And his mind went back to a conversation he and
his brother had had years before, the mere recollection of which had power to make him silent for a
time.

On that occasion, Tom, who had then some lingering faith in Reginald's reformation, had tried the
effect of desperate remonstrance, and had come to
a definite understanding upon another point. Leading a very busy life, and going only occasionally into
society, Tom did not know, and did not care to know,
the details of his brother's existence. But exact facts
are not needed by acute perceptions; and sin leaves
its dreadful signet, whose impress can be read like a
written page. Character is formed by accretion; and
a man's associates, and the story of his life, tell themselves without words. Reginald was too well bred

to use a coarse expression before a lady; but the unconscious, indefinable tone of his conversation, the sentiments and opinions he sometimes let slip, made Tom flush with anger at his end of the table, while Maria colored with shame and sorrow at hers. Generally, she managed to keep silent on such occasions; but, every now and then, the pent-up, growing indignation of weeks would flash out in some biting sentence, which would have cut his conscience to the quick had he possessed such an uncomfortable adjunct. Being exempt from such weakness, she merely disturbed his nerves; and he would regard her for a little while with a sort of mild detestation, blandly indicating at the same time his pity for her defective temper.

It was after such an occasion, rather more marked than usual, that Tom spoke out.

He waited until Reginald dropped into his counting-room for the customary morning visit. Leaving his writing-desk, he came and stood with his back to the fire, looking down at the handsome face and figure sitting with such elegant grace in the arm-chair before him.

"Reginald," he said presently, "I want to say something to you."

The other glanced quickly up with that radiant smile which seemed shared between his white teeth and his brilliant eyes, and saw in a moment where the trouble lay.

" Well, old fellow, what is it ? " he exclaimed, attempting to carry this off, as he did all things, by his genial laugh and lordly presence.

" I am not," Tom went on steadily, looking him straight in the eyes, " moral dry-nurse to you or any other man ; and I don't attempt to preach to you, as I suppose it would do no good. You are my brother, and have a right to share my home ; but I swear to you here, that, if ever again you bring into it even the shadow of your outside existence to insult those who live in it, you walk out of my door, never again to enter it while I breathe ! "

" Why, you take matters seriously, my dear boy," said Reginald airily. " I have no desire either to insult or to incommode Maria ; but she is so ridiculously narrow-minded, you know."

" Maria is right," Tom broke out hotly, his eyes glowing, and the anger he had been visibly restraining getting the better of him. " I would to Heaven there were more women like her ; for then your trade would fail. Reginald Archer, if you were not my brother, bound to me by ties which I can not and ought not to break, I would never speak to you ; I would never touch your hand ; I would cast you off as an object utterly loathsome to me. Why, man, a dog has instincts above yours, and would disdain the life you lead : even that brute can love and cling to one object, can hold to one master."

" Tom," said the other slowly, gathering himself up, and standing before his brother in all his splendid physical superiority, and planting himself, as it were, upon it, " you and I have entirely different aims and pleasures in life. You like to work, and I like to play ; and I am sorry that you will not or can not share my enjoyment."

" Enjoyment ! " cried Tom. " Do you call it pleasure to cultivate the lowest elements of your nature ; to wallow in filth that a clean animal would reject ? Do you desire such a present for me, and such a future as it must inevitably produce ? Man, I hope one day to marry a good, innocent woman. What right could I have to ask of her the pure heart and clean hands I could not offer her in return ? Do I want to give my wife her first lesson of evil in actual life ? Do I wish the ghost of my wicked past to haunt my bed and board ? Could I bear to see the woman I loved shrink from me in uncontrollable physical loathing when the slightest taint of what had gone before re-appeared ? I believe in a moral arithmetic, which keeps unfailing account of every action ; and, in footing up the sum of life, facts will no more lie than figures. I can't think that man wise who makes such a provision for his old age ; and, if that is what you call happiness, keep it to yourself, for I want none of it."

"Tom," said Reginald, gazing at his brother with a grave, blank expression, which the other had never before seen in his face, " either you are a fool, or I am one ; and excuse me for saying that I do not much doubt to whom the honor belongs. However, if you happen to be right, I am most infernally wrong. At any rate, if I were not myself, I would be you, — one thing or the other, and not a flimsy compromise between the two."

" Reg," exclaimed Tom, with a thrill through his voice, " do you ever remember our mother, and the pure home she made for us ? Doesn't it sometimes fill you with shame and remorse to think of the good women who have loved you there ? "

" No," was the cool, quiet reply. " I am not a woman ; and I can't measure myself sufficiently with them for their influence or example to have much effect upon me. But I think of you sometimes, old boy, because you are a man, with the same liberty and the same lot as myself ; and I confess you are a fact in Nature which I can't quite get over."

And he laid his hand on his brother's shoulder, and looked down at him, not only with acute mental appreciation, but with something so much like human feeling, that Tom flushed with pleasure and surprise. He knew ever after, that, if Reginald had possessed a heart, he would have had the first place in it; that, as much as the man was capable of giving, he received.

He never quite forgot that grasp upon his arm. Its memory lingered with him even in the heat of the battle he and his brother were destined to fight: it came strangely back to him when it was the touch of a vanished hand; when the valley of the shadow of death lay between them.

CHAPTER III.

THE old saying runs, that there is a woman at the bottom of every thing If there be an exception to this rule, it certainly is not in the case of novels. In them, at least, the female element is sufficiently felt; generally forming, not only the foundation, but a·large portion of the structure, of the tale. Your heroine is a necessity; and the motive-power " which makes the world go round" here appears in its full proportions: here, at least, women and love receive credit for all they accomplish. Be the lady what she may, she is, *ex officio*, the centre of the story; and the person about to be introduced to the reader claims attention by that position.

It was when the lives and characters of the Archer family had reached the phase described that she reappeared to influence the existence of these brothers; to win the love of one, and the hand of the other. Connected with their boyhood, and then forgotten, Fate brought her back to mould the manhood of both; used her small hand to shape the career and develop the nature of each.

"I saw a gentleman from California last night," said Tom, one morning, as he took his place at the breakfast-table; "and he told me that old Col. Macalaster died a month or two ago. It carried me back to the old times to hear the name. Don't you remember the stately way in which he and father used to call each other cousin? though I defy either of them to trace the relationship. It is rather odd that we have not heard of his death before. But perhaps Christie has almost forgotten us; and there was, probably, no one else to let us know."

"She can scarcely have forgotten us," remarked Maria: "she saw too much of us when she was a little child for that. Why, when they lived in the South, they were here every summer, on their way to the Springs. Perhaps, on the other hand, she may think she has gone out of our recollection. Poor little Christie! she is entirely alone in the world now. I think I will write to her to-day, and tell her how sorry I am for her."

"By all means," said Tom. "She used to be very fond of you, Maria."

"Little Christie can't be little Christie any longer," quietly remarked Reginald, who had looked up with quick interest at Tom's announcement, but had not yet spoken. "I wonder how old she is now."

"That is very easily determined," answered Maria; "for she is just Ellen's age."

" And how old are you, little woman ? " asked
Reginald of his sister, who sat lazily eating her breakfast, her sympathy in the sorrows of others being
much too mild to affect her appetite even momentarily.

" Eighteen," she replied.

" Then," said Reginald slowly, " Christie probably
has that immense fortune in her own right, and under
her own control."

Tom lifted his head suddenly, caught his brother's
eye, and read his thought perfectly.   When he looked
down upon his plate again, it was with a rather sar-
donic smile upon his lips.

" Ah, that is your idea ! " he thought.   " No doubt
the money would suit you exactly.   But, thank
heavens ! she is on the other side of the country ; and
I hope most devoutly that she will stay there.   If
she ever comes within your reach, she will have
about the same chance that a bird has before a
snake."

" Christie used to be pretty," Reginald went on
presently.   " I wonder how she has grown up.   I hope
she is as much like Ellen in that as she is in age," he
added, nodding pleasantly to the person in question,
and instinctively using the language of compliment
to a woman, even though she were his sister.   In
this case he spoke the truth ; for Ellen was as pretty

as a lazy little pink-and-white doll could possibly be. Between herself and Reginald there was a decided resemblance both in disposition and appearance; and, as their tastes for pleasure and comfort agreed, they rather liked each other, and always coalesced in family discussions.

"Christie could never be ugly, with those great dark eyes of hers, and that lovely curling hair, even if her features have changed," said Maria, smiling as the recollection of the pretty, merry child came back to her.

"I wonder whether she tears her dresses still," laughed Tom. "What a wild, little thing it used to be! She kept me in perpetual terror for fear she would come to grief and break her neck."

Poor Tom! He little imagined how soon his fear for her would be upon him again, or that this time his terrible dread would be that she would break her heart.

"Don't forget to write to her, Maria," he said, as he lighted his cigar, and left the breakfast-room to go down town to his counting-house; "and give my love to her when you do so."

Reginald lingered over his tea and toast, as was his custom, for some time after his brother's departure. He had a certain purpose to accomplish; but he took his own time, and the means he judged best, for securing it. He never hurried, and therefore never lost his acuteness nor his composure. He had seen and understood Tom's look at his mention of Christie's money, though he kept any shade of comprehension from his eyes ; and he knew he must effect his object without his brother's knowledge, and secure its fulfilment before the other could interfere.

He waited until Maria had made her household arrangements for the day and was about to leave the room. Then he spoke.

"Maria," he said when her hand was on the door-knob, "I shall not go down town before mid-day ; and, if you will write your letter to Christie before then, I will post it myself."

"Thanks," said his sister, quite touched at this unusual desire to oblige some one besides himself.

"By the way," he went on, as though the idea had just occurred to him, "don't you think it would be well to ask Christie to pay us a visit ? She is free to go where she pleases; and I should think she would like to come back to the Atlantic States, if only for change and variety. We are her nearest connections, and ought to show her some kindness and attention. Besides, it will be so pleasant for Ellen to have some companion of her own age ! Poor little Nell doesn't have much fun in life ; and she shall have a good time when Christie comes."

And he stooped down, and smoothed Ellen's curling hair with a real appreciation of its beauty, and an apparent brotherly attention before which he knew Maria would melt like wax. Ellen's welfare was an unanswerable argument with her; and consequently he fully expected the reply he received, — at least, the first part of it.

"I think it would be an excellent plan. Christie can only say ' No,' if she does not care to come; and, if she would like it, we should be charmed. But," she added, suddenly hesitating, " don't you think we had better speak to Tom about it first ? You know, after all, it is his house."

" Nonsense ! " exclaimed her brother. " Tom always liked Christie; and he is as hospitable as he can possibly be. He will be delighted to have her here," — deliberately lying with a smooth grace that was inimitable. " Go up stairs and write your letter ; and, as I have said, I will post it for you."

And, thus urged, Maria complied.

Reginald sat back in his chair, and held up his newspaper as though he were reading it. But he could not have made much progress; for his eyes rested upon the same spot; and there was a quiet smile in their depths, that told of a satisfaction as deep as it was undemonstrative.

He did not return to dinner that day. He wanted

Tom to hear of the invitation which had been sent and to realize his powerlessness to prevent its acceptance, before they again met, thereby escaping explanation or outbreak with his brother. ·

It fell out just as he had calculated.

" Tom, I have written to Christie," Maria said as soon as she saw him that evening.

" I am glad to hear it," he answered. " What did you say to her ? "

" Oh ! I told her how much we sympathized with her, and how well we remembered the old days when she used to stay with us; and I asked her to come and stay with us again."

" You did ! " cried Tom, whirling round on her, with a flash in his eyes and a breathlessness in his voice that startled her.

" Yes," she answered nervously, with surprise at his evident objection to the invitation. " I had no idea that you would not be pleased. Why do you dislike the plan ? "

" How came you to ask her ? " he demanded, disregarding her question, and following his own thoughts.

" Why, I supposed it would be delightful for us all ; and then Reginald said, what was very true, that it would be so pleasant and useful to Ellen to have a young companion ! "

"Ah! Reginald suggested it, did he? I might have known it!" he exclaimed. "Well, that will do," he added hastily, a moment after, evidently to cut the matter short. And he turned to the window, and gazed out of it for the next five minutes in perfect silence.

"So Reginald played his trump as soon as my back was turned, and won the trick," thought Tom hotly.

As his brother had foreseen, he was too acute not to recognize instantly his helplessness in the situation. He was quite sufficiently human for his vanity to tingle at being thus quietly outwitted; but it was a much higher emotion than injured self-conceit which filled him with sore indignation against the man who had circumvented him, and which made his heart sink with pity for the pretty little girl he remembered with such curious old-time tenderness.

"Will he win the whole game in the same way, and with the same ease?" And his own dread answered him.

"Maria," he said quietly when he presently took his place at the table, "if Christie comes, of course we will all welcome her as cordially as we did years ago. But I must tell you, once for all, that I cannot let Reginald direct the affairs of this household in any thing. I am sorry to say, that you know as well as I do that his guidance would contribute neither to the good nor the happiness of any one in it."

As Reginald well knew, he was safe from any marked outward sign of defeat from Tom. Consequently, he entered the breakfast-room next morning not only with perfect external ease, but much inward comfort. His brother's manner towards him had a quiet little chill in it, which would have affected the nerves of a weaker man. But Reginald carried to perfection the great art of never seeing that which he did not wish to see, and merely noticed the change so far as to cover it with increased gayety and good humor. Then, as often before, he seemed to turn the ordinary meal into a banquet by his æsthetic appreciation of the viands, and the intellectual feast he spread before those surrounding the table. He carried Ellen, Arnold, and Maria completely away with him; and even Tom could not help looking at him with a strange love and pride mingling in his sorrow and anger.

By the earliest return mail, Christie's answer arrived. It read as though tears and smiles had been shed upon it. The poor little woman eagerly grasped, perhaps, the first tender, well-known hand which had been extended to her since her father's death.

" Of course she would come," she wrote, " if they were good enough to love her still, and care to see her. Did they think she could ever forget how kind they had once been to her? If they could only know how lonely she had been during the past months, they would understand her eagerness to be with those who had once loved her father and herself."

And then she went on to recall each member of the family with the minuteness of a child's recollection, showing how fresh their memory remained in her warm, innocent heart.

" She is just the same impetuous little creature she always was," said Tom, laughing softly over the letter. " Just look at the headlong handwriting! I wonder how many, or rather how few, i's are dotted, or t's crossed, in the whole document."

Except for his intuitions as to Reginald's designs upon the girl and her fortune, Tom thought how gladly he would have welcomed her to his home. Even as it was, when he could partially forget his fears, or persuade himself that he had been over-certain of the result, he would look forward with delight to the prospect of seeing her, and grow as eager for her coming as the remainder of the household.

As for the rest, except Reginald, they talked of little else. He, having gained his purpose, covered his further intentions by apparent indifference. Maria

and Ellen spent much of their time in refurnishing
the pleasantest spare-chamber for her occupancy, and
daily added some small ornament or engraving to
beautify it, or some article of furniture with which
to render it more comfortable.

As for Arnold, he labored for weeks, with an incal-
culable amount of industry and skill, upon a wonder-
fully-carved cage, in which his sweetest-voiced canary
was to hang in Christie's room. He wished to sacrifice several other small animals at her shrine ; but
Maria was compelled to protest, and they compromised upon the bird.

The manufacture of its cage afforded entertainment
for the whole family. Such was its elaborateness, and
the pains Arnold lavished upon it, that he found himself so pressed by business as scarcely to have time
to partake of his meals regularly. Carrying bits of it
about with him, and applying himself thereto regardless of time or place, Maria could not help faintly
intimating, that, considering the chips, dust, and injury to tables and chairs, it would have been a decided saving to buy a handsome cage. But Tom gave
her a quick look, which silenced the sentence before
it was half out of her lips.

He would listen to Arnold's explanations on the
subject with the greatest apparent interest ; and
would sit and watch him carve, with a loving smile in

his eyes which was beautiful to behold. Reginald would stand and gaze at both with the queerest laugh in the corners of his mouth. Tom's delicate generosity and tenderness always touched his brother's æsthetic perceptions; and the whole situation curiously stirred his sense of humor. Added to this, it amused him that they should show such earnestness over an arrival which meant so little to them, and so much to him; that they should be so eager and occupied, and he so idle, and apparently uninterested.

The time that went by was filled to them all with a pleasant sense of expectation; and scarcely a day passed without some one reckoning the shortest period which must necessarily elapse before Christie could be with them.

CHAPTER IV.

TO society, Christie Macalaster was merely remarkable for being the sole heiress to her father's great estate. Her personal attributes were unknown, as she had been brought up in perfect seclusion. Motherless almost from her infancy, Col. Macalaster found his darling child a heavy responsibility. Feeling a busy man's inability to give his daughter a proper woman's training, without time or power to select her associates and shield her from harmful influences, he had adopted the negative system of shutting her out from companionship of almost every kind. Left at first to the care of a faithful nurse, and passing afterwards into the hands of masters and professors who taught her all that educated young ladies are supposed to know, she had grown up entirely apart from the world and ordinary social existence. Her ideas of human nature and life were gathered from poetry, and novels of the better sort; and what relation they bore to facts may be imagined.

Col. Macalaster's secret dread had been, that his daughter would be married for her wealth; and he had sought to put off the possibility by delaying her introduction into society as long as possible. The girl's disposition and childlike appearance assisted him in this, and enabled him to regard her, almost to the end, merely as his little pet, requiring from him only love and tenderness.

A consciousness of her womanhood and his altered duties had just begun to force itself upon him, when death relieved him of this and all other cares; leaving his child to face the world, of which she knew absolutely nothing.

In those days, the Pacific Railroad was not; and a journey from California meant sailing through two oceans, instead of flying across a continent as now. Consequently, it was many weeks before Tom received a telegram from New York stating that Christie was in that city, which she would leave in time to be with them that evening.

Tom carried home the telegram in triumph, and, after warning them to kill the fatted calf, drove down to the station to meet the train. He felt sure he should know the girl, unless she had entirely changed since childhood; and her letter had been so like her old self, that he could not believe the physical alteration had been very great.

He was walking down the car, examining the faces he passed, when a little figure in black sprang up, and, eagerly putting out its hands, exclaimed, —

"Why, it's Tom! I should have known you anywhere!"

"And I should have known that you were Christie, if only by your eyes. They are as big and brown as ever," laughed Tom, as he grasped the little hands in both of his.

"I am so very, very glad to see you!" the girl went on, her innocent pleasure overflowing at lips and eyes.

"Not half so delighted as I am to get you back," Tom answered eagerly; and he was surprised at the fervency with which he spoke and felt the sentence.

Half an hour before, he might have said the same words, and meant them; but those clinging hands, and that sweet, upturned face, with its changeful color and shining eyes, had put a something in them which they would not then have possessed. He gave the girl his arm, and conveyed her to the carriage.

"It makes me feel like a child once more to have you taking care of me, Tom," she said, after he had made her as comfortable as possible, and they were driving along the streets toward home.

"I am sure you look like very little else," he answered gayly: "and I shall have to pet you and take care of you accordingly; for you evidently can't do it for yourself. See, your furs are falling off now!" and he drew her wrappings close and warm about her.

She nestled down into them with a soft little laugh, which Tom thought the sweetest sound he had ever heard.

"You must be very tired, Christie, with travelling so many hours," said he after some further talk, his remark suggested by a smothered gap on the girl's part. "Lay your head on my shoulder, and try to rest for a few moments. I want you to be bright and fresh when we reach home; and we shall be there in about half an hour."

The girl laughed, winking like a sleepy kitten; and finally did as she was told. In a little while, she had dropped into a doze as unruffled as an infant's repose. Tom looked down at her with a curious tenderness stirring his heart. The street-lamps, shedding their light into the carriage from moment to moment, showed him the fair, innocent face in all the soft warmth of slumber. It was a delicately formed and tinted countenance. The small features were so rounded by youth and health as to seem scarcely those of a woman; while the long lashes resting upon the pink cheeks, and the lovely rings of curling brown hair, showed that she was a remarkably pretty one.

"I shall have to wake this poor little baby," thought Tom as they approached the house, with unspeakable annoyance at the idea of any change in the situation.

But Christie spared him the trial; for, when the carriage stopped, she raised her head, rubbed her eyes, and was herself again almost in a second.

" Why, you are as gay as a bird!" exclaimed Tom in astonishment. "So you can fly out of your cage," he added as he took her hand and she sprang to the ground. "Here are the family at the door waiting for you."

And, in another minute, Christie was quite lost in the mingled embraces of the two girls.

" Christie dear, I am so delighted to see you, and so glad you are as pretty as ever!" cried Maria from the depths of her honest, generous heart.

" Beginning to spoil me already, just as you always did, you dear old thing!" returned the other, reaching up to her shoulders, and giving her a shake which set them instantly upon their old footing.

Ellen had also noticed Christie's beauty, but had scarcely shared her sister's sentiment regarding it. However, their styles being exactly opposites, she consoled herself with the idea that they would be effective contrasts rather than eclipsing rivals. Consequently, by the time it became her turn to kiss Christie, she could do so with all the good will and enthusiasm of which she was capable.

Arnold stood disconsolately on the outskirts of the party, intensely conscious of himself, and his inability to make himself felt and heard. He beamed upon the new-comer most blandly, but was quite unequal to any further unassisted expression of his feelings.

"Christie, here is Arnold," said Tom; as usual, quick to come to his brother's rescue. "Don't you remember him?"

"Perfectly," she replied; "and his cats and dogs too. Do your birds still sing more sweetly, and your flowers grow better, than any one's else?" she asked as she smiled brightly up at the man.

Arnold went into an ecstasy of blushes as he managed to tell her that his pets still existed; and that, in future, the birds should sing, and the flowers bloom, for her and her pleasure.

"Why, you are working miracles already, Christie," laughed Tom, patting his brother's shoulder, "in setting Arnold to making gallant speeches."

Whereat Arnold became more celestial rosy-red than ever.

Then Christie was taken up stairs to make some preparation for dinner.

While this scene had been going on below, Reginald had been standing in his bedroom, before his dressing-glass, gazing at the magnificent figure and face reflected therein, and giving little effective touches to his evening toilet. The occasion had seemed to him of sufficient importance to make him waver in his choice between two cravats, and only to reach a decision after trying both. He was aware of Christie's arrival; had heard the ascending sounds of her greeting: but it was no part of his plan to mingle his welcome with that of the family. He knew the power of a first impression, and he intended to use it. His purpose was to appear before her in all his glory, and stamp his image and superscription upon her nature once and forever. Had she been a poor, pretty girl, with whom he was to be thrown, Reginald would have attempted her conquest as a matter of vanity and habit: being the heiress to nearly a million of dollars, he put his hand to the same work as an affair of business, and very serious business indeed. He had no doubt as to the result; but he did not wish to risk mistakes or false steps. He well knew that such a fortune is not to be secured every day, even by such a man; and that it behooved him to do quickly that which he had to do. Fate, — he was in such a good humor, that he was almost inclined to call it Providence, — aided by some slight intriguing on his own part, had brought the girl into his hand. Thus placed, he thought, if he did not win her, he deserved to lose her and her fortune. His expenditures had been unusually heavy that year, and he was rather tired of extracting cash from Tom: even that slight exertion bore a faint resemblance to working for his living, which made it constitutionally objectionable to him. He had now an opportunity of permanently and splendidly providing for himself; and he intended to improve it. The largest " piece of bread and butter " he had ever been near was now within his reach; and, true to his nature, this little pig intended to " get " it.

" Is Reginald away from home ? " asked Christie while she was dressing, speaking of him in the same familiar tone in which she had addressed the others. " He is the only one of the family I haven't yet seen."

" No," answered Maria : " he is in the house now. You will meet him presently, at dinner."

" I remember him as such a tall, handsome boy," Christie chatted on at her ease.

" Reginald is even more beautiful now than he was then," replied Maria complacently, sharing the family pride in her brother's superb aspect.

"Beautiful!" exclaimed Christie. "That's a queer word to use in speaking of a man."

"You won't think so when you see him. He is not like anybody else; and you can't talk of him in the same way."

The girl's only reply was a slight movement of the head, as though she were thinking that she scarcely expected to be overwhelmed, no matter what degree of beauty she encountered. Poor child! she little knew with what she was measuring herself; that her chance was that of a kitten within stroke of a lion's paw.

Dinner was served; and the brothers stood in the dining-room, when the girls came laughing down stairs, and entered the apartment.

Just before they crossed the threshold, Maria, who was in front, said, —

"Here is Reginald: now you will see him." And Christie stepped forward, intending to greet him as freely and frankly by name as she had done the others.

He was standing rather apart from the rest, the gas-light blazing upon him, — a position he had deliberately chosen.

The girl gave one eager, upward look at him, and then suddenly stood still; while the unsophisticated little creature's eyes grew larger and larger with ineffable astonishment.

Reginald smiled, partly to himself, and partly upon her. He had seen too many worldly women dazzled by his splendor not to think its present effect quite natural upon an inexperienced girl: he was too well accustomed to it to be even flattered. He considered this hop-o-my-thumb very small game; but its acquisition was necessary to him, and he was well pleased with the success of his initial step. The second after she paused, he came forward with out-stretched hand, and said pleasantly, indicating that her hesitation had been caused by imagining him a stranger, —

"I am entirely forgotten by Miss Macalaster, I suppose. If so, I appeal from her to the Christie of other days, who, I feel sure, will acknowledge me as an old friend."

She gave him her hand, glancing shyly at him, while the bright color flushed over her face; and said, with a quaint reserve in her manner, —

"You have changed more than any of your family, Mr. Archer; and I confess I should not have known you. I don't recognize at all the boy I used to know."

The thought of her intention to call that magnificent individual by his Christian name would have horrified her, had she even remembered it.

"Then I am so unfortunate as not to be able to

appeal to the past for aid : so I shall have to begin anew, and make friends with Miss Macalaster." And he put out his hand gayly, and took hers again, as though welcoming a new acquaintance. "But I warn you that I shall claim a double measure of friendship from her to compensate for the loss of her predecessor."

He softly held her hand for a moment longer than was necessary, bowing over it with an exquisite grace which had enchanted women immeasurably beyond Christie Macalaster in strength, and knowledge of life.

As he lifted his head, he caught his brother's eyes, and saw in them just the expression they had held when Christie's name had first been mentioned in that room months before. Again Tom had recognized his purpose, and again it had filled him with disgust and indignation. He did not analyze his emotions: but he saw innocent helplessness within the power of malign strength ; and, more than ever, the child he had loved seemed calling upon him to protect her.

Reginald placed Christie between Tom and himself, and undertook the task of her entertainment, quietly conquering her shyness towards himself. His manner was truly perfect ; so unaffected, so almost boyish in its fresh, genial ease, that, even when he fell into fine speeches, they sounded natural from his lips. It was impossible to realize that Art had any thing to do with what seemed a triumph of Nature's handiwork. Too profoundly, placidly self-satisfied for self-consciousness, which is the outward evidence of secret self-doubt, his mind always seemed full of you, instead of himself. Too well accustomed to his own beauty and grace to remember them definitely, you were constantly crediting him with singular modesty and forbearance in apparently forgetting that which it was impossible for you to forget: you mentally gave him humble thanks for not openly triumphing in a loveliness which held you in bondage even against your will; which subjugated you afresh each moment by some fresh phase. With a right to overweening vanity, it was no small element of his fascination that no shade of it appeared in his manner: even in his early days, when his inward elation must have had the force of novelty, you would have searched in vain for outward evidence of it. Thus, as Tom watched him, he could find no flaw in his brother's armor: his acute intellect compelled him to share the girl's admiration for the man's outward seeming.

Christie answered Reginald's remarks as easily and brightly as she could; but the shyness remained. He understood its cause, and was well satisfied with it. She had evidently set him upon a pedestal; and he knew the advantages of the position too well to wish to descend, and looked upon her unwonted diffidence as a point gained.

On the other hand, the girl kept turning to Tom, — taking refuge with him, as it were ; drawing him into the conversation as some one with whom she was perfectly at home.   All her mild little sallies were addressed to him : she made gay attempts at repartee, and had all her abilities under her control in speaking to him.   Her manner and tone changed so completely, that she seemed two different persons in talking to the two men.

Tom talked, and talked well ; in fact, with a shrewd wit, an insight and originality, which were beyond the inexperienced girl's comprehension.   Had she been a broad-natured woman of talent, with a deep, wide knowledge of men, she would have turned from the gracious gentleman on the one hand, to the strong, virile nature on the other, — choosing, as one might, between cloying sweet and appetizing salt ; she would have perceived instantly that Tom's conversation exceeded Reginald's in matter as far as his brother's excelled his in manner.   But Christie was much too young for such clear-sightedness : and indeed I fancy that in early life we all prefer confectionery ; that a taste for sugar-plums in every form is indissoluble from extreme youth.   In persons naturally constituted and developed, maturity is required to appreciate and enjoy the strong meat of the word. At a certain age, the mental digestion rejects genuine humor, and vigorous, sinewy statement; just as the physical palate has no relish for rare roast-beef and dry wine. One almost imagines that a liking for good sense is an acquired taste, not to be gained before a given age or without a given discipline. Consequently, all that gave Tom's conversation its extraordinary merit fell upon ears unfitted to perceive it; at least, as far as Christie was concerned.

With Reginald it was quite the reverse. As usual, he delighted in his brother's talking; answering, and drawing him out, as was his wont. Between his attentions of such different kinds, he was like a juggler who keeps two balls flying in the air; one hand fondling Christie, while the other fenced with Tom. Thus he passed a most agreeable evening. The girl, as he well knew, would have failed to hold him interested for that length of time; but being mentally excited by some one else, and having made very satisfactory progress towards the end he had in view, he went up stairs that night in perfect humor with himself and others.

"She'll do very well," he coolly thought. "She is not brilliant or imposing, to be sure; but she is extremely pretty, and her eyes and eyelashes would be worth looking at in anybody. She's a refined little

creature, and I shall never be ashamed of her; which
is very fortunate, as I should have felt obliged to
swallow her, no matter how unpalatable a morsel she
had been. I have had a lifelong horror that I should
be compelled, in the end, to marry an ugly woman, or,
what is infinitely worse, an underbred one; though I
don't think I could have survived that. Christie
lacks style fearfully; but I can train her to it. I shall
tire of her terribly in a few weeks; but that would be
the case no matter what sort of woman I married,"
he candidly admitted to himself. "I am only thankful that she has so many advantages; and, upon the
whole, she will do very well," he added, ending where
he had begun.

Settling this matter, he went off into that balmy
sleep which seems to prove, in such men, the superiority of a good digestion over a good conscience. In the
long-run, and at the final settlement, a well-ordered
conscience may probably prove the best investment;
but, for the present, a well-conditioned liver certainly
appears the true secret of happiness and comfort. It
seems the real seat of sensation; and there is force
in the view of existence taken by the dyspeptic, who,
for the future state, desired rather a new liver than a
new heart. Lord Byron said he " was as good a Christian as his stomach would let him be;" but upon
that point one might claim leave to disagree with his

lordship, as there are a goodly number of dyspeptics on record who differ strikingly from the noble lord in moral character.

In Reginald's case, health really was, for this world, like faith, " counted to him for righteousness ; " making him better tempered than many better men. Escaping all pangs of conscience by possessing none, his perfect constitution saved him from physical qualms, which would have disturbed and might have checked him. As it was, he possessed the double power of sinning like a man, and sleeping like an animal ; and he passed the night in a sweet repose, which his brother Tom, excited and troubled, could not gain, and would have sincerely envied.

" Maria," exclaimed Christie as the other bade her good-night, " I am so very, very glad I came ! " And the enthusiastic girl threw her arms around her friend, and kissed her again and again.

Her eyes were shining, and her cheeks glowing with a strange, new life ; while her heart and blood throbbed with a tumultuous sense of pleasure as bewildering as it was unwonted. A fresh element had entered her quiet, girlish existence ; and she understood neither it nor its effect. She tossed restlessly in bed for an hour or two before carrying her dream of happiness from her waking to her sleeping moments, — a dream, alas ! baseless in both.

4 *

CHAPTER V.

A S that first evening passed, so, in varied forms,
passed each evening of the following mouth.

To the delight of his sisters, Reginald made his appearance every day at the dinner-table, and remained in the house until the ladies retired for the night; then away to the club, or elsewhere, to stretch morally, as it were, after the restraint he had imposed upon himself.

Christie's mourning precluding her from outside entertainment, the family devoted itself to her amusement; while Reginald gave his time and attention to the accomplishment of his purpose. Concerning the morning-hours, he acted with his usual perfect tact. After the first day or two, when he had made the desired impression, and satisfied himself that he had gained an immeasurable start in the race, he ceased to breakfast with the rest of the family.

"I'll give Tom a chance, especially as it can be of no use to him," Reginald thought, laughing to himself. "The foolish fellow has tumbled over head and ears in love with that child; though I doubt if he knows it himself. Tom is so plucky, that you can scarcely tell how hard he is hit; but the sharp pain will look out of his eyes sometimes, when Christie is gazing up at me as though I were a great shining angel come down for her special benefit. Somehow, I find I am generally regarded as an angel,—from one direction or the other," he meditated, gazing reflectively at his image in the full-length club mirror to see from what the impression was gathered. "I am sorry Tom is going to make a fool of himself about this matter," he thought, coming back to the original subject; "but I suppose it can't be helped. I can't afford to have him working to defeat me, though: so I will throw him off the scent by apparently letting him have his own way. I'll cast a sop to Cerebus, and allow him to have Christie to himself over the breakfast-table."

Consequently, the sun always shone for Tom in the morning, let the weather be what it might. Christie would come down stairs rosy and bright, and chatter to him over his morning-meal until he tasted her sweetness in every morsel, and drank from his cup an elation far more subtile than Mocha can give. At such times she was so thoroughly a part of his home, so near and dear to him, that he forgot his brother, and ceased to fear for her. He was not yet conscious that he was in love with her; but she seemed to belong to him too completely for any one to dream of taking her away, or to dare attempt it.

Yet with Reginald's coming, and the falling of night, the old shadow would surely appear; in which would gather darkly, and take form, like a spectre, his dread of his brother and of the future. Had he been aware of the exact truth, his pain and fear would not have been reserved for the latter part of the day; but he did not know, that as soon as he left the house, carrying with him a vague, sweet happiness, which made all things, even the drudgery of his business, a pleasure to him, Reginald descended to receive his share of the feast, spiritual and material. Of course, he demanded that Christie should do for him what she had done for Tom, — should sit by him, and entertain him; should perform pleasant little table-offices for him: all of which she did with a very different feeling and manner from the kindly gayety with which she had served the elder brother. They would linger over the meal for hours, which seemed to Christie like enchanted moments; and the girl had fallen so completely under his fascination, that she would remain indefinitely at his bidding, until Maria was sometimes forced to order them good-naturedly out of the room, that the household arrangements might proceed.

Then Reginald would take Christie and Ellen to walk through the gay streets or through the pleasant suburbs; but, let the road or the place be what it would, Christie walked in a lovely fairyland, which shone with a glory and light beyond the splendor of the sun.

Lloyd Truxton, Reginald's double, was usually attached to these expeditions. To his care Ellen was committed; this enabling Reginald to devote himself to Christie.

Tom heard of these walks but rarely, through Ellen's vague mention, which was too indefinite to arrest his attention. Reginald had his own reasons for not bringing them to his brother's notice; and as for Christie, she could not have forced herself to speak of them. She was too delicately refined, and too thoroughly a woman, to be able to talk of her love, or any thing connected with it. The charm of those weeks was hidden deep in her heart, only to be brought out in secret in the long, still watches of the night, for her own blushing delight. Thus Tom remained ignorant of much that was happening around him: he lost a knowledge of facts which might have spared him, in some degree, the terrible

shock which was coming upon him. Had he known
all, the blow, hard and cruel as it must have been
under any circumstances, could scarcely have been
such a thunderbolt.

One growing change Tom noticed in Christie,
without definitely tracing it to its source.   The
girl's appearance of extreme youth arose not so much
from her size and soft outline as from the expression
of her eyes.   It was a child's utterly unawakened
soul and heart that looked out of them.   They were
all smile and shine on the surface ; but their clear
depths were destitute of any variety of thought or
emotion.   The girl's nature had the blankness, as
well as the fair whiteness, of an unwritten page.
Growing up in perfect seclusion, she had the experience neither of feeling nor observation.   But Tom
noticed an alteration in those eyes.   They had become capable of other changes than from smiles to
frowns.   A soft light had grown into them, like the
illumination from some hidden, happy thought: the
new-born heart of the woman was casting its reflection into them ; and you saw how warm and true and
pure was its image.   The infinite variety of expression which was one day to be their highest beauty, Christie's eyes were, as yet, far from possessing.
The soul, like the body, can only come into existence

through travail; and sorrow and trial and anguish had not yet wrought in her that spiritual birth. What Tom perceived in her was the bright dawn of a new day. That which its meridian would bring forth, or its evening light and shadow disclose, was as darkly hidden in the future from him as from her.

CHAPTER VI.

THE month had quickly flown by; and Reginald had begun to weary of the work he had set himself, to which he had at first applied himself with some interest. He had read Christie's heart with the ease of a man who was familiar with every language into which emotions can be translated; and he felt certain of the result. He considered that he had now served long enough for his wages, and that they ought to be paid him. His creditors had become more pressing than ever, and he felt that what he had to do he had best do quickly. The apple being perfectly ripe, it behooved him to pluck it as speedily as possible.

Consequently, entering the house late one afternoon, and catching sight of Christie standing alone in the parlor, he coolly resolved to bring matters to a close on the spot.

The girl had come in from a walk, with her hands full of beautiful flowers she had purchased; and while Ellen, her companion, had passed on up stairs, she had entered the drawing-room, and was placing the gay blossoms in vases as a pleasant surprise to Maria. Reginald saw instantly that she was looking even prettier than usual. He was thankful, as rendering his task so much the easier; though love-making was, with him, too wonted an occupation ever to be difficult work. Exercise had brought the bright color into her cheeks; and, having thrown aside her hat, the little curls into which the wind had blown her hair were left visible.

Reginald came softly behind her, and spoke her name before she knew any one was near her, though she had heard some one enter the front-door. She started slightly, though she did not turn; but the deep blush which dyed her face, and even her throat, showed that she well knew who was speaking.

" Christie, are you afraid of me ? " Reginald said, softly laughing in answer to her movement, bending over her shoulder as she bent her hot face over the flowers.

" No, no," she replied nervously, turning partially towards him.

" Let me see if you are telling the truth," he went on : and, gently touching her face, he drew it upward until he could look straight down into it with those wonderful eyes which had beguiled so many women to their ruin; for love of which they had sacrificed

all that is worth possessing in this world or the next, —
honor and purity here, and salvation hereafter. No
wonder she gazed at him, not only as though her free
will, but her very life, were being drawn from her.

Reginald resolved to make short work. He put
his arm about the unresisting girl, and drew her to
his breast.

" My darling," he whispered, "if you truly are not
afraid of me, will you trust yourself with me forever ?
Will you be my little wife ? "

Had he really loved her, could his tones have been
so exquisitely musical ? Could aught but perfect
coolness and infinite practice have enabled him to
modulate his voice to such lingering tenderness ; to
convey such a world of meaning in every word?

The sudden, almost unconscious relaxation of the
figure in his arms, the absolute surrender of body
and soul which it expressed beyond the power of
words, gave Reginald the answer he wished.

"My precious love, my darling wife!" he murmured in return, pressing her close to the calm
heart, which never altered its beat for a second, but
speaking again with that intonation which thrilled
the girl to actual pain.

She clung to him passionately for a moment, giving
mute reply, and mutely expressing all the immeasurable love which was throbbing through her heart and

coursing through her veins, and then hid her face more closely than ever in his breast. He stooped, and kissed her again and again; deriving a very pleasant sensation from the dewy ripeness of the lips and the outlines of the supple young form. The feeling that he had gained the money and accompanying power he had always coveted excited him like wine. He was triumphant, as a man who had reached the aim of his life. He had won, and was in the best possible humor with himself, with her, and with all the world.

Suddenly the sound of a latch-key in the front-door broke the stillness.

"That's Tom!" Reginald exclaimed; and the situation flashed upon him.

He resolved in an instant to meet and brave it then and there. What must be done eventually had best be done on the moment. His plan would extricate him neatly from his present position, which he felt would soon bore him; would relieve him from the *ennui* of playing the part of lover and engaged man for the evening; would obviate the nuisance of explaining the affair to his sisters; and, above all, would carry him swiftly through the announcement which must be made to his brother.

"Good-by, dearest!" he said, kissing her. "I had better go now; but I will see you to-morrow morning. I will tell Tom of our engagement as I go out." And, turning, he left her.

Tom had taken off his hat, and was walking down the hall, when he saw Reginald coming towards him, not only with his accustomed imperial bearing, but with such a light in his eyes, and smile curving his perfect lips, such triumph and security radiating from every line of his beauty, that the truth broke upon Tom like a revelation.

Then he knew by the awful pain at his heart, as though some hand had clutched it and was tearing it from his body, that he loved Christie Macalaster with all his strong, long-restrained nature; with the height and depth and breadth of a passion only possible in that rare, exceptionally-powerful man who can love one woman, and her alone for life. This he learned, and, in learning it, knew also that he had lost her forever.

He stood perfectly still, and awaited his brother's coming, and the words he could almost see upon his lips, as a brave man might stand to receive his executioner and his death-blow.

Reginald's keen perception showed him instantly that his brother had perceived the truth; showed him also what that truth was to him. A sentiment almost like human regret passed through his mind, though it did not accord with his plans to let it become very evident in his manner.

"Tom," he said gayly, facing his brother's resolute

eyes with some of the same cool gallantry with which he would have charged a battery of guns, " Christie has promised to marry me ; and you shall have the honor of being the first to congratulate me."

Tom waited a moment until the horrible pain should allow the breath to come back to his lips. Then he spoke, — a little slowly, but just as steadily as ever.

" Reginald," he answered, " I can give you no congratulations, and you know it. There is no use in our lying to each other. Christie had better be in her grave than become your wife ; and no one is so well aware of it as yourself. You have taken her from me : but take care how you treat her ; for, by God ! as you deal with her, so will I deal with you."

" Tom," replied the other, " I am sorry for you ; and I regret, that, in this particular contest, two cannot come off conquerors. But you really ought to have known better than to attempt to play against me. It was an open game ; and I am the winner, at your service ! " And, taking up his hat, he made his brother a superb bow, and passed out of the house.

The sound of their voices could be heard in the parlor, but not the words spoken ; and these two men alone knew, then or thereafter, what had passed between them.

A moment after, Christie's figure flitted through

the parlor-door, and came swiftly towards Tom, with
glowing eyes and blushing face, and eager hands
extended to him. This motherless, fatherless child,
whose very lover had not cared to receive the sweet
overflowing of her tenderness upon his breast; who
had not one of her own blood to whom to turn in
depth of sorrow, or height of joy,— this girl, so rich
in gold, and so poor in all else, demanded some out-
let for the tide of feeling that was within her, and
claimed as confidant the first kindly nature near her.
With the strange sarcasm of circumstances, she
turned with unconscious cruelty to the one heart
which loved her but too well. Coming up to the
man, she threw her arms about him with the frank-
ness of a child, but with the passion of a woman.

"Tom, dear Tom!" she cried, her voice vibrating
with the weight of unutterable happiness, "he says
he loves me!"

She could scarcely realize her own blessedness: it
seemed too wonderful to be true; as, alas! it was.

Tom stood like a stone, his teeth set, and every
muscle tense and rigid. He knew to whom this
warm, clinging embrace really belonged; he knew
whence its fire and sweetness were drawn; and he
sickened and grew faint at the thought. He would
share this with no man: all, or nothing; his, and his
alone, or he would none of it. He would stand as

proxy to no one. Let Reginald take his own kisses : he scorned and flung them back even from the woman he adored. The refinement of torture was too much. He took the little hands from about his neck, and, firmly holding them in his own, put her at arm's-length.

" Tom," she said piteously, " you don't love me ; you don't wish me joy ! "

She was pushing him too far: it was more than human nature could endure.

" Christie," he exclaimed in desperation, " I pray God to give you all the joy he can bestow ! My darling, my darling ! " he suddenly cried out, breaking down entirely before those appealing eyes, " I pray that he may love you and protect you as I never can ! "

His strong will was swept utterly away. He caught the girl in his arms, and tasted, for one wild, sweet moment, that bliss of living and loving from which he seemed parting forever. The touch of her hands, the curves of her form, the softness of her cheek, the sweeping lashes and falling hair, thrilled his blood and bones with a mad joy that was the very elixir of life. What could Reginald's bald, worn being know of passion, compared to this nature, which united the fresh, pure vigor of a boy to the deep, broad maturity of a strong man. Tom's na-

ture was capable of a fire, of an intensity of enjoyment, which Reginald had never experienced; his
senses brought him gifts and pleasures for which
the other sighed in vain. He tasted the fulness of
this joy so completely, that, for a moment, he forgot
it was not to be his.

But the bitter truth came back upon him full soon.
For a second time he put the girl steadily from him,
and gathered his nature again within his grasp.

So young and inexperienced was she, and, above
all, so absorbed in her new-found love and happiness,
that she entirely failed to interpret his emotion and
its changes. He had kissed her as though he loved
her; and she was satisfied, never dreaming of ana-
lyzing the quantity of his affection. To her he was
the dear friend of her childhood, and, above all,
Reginald's brother. All persons and things pertain-
ing to her splendid lover were exalted in her eyes;
and she emphasized her relation to them, as bringing
her nearer to him. It was this feeling which dictated her next words.

"You will be my brother, then, Tom, my dear
brother, when I belong to Reginald!"

He looked straight at her, still holding her at arm's-
length; but his face suddenly changed and shrank,
as though the words had been a blow. The sentence
and the epithet carried a different meaning and les-

son to him from that she had intended. Even in that moment of bitterest trial, he was man enough to know his duty, and to do it. Then and there he made a vow to God, which he kept faithfully until death absolved him.

" Christie," he said slowly, " you have said it: I will be your brother. Remember that, if you ever need me ; for I shall never forget it."

Then he dropped her hands, and walked up stairs without another word.

The girl stood for a moment with that beautiful smile of ineffable happiness upon her lips ; and then, all other recollection being swallowed up in her great joy, she stole away to Maria and Ellen to confide it to them, and to receive her warm welcome as their sister.

5

CHAPTER VII.

TOM entered his room, and, turning the key in the door, sat quietly down, determined to settle this matter with himself.

"Her brother!"—that was the word which kept repeating itself in his brain; that was the standpoint from which he compelled himself to look at every fact and feeling as it arose before him. In spite of the horrible pain at his heart, which never ceased for a moment, he held his will and his intellect to the work of deciding his course apart from all desire or emotion.

Knowing what he did of Reginald and his life, and what such a marriage must inevitably bring upon Christie, ought he not to make some effort to prevent it? That was the question he had to settle, and settle immediately. The strength of the temptation to separate at any cost the woman he loved from the man he hated; the fact that Reginald's loss would be, in a certain sense, his gain,—would have made Tom resolve to cast such impulse behind him as savoring too much of low revenge and mean cowardice, except that, in this case, self must not be allowed to enter, however disguised. He must let his personal feeling influence him no more on one side than the other. Here he had no right to be generous towards Reginald, and self-denying towards himself, if the result were lack of justice to Christie.

Yet, reason with himself as he would, he could not help revolting from the work whose motive might appear so mean: he could not but sicken at the purpose Reginald would probably attribute to him if he made up his mind to oppose his plans. It was very hard for Tom to do even a seemingly ungenerous act: it was almost like moral death to him even to shade that sense of honor which he had kept so pure and high, that, like all his strong sentiments, it had become a passion. Struggle against it as he would, it was this intense, high-toned pride which influenced him in the end: it was that, at least, which made him perceive so clearly all the arguments against interference.

"She loves him," thought Tom bitterly, with a thrill through every nerve as he remembered the light that had been upon the girl's face, — "she loves him with all her heart; and what can mortal man effect against that power? If I could bring myself to tell her in plain terms the loathsome truth, she would never believe me; still less would she comprehend me: for what can an innocent woman know of such things, and their inevitable effect? Pure as she is, what can she know of the true nature of sin? No matter what I told her, it would be to her mere words with vague dictionary meanings. She is too absolutely unacquainted with evil to recognize it as such when it is presented to her. I suppose she would dream that she could purify and save him; as though a man could ever be raised by any outside process by any thing but 'working out his own salvation.' These pitiable, blessedly ignorant women believe, that as a man can thrust his hand in filth, and afterward wash it white and clean, he can dip his soul and body in sin, and not absorb it into his very essence. My God! she will learn differently one day, when she is brought into contact with it, and is forced to see and know the truth. I don't think Reginald will maltreat her; I don't think he is capable of that: but he will either break her heart, or he will degrade her nature gradually to his own level. My poor little darling, my poor little innocent darling!" the man moaned out, in such an agony of pity, that his personal pain was for the moment forgotten.

Tom was right in his idea that he could not have made Christie really comprehend Reginald's past life. A perfectly pure-minded girl who has

been reared in an innocent home, who carries about
with her a spiritual atmosphere into which evil cannot enter, has not the power to take in or understand
the actual quality of wickedness.   To talk to her of
such things is to speak a foreign tongue ; and the
words fail to convey their true sense.   A knowledge
of the worst side of life may be forced upon a woman,
or she may roll impurity as a sweet morsel under her
tongue ; the fruit of the tree of the knowledge of
good and evil may be held to shrinking, recoiling lips,
or to those which long after and seize the horrible
tainted food : but she must in some way have become acquainted with it before any description can
appeal to her perception in the slightest degree.
That dreadful introduction to sin must have been
undergone before she can recognize it, sadly or gladly
as it may be in her nature to do.   When Wordsworth
sang of that little girl, who, though she had seen the
graves of her brothers and sisters, could not take in
the idea of death, and believed that they seven were
still an unbroken band ; when the great poet told
that simple story, he conveyed the same deep principle of life, — that we have but the ability to comprehend that which in some degree corresponds to our
experience and our nature.   Tom knew by instinct
that he could no more teach Christie the essential
quality of evil than that child could be made to
realize death by the mere telling.

Still further: he felt that he could never make his word stand with her against that of her lover; that what he could affirm Reginald could deny; and, upon a question of veracity, he knew beforehand which side Christie must take. The more he scrutinized and viewed the matter in every light, the more inevitably he came to the conclusion that all opposition was useless, and worse than useless. It could not be his duty to make an attempt which would pain Christie severely without benefiting her; which would put him forever in a false position towards her, and prevent her from turning to him in that time of trial which he felt would come as surely as that the sun rose and set.

"But Reginald ought not to be allowed to control her fortune, and to squander it, as he is quite capable of doing," Tom suddenly thought. "It ought to be secured to her; and, as there is no one to see to it, I suppose I ought to. She has no more idea of money than a baby; and I can't stand by, and watch her run the risk of being beggared. Reginald always has a certain respect for the person who holds the purse-strings; and the poor child will need that defence, and every other, when she is in his power. I suppose all I shall get for my effort will be that she will think me mean-spirited and mercenary to take such things into consideration at such a time, — not at all like her romantic lover, who is far too fine for such commonplace trifles as forethought and honesty and justice," he went on in the bitterness of his soul.

"But what difference can it make now as to what she thinks of me? Almost any one can act the part of her brother, — 'her dear brother,' she called me." And the man's blood throbbed and tingled to his finger-ends as the sensation of the embrace which had preceded her words came suddenly back upon him; but the warm thrill died away, leaving the same pain at his heart, — a pain now sunk to a dull, sickening ache, worse than the sharpest pangs.

Tom rose slowly to his feet, and prepared to face again his ordinary work-a-day life, — with what change in himself, he alone knew. He had settled his account between conscience and circumstances; he had determined on his own line of conduct from thenceforth; and, so doing, he took up that heavy burden of duty which he bore so simply, so faithfully, so bravely, until death's dread hand lifted it from his weary shoulders.

Going down stairs to dinner, he had to undergo the long-drawn torture of listening to the amplifications of pleasure with which Maria and Ellen overflowed; still worse, he had to endure the sight of Christie blushing, and casting down her long lashes in her vain endeavor to hide the radiant happiness that beamed in her eyes.

Tom bore it steadily and well, as he sat, only rather quiet and weary-looking, at the foot of the table ; but it was very, very hard to bear, when Maria kept appealing to him for sympathy, and for expressions of joy over the aspect their family-affairs had taken.

" Won't it be delightful, Tom," she would say, " to have Christie near us? She will never go away now that she is to be our little sister." And Tom tried to smile pleasantly in reply.

" I haven't heard you wish Christie joy yet," she remarked soon after ; so full of the subject, that she said any thing which occurred to her, merely for the gratification of talking upon it ; thereby torturing her darling brother as his worst enemy would scarcely have done wittingly.

" I have told Christie how much happiness I wished her, though I scarcely think she needed telling," he managed to say, turning to the girl, who sat on his right hand.

" No, indeed! you have been too good and kind always to fail me now." And the impulsive, happy child made a little movement, as though she intended to spring up and kiss him again in her loving gratitude. But something in Tom's eyes checked her, she scarcely knew why ; and she returned to her pretence

of eating her dinner, — her meal being from the beginning a mere farce.

Again Tom utterly refused to take " the crumbs
which fell from the master's table ; " not daring,
moreover, to trust himself to receive such a token in
the way in which he must then and there accept it.

Christie's momentary sense of defeat passed away
as a ripple disappears from the surface of a flowing
river. She could not then have felt angrily towards
an enemy ; and, in another second, Tom was to her
just the Tom of old.

But he was thankful indeed when the meal was
over.

" I will leave you ladies to talk over your plans
and ideas this evening," he said as they rose from
the table, " as I have some work for to-night. You
can tell me of the result to-morrow morning." · And,
smiling good-by, he left them, and went to his own
room.

" Work to do ! " Yes, he had that work appointed
for every human creature, — the struggle with and
conquest of his own passionate heart and nature ; he
had to silence the crying-out of his whole being for
gratification which was no longer lawful; he had to
do battle for his own soul. But not in a single night,
not in many coming hours of darkness, could that end
be attained.

5 *

For the present, mere existence seemed to demand all his strength. Hour after hour, he lay motionless upon his sofa, without definite thought, with the vague hope that the pain at his heart would gradually become less unbearable. Had there been any exertion to make, it would have been a relief to employ his thoughts and energies, however trying the action. But there was nothing except to endure. To this quick-thinking, swiftly-executive man, it was the severest form in which trial could have come. Lying there so silent, so still, it was as though he were firmly holding with his hand some physical wound, in the hope that the life-blood would cease to flow.

But the long hours that went over him brought little relief. The labor of a lifetime demands a life-time for its execution.

CHAPTER VIII.

THE next morning, Tom came down stairs before his usual time, and swallowed a hasty breakfast, saying that it was necessary for him to be at his counting-room at an early hour. He could not have gone through that meal in its usual form. It had been to him the brightest part of each day; but now the mere recollection of it made him set his teeth to think how he had befooled himself with false happiness.

For that, and many other days, he took refuge in his counting-room, toiling there from morning until night until he grew thin and haggard from the strain upon mind and body. He gave his managing-clerk holiday to leave the city; and did his work for him, in the mean time, as such work was probably never done before. He went into the minutiæ of his affairs, and pushed his business, until his employees wondered and admired, and imagined that he was ambitious of making a fortune in a single year. He was willing to relieve any one of a share of his labor. He seemed

to crave routine, and to seek drudgery ; any thing to
prevent him from looking backward or forward, — to
the past which held so much, or the future which
held nothing. It would be difficult to say which he
found it hardest to face, — the rich fulness of one, or
the blank emptiness of the other.

To occupy himself with the dull detail of the present moment was his only relief. When all else failed
to keep thought and brain bound down, he would fall
to casting up accounts, to adding up lines of figures,
with the vague hope of gaining some of the insensi-
bility of a machine by imitating its regularity.

" My best friend in life has been the multiplication-
table," Tom Archer said years after, when he and all
about him had changed completely; looking back
upon his life, and summing up its results. " It has
been my salvation in many ways. There have been
times, when, without it, I do not think I could have
lived to talk of it at this moment. I have always
held that it was the law of God, and that a sufficiently enlightened knowledge of it was a great code of
morality. When a man has it well grained into him
that twice two will go on making four to all eternity,
that it is the fundamental law of the universe, he will
hesitate before committing acts which will inevitably bring certain results and certain penalties. He
can never deceive himself into thinking that cause

and effect can be divorced, or that a soul can sin
without suffering for it at some period of its existence. The religion of the multiplication-table may
appear a stern one; but it seems to have a very rocky
foundation. I think Christ preached that sermon,
and gave out its great text, when he said, ' With what
measure ye mete it shall be meted to you again.' An
individual who has this article in his creed is compelled to hold himself to a terribly strict account, and
to recognize just what he is doing when he sins against
God and man. The moral aspect of the multiplication-table, its extension into the region of right and
wrong, is to me its most appalling power. When I
think that spiritual consequences, like material results,
are absolutely relentless; that no amount of pardon,
mercy, or reconciliation, can restore a criminal to what
he was before he stained his soul; that nothing can
take away from him that dreadful acquaintance with
evil, and awakened appetite for it, which tasting the
forbidden fruit must give, — I get a realization of the
awful quality of sin which nothing else gives me.
When I see that moral law of inheritance, that ' the
sins of the fathers shall be visited upon the children,'
being executed around me every day, the mathemati-
cal accuracy with which Nature keeps her accounts
fills me with dread of the least deviation from her
straight line. If we were sufficiently clear-sighted

and far-sighted, we should do right, if only from sheer selfishness; we should tremble before our own wrong-doing as before nothing else in heaven or on earth. The multiplication-table is microscopic as well as telescopic in its working; and, like godliness, it is profitable for this world and the world to come. I suppose it will take far more than a lifetime really to comprehend it; but even a faint appreciation is a great advantage. I have tried to serve it faithfully; and it has been my strength and my support, even when every thing else seemed to fail me."

And these were indeed times when all save the multiplication in its lowest form, the laying-together of dollars and cents, appeared to have failed Tom Archer.

Reginald descended the morning after his engagement, and for a few hours played the part of devoted lover to perfection. Beautiful, tender, and ardent, he could have made Christie grant almost any request; and, when he pressed eagerly for the earliest possible marriage, what could the girl do but acquiesce? His earnestness and impetuosity could only flatter and charm her; and, had there been any reason to oppose his wish, her purpose would have melted before his soft pleadings.

"When is my darling to be mine forever?" he murmured as the girl lay in his arms. "I shall be miserable until I have her entirely to myself. My pet, I am so silly about you, that it makes me wretched to see any one else interest you, or, indeed, come near you."

This last statement was so purely a flight of fancy, that Reginald was rather pleased with himself for having thought of it, and paid the idea the compliment of using it again. It struck him as too good a string not to harp upon.

"If you loved me as I love you, dearest, you would understand and pardon my foolish jealousy, which makes me want to claim every iota of your nature, and claim it instantly. I am haunted by a fear that circumstances, or even death, may come between us, may rob me of you," he went on ardently, even tragically, as he clasped her in his arms; listening to himself meanwhile with a delighted sense of humor, and much inward approbation.

It tickled him rarely to think how nearly he had spoken the truth in his last sentence, and yet how far he had been from conveying his real meaning: it amused him to see how openly he could state his dread that her fortune would slip through his fingers, without her being any the wiser for his words.

The girl must have been a stone to have resisted such tender passion and fire as vibrated through his tone, and even through his frame, as he spoke. He was extremely anxious to bring this matter to the speediest conclusion, thus extricating himself from his financial difficulties; and he spared no pains to gain his end.

"My darling, nothing shall part us!" she exclaimed in reply, raising herself, and throwing her arms about him with all the passionate devotion of her pure heart. "I should die if you were taken from me!"

"Will you marry me immediately, next week?" Reginald instantly asked, descending from his romantic elevation, and becoming practical in a second.

"Yes," she answered freely and fervently: "whenever you wish it. I will do any thing to show you that I love you as deeply and truly as you can love me."

Reginald smiled the sweetest smile of absolute satisfaction that probably ever sat upon mortal lips. He fully appreciated the unconscious satire of her last words; but he kept all shadow of amusement out of his face; and the girl seemed fully justified in her belief, that, as he kissed her, his joy was too deep for utterance.

He was in such good humor, that, even after he had accomplished the business of the day in winning her consent to an immediate marriage, he wasted fully an hour of his valuable time upon her without any particular compensation; giving her loving words and caresses with somewhat the amusement with which one feeds a child on sugar-plums. When at last he went away, it was with the definite agreement, that their wedding was to take place on the Thursday of the following week; leaving less than ten days for preparations.

Christie's wealth rendered such considerations no obstacle; as a *trousseau* of almost any magnificence can be provided as by magic, if one be willing to pay the required price. Christie and Maria and Ellen were kept busy from morning until night. The first was little more than a lay-figure upon which to try clothes; but she was so constantly needed in that capacity, and to give the final decision in all matters, that she had scarcely an unoccupied moment at her command. Even Reginald saw little of her, except in the evenings, — a fact which he outwardly deplored and secretly rejoiced over, as saving him much attitudinizing and speech-making, much weariness of mind and body.

They breakfasted together each morning; and the meal was the same pretty play as usual. Then would follow an hour of lovers' talk and caresses, from which Christie would finally tear herself away, as though she were taking sweetest food from her lips, but from which Reginald departed to his accustomed amusements and occupations with a sense of relief.

"I could not let you go, dearest," he would whisper with the softest accent of regret, " except that it will bring you to my arms the earlier. It is only by remembering that we shall soon be together forever that I learn to bear the separation now."

Then he would leave her with a delightful sense of freedom until the dinner-hour called him back to temporary servitude. At times, the work was heavy; but he consoled himself with the business-like consideration, that he was purchasing a fortune cheaply, and could well afford to pay the small required price for a week or two.

He announced his rapidly-approaching marriage at the club and in general society; and in both it created a profound sensation. The gay women whose company he most affected rather regretted that he should fetter himself, even slightly, with the bonds of matrimony; but were more than consoled when they reflected that they would have a rich lover instead of a poor one. He would keep up a magnificent establishment, and could *fête* them to their hearts' content; not to mention other advantages, less openly displayed, which they would derive from the increase in his income. They soon ascertained the particulars of his engagement, — that his intended wife was a mere child, whom he was marrying for her wealth; whom neither he nor they need fear in any respect. She would be a very pleasant member of their set; too innocent for perception, and too child-like for criticism and contention; a person to be kept in good humor by caresses and careless compliments, and, in the mean time, to be used as freely as possible. They made up their minds to ride in her carriages, to eat her fine dinners, to hint presents out of her, to manage her to their utmost advantage, and to maintain their old relationship towards her husband under her little nose. This course of conduct would suit both Reginald and themselves: and, if Christie fell into it gracefully, they would treat her extremely well; in fact, be her dearest friends.

Among men, Reginald's avowal of his intention produced mingled emotions.

When he spoke of his engagement at his club, he was, of course, congratulated by all present, as though his success in life were their darling hope and fondest desire. They were aware of Christie's wealth; and some had, perhaps, anticipated the result when they heard of her arrival; but none had expected the campaign to be conducted to such rapid and brilliant victory. Many pleasant and flattering things were said to Reginald as the hero of the hour; and they could not help regarding him with a certain new deference, as the prospective owner of so much money. But scarcely was his back turned, when there broke out audibly that curious discontent which fills the mind of man at any unusual and unexpected success on the part of his brother-man.   A certain secret sense of injury, a feeling that one has been taken and the other left without legitimate reason, will insinuate itself into human nature under such circumstances.   The other's gain does, in some shadowy way, become your loss; and you feel aggrieved in so much as something which might possibly have become yours has been secured by another.   You resent the partiality of circumstances, and feel wronged by fate; and you vaguely express your sentiment by being in a bad humor with the world in general, and the fortunate individual in particular. You regard it as a species of swindle that he should fare so much more softly than yourself; and your soul is fired with righteous wrath that he should be so much better paid for being no better than you are.

"Hang that fellow! did you ever see such luck?" exclaimed one of the young men the moment Reginald left the room, speaking with an anger and disgust which were comical enough to witness, but in which he was perfectly serious and sincere.

Those around him shared his feeling too entirely

to see any thing amusing in his mood or his remark; and all broke out in the same strain.

"Now, I want to know where is the justice of Heaven in letting Reginald Archer draw such a prize," cried out another indignant young person. "He is the worst man I know; and here he has been given the very thing of all others that he wanted. The greatest heiress that has been about these parts for years is brought into his very house; walks right into his hands. I confess I don't understand the dealings of Providence: for that looks to me like putting a premium upon wickedness; giving a high reward to an evil life."

The young man's virtuous indignation gained point from the fact that he had modelled his social existence upon Reginald's, and so might reasonably have expected to share the benefits conferred on such a course.

"I fancy it will be some time before any of us get such a chance of settling ourselves in the world. I suppose we are not quite wicked enough; that it is only the eminent sinners who get paid so largely," he wound up angrily.

"So it is Col. Macalaster's daughter whom he is to marry," remarked an elderly gentleman of the old school, who came to the club for a game of whist because he had no family with which to take refuge, but had nothing in common with the young men around him. "I used to know him years ago; and this daughter can be little more than a child now. It would have been well if he could have taken her with him when he died, instead of leaving her to that man's mercy," he added sadly.

"I suppose Reginald will give up his pretty ways, in mere decency, when he is married; he will be ashamed to go on as he now does," suggested one of the company.

"My young friend," replied the elder gentleman, "neither a man's nor a woman's nature is changed by having a few words said over him or her. What is born in the bone will come out in the flesh. If a man has not sufficient conscience and honor, and fixed standard of right and wrong, to restrain him before his marriage, the wedding-ceremony is no miracle to give them to him. If a far less abandoned man than Reginald Archer plant certain seeds in his nature, they will crop out from time to time in spite of himself; at least, sufficiently to make his wife a very miserable woman, if she possesses conscience, a heart, and high-toned honor, and, above all, is striving honestly to keep her marriage-vow to 'love and honor and reverence him.' No: I say again, that that poor innocent girl had better be lying peacefully by her father's side than be bound for life, not merely to Reginald Archer, but to any man who has even put his foot upon the course he has walked so long."

The elder man, who had tried life and proved it, and knew whereof he affirmed, stood facing the whole circle as he spoke, with glowing eyes and vibrating voice: for he was thinking of his own dead daughter, who might have lived for such a fate; whose loss had once been his heaviest sorrow, but whose death he had learned to cease to regret through watching the fate of other women. The intense feeling, and, above all, the immeasurable conviction, with which he spoke, and the application of his words to every individual present, made a strange quietude and very uncomfortable sensation creep over that company. It was as though each one had had his own sin and its inevitable consequences presented before him, and found it hard to look it full in the face.

There was silence for several moments; and then the elder man, speaking more quietly, said,—

" I remember this girl as a child; and, if she be of the stuff I take her to be, she will not live very long under the circumstances. She has, at least, that way of escape from him; which sometimes strikes me as being the only certain resource women have in this world."

And, having said his say, he took up his hat and left the room.

There was an uncomfortable pause; and then one of the young men said, with an uneasy laugh, —

"Takes things rather seriously, doesn't the old gentleman?"

"Yes," answered several others, glad of any thing which broke the constraint which was upon them all. "He always was a queer fellow, and had odd, old-fashioned notions of things."

"It's enough to give any one the shivers to hear him talk!" exclaimed another.

"He must have known a very different set of women from that which we live in, to be able to speak and think of them in that manner," remarked one of the party, rather older than the rest, looking gravely and quietly before him. "I should like to see a woman who was worth all that faith and feeling from such a man; for he is no fool, I can tell you, and knows the world well. I only hope that what he says is one of his peculiar whims; because, if he be right, we have laid up a pleasant prospect for our old age; and I suppose most of us have an idea of being good boys one of these days," he added, breaking out into somewhat bitter laughter. "However, we have made our beds; and the best thing will be to lie on them as gracefully as possible."

"There is one person who will be pleased at this marriage," exclaimed another of the young men, glad to take a different view of the subject; "and that is Tom Archer,"— naming the man, of all others, who would have died to prevent it.

"I wonder how much Reginald has cost him in the last ten years," suggested another.

"Quite a pretty fortune, I imagine," was the reply. "Reginald has supported himself for a long time by a dexterous system of taxation both at home and abroad,— high tariff and internal revenue; and Tom represents the latter. I wager you one thing,— that it is a tax punctually collected."

And, with a general laugh, the party broke up.

Each went his own way; but each took with him the same vague sense of ill-will towards Reginald, and the same fixed determination to hold to him faithfully until his last dollar should be spent. "Bound together by the strong cohesive attraction of 'private' plunder," they felt it to be their duty and privilege to obtain, severally and collectively, as large an amount of the great fortune as could be extracted from its owner. They had stood by Reginald in his comparative adversity; and, in his prosperity, they did not intend to desert him. The possession of a rich friend is the next thing to being rich one's self; and they had no idea of letting any foolish reticence withhold them from any advantages which might arise therefrom. Reginald's associates eminently belonged to that class of persons who consider Christ's injunction, " Ask, and it shall be given unto you," so good and fitting, that it ought to be applied to this world as well as to the next, and acted upon in reference to their fellow-beings as well as to a higher power. Among the host of individuals whom he called his friends, there was scarcely one who had not already definitely or indefinitely determined to improve his or her fortunes by the other's good fortune. With all the splendor attending the preparations for Christie's wedding, she seemed truly but a poor little lamb being made ready for sacrifice; and the vultures and cormorants were even now gathering in the distance, scenting their prey.

CHAPTER IX.

LLOYD TRUXTON, having assisted at Reginald's courtship from the beginning, had an interest and a sense of triumph in its successful conclusion. He had a disinterested, doglike attachment to his leader, and a pride in his power and fascinations, which made him delight in his victory, apart from personal considerations; though these latter were very strong. Reginald having been perfectly free-handed with Tom's money, the inference was that he would be so with Christie's; and Lloyd naturally concluded that there was a rich harvest in store for him. He had almost the sensation of having made a wealthy match himself, and realized more than ever that his best investment in life was sticking close to the Archers. He was with them so constantly, that he felt like one of the family, and plumed himself not a little on the connection it was about to make.

"See here, Truxton," said one of the young men at the club, after they had all borne his vicarious elation for several-days in silent irritation: " what have you got to do with this wedding, that you are so set up about it? If Archer were to put on airs,— which, I must confess, he doesn't,— I could see some reason for it; but why you are holding up your head so high, I really can't understand."

" I am sure I was not conscious of putting on any airs," returned Lloyd, suddenly lowering his plumes like a drenched chicken; " but Reginald is almost like a brother to me, and of course I am glad to see him provide for himself so well."

It must be admitted that he did not shine in retort.

" I suppose you intend to make him your brother in reality one of these days, which would account for your deep interest in the family prosperity," suggested another speaker. " I saw you playing the devoted to that pretty little sister of his the other morning; and it struck me as rather a bright idea on your part. I really should not have given you credit for so much perception, or for such a neat combination of your pleasure and profit. Two rich, generous brothers-in-law are not a bad provision in life for such a fellow as you, who will never work for a living, and never be clever enough to marry a fortune," he went on, with that half-contemptuous truthfulness of statement to which Lloyd's friends generally treated him.

Lloyd Truxton sat and looked at the man in silence for several minutes, as though an idea were dawning upon him, — were gradually penetrating his brain. From his appearance, one would imagine he found it necessary to open his eyes very wide to take in the new-comer.

" You are very complimentary, I must confess," he presently returned rather meekly by way of reply, not knowing what else to say.

And, finding that they had reduced him for the present to a convenient and proper level, his attackers drew off their forces, and allowed him to remain in peace.

He sat quiet for some time, apparently thinking; but presently took himself away, carrying with him the suggestion he had received during the discussion; for he had, indeed, gained a perfectly fresh thought.

Ever since Christie's coming, when Reginald had introduced Lloyd into his home for his own purposes, the latter had been carrying on a mild flirtation with Ellen Archer, upon his general principle of flirting with every pretty girl he came near. Their tastes and inclinations agreed; and, being constantly thrown in her society, he had come to care for her about as much as he was capable of caring for any one except himself. But, having predetermined that matrimony must be the means of securing him a final support, the idea of marrying Ellen, or any other girl without fortune, had not entered his mind.

That little conversation at the club had, however, presented his fancy for her in a new light; and he was now by no means sure that gratifying his inclination would not be his wisest as well as his most attractive course.   That he could neither make money nor marry it, he was beginning strongly to suspect; and to have the same opinion authoritatively pronounced by others settled the matter with him, as it settles all such questions with weak men who cannot help rating themselves at the valuation of others.   Having no inward consciousness of reserved strength, they cannot withstand, even in their own eyes, the decision of their circle: they unconsciously appeal to those around them to learn their own mental and moral weight and measure.   Naturally, Lloyd easily acquiesced in an opinion towards which he had been experimentally led for some time past.

It was strongly borne in upon him, that it would be better to secure a certain advantage than to go on striving after an imaginary good which failed to make its appearance.   With all his diligence of pursuit, no woman uniting the two essentials of social position and wealth had yet smiled upon him ; nor did it seem likely that one would be found of sufficiently peculiar taste to do so. Tom and Reginald in the positions of brothers-in-law — with his hold of old friendship upon one, and of family pride and honor upon the other — appeared more stable supports than the supposititious heiress who was to rescue him from his slough of despond. He wondered that he had not immediately taken this view of the affair; and was really thankful to his brother clubman for his sound and sensible advice, even though it had been given in a somewhat insulting manner. That his wishes and his interest should run parallel charmed him; and he determined to devote himself from that time forward to attaining their common end.

Perhaps, with all the advantages of the plan, he might not have made up his mind to immediate matrimony but for the curious contagious power of a wedding in the family or connection. Let one person take that plunge, and the other members of his circle seem drawn by some mysterious influence to follow him. He appears to create a species of moral eddy, into which they are attracted almost against their will. Matrimony is certainly, at times, epidemic in its nature, or may be caught, like the measles or the small-pox. Reginald's example influenced Lloyd as much as the pecuniary benefits of his scheme; and, the elder man having led the way, his trusty adherent felt, in a measure, bound to follow him. As soon as

Reginald declared his intention to marry, the other felt it to be fashionable, — a species of social duty which he must neglect no longer; just as he had previously supposed gay bachelorhood to be the finest form of existence.

It must truly be a wonderful relief to have one's life squared and measured by the simple rule of following the lead of some one else ; and the ability and necessity of thinking for one's self has serious penalties, from which, at times, one would willingly be exempt.

To whatever Reginald announced as the proper course, Lloyd responded amen, — even in so grave a matter as taking a wife. The more he considered the plan, the more feasible and pleasant it appeared, until he worked himself into almost an enthusiasm on the subject. Meeting Reginald soon after, he accompanied him home, and devoted himself almost as openly and ardently to Ellen as Christie's lover did to her.

Thus he laid siege to the fortress he intended to capture.

CHAPTER X.

THE fourth day before the time appointed for tho
wedding had arrived, and still Tom had not
brought himself to speak to Christie upon the subject
of securing her fortune to herself ; indeed, had scarcely found strength and courage to speak to her at all.
But he felt that the attempt must be made ; that in
this matter he had no right to spare himself any
longer.

He had managed so successfully to avoid meeting
her, that when he came home an hour earlier than
usual, and sent word he wished to see her, the girl
came down stairs eagerly and gladly to greet him.

" Tom," she exclaimed, entering the room, her face
all smiles and brightness, and her voice thrilling with
pleasure, " I had begun to think I should never see
you again. Have you been so swallowed up in business that you could not give me a little of your time,
even during the last week I shall be here ? " she
asked, with the old quick gesture of putting out her
hand as she spoke.

Tom had been standing with his clasped behind him, gazing out of the window, when she entered. At her words he turned round, but kept his hands tightly locked as before ; thus securing the resistance of the temptation to take the soft palm which was offered him.

"I am very glad to see you, Christie," he said quietly ; and then stopped a moment, thinking how far too glad he was, and wondering whether the gnawing pain at his heart would grow utterly unendurable, or whether he would be able to bear it during the five-minutes' conversation which would probably ensue.

"I have not been able to spend much time with you lately, as I have been very much engrossed," he went on steadily, after an almost imperceptible pause, disregarding, as far as he could, the sorrowful shade of disappointment which came into the large, uplifted eyes at his reticent, cool address ; " but I have come home this afternoon to say something to you which I think ought to be said.   Will you sit down and listen to me ? "

He placed a chair, and she silently took it, surprised at his expression, and vaguely wondering what might be coming.

Standing before her with that concentrated look in his face, as though holding himself to his purpose, ho went on to explain his meaning.

"I told you, Christie," he proceeded slowly, as though he had thought over and predetermined his words, and wished her to take in their full force, "that I would be your brother; and, in what I am about to do, I ask you to believe and remember that I think I am acting a brother's part. If your father were here, he would settle that which it now falls to my lot to arrange. But you are alone in the world." (It was fine to see the girl's eyes flash, and her cheeks glow, to hear herself called alone in the world, — she, the elect of all women, the beloved of Reginald Archer; who, in possessing him, possessed all things.) "I am compelled to seem to meddle in your affairs. I am constrained to take up that, which, let me assure you, is a very unpleasant duty."

He was emphatic upon that point in his concentrated earnestness; for he grew more sore every moment to think that he was forced to appear before her in the light of a coarse intruder; that she would remember him as a shadow upon her happiest hours; as one who had brought sordid, pecuniary considerations into her holiest, highest sentiments.

He had determined to state his purpose as immediately and in as few words as possible; and he proceeded to do so.

"Before your marriage, I want you to let me have your fortune settled upon yourself, so that no mischance can ever reduce you to poverty; so that you may have a certain independence of action always secured to you. I ask you to empower me to act in your father's place, and to see that his child's future is made safe against all hazard."

The girl rose to her feet. There was such splendid indignation in her eyes, such an enthusiasm of contempt for his proposition, that Tom's heart swelled with admiration for the fair, generous young creature before him.

"If you think my father would have asked me to do that which would imply an utter lack of faith and trust in the man I profess to love, you must have known as little of him as you seem to do of his daughter," the clear voice rang out. "Do you imagine I would offer Reginald such an insult? that I would even appear to divide our fates? Why, it is my privilege and my glory that I can give him all I have in the world, and that he thinks it worthy of his acceptance. Do you ask me to deprive myself of this happiness? When I give him myself, would I withhold any miserable money I can bring with me? If you think such a thing possible, you understand me very little; for it can never, never be. And Tom, Tom! to think that you should ask me to do any thing mean and faithless! — you, whom I believed in so entirely!"

And the girl's voice broke down from its proud anger with a little wailing sob, which smote her listener to the heart.

It was the first jar upon her faith in humanity; the first abrasion of her trust in mankind, which was to wear away so surely and steadily; the first striking of a bare nerve, whose constant thrill was to be the most familiar suffering, the true torture of her life.

"Christie!" Tom broke out, "I knew you would misjudge me in this way; but I thought it right to warn you, regardless of any personal pain. I entreat you to remember that I am older than you, and know men far better; and, in the face of all you have said and can say, I implore you to follow my advice."

"Why will you go on insulting me in this way?" she flashed out, her anger rising again, and what she held to be her righteous wrath overcoming her sorrow. "If I were capable of such an act, I should despise myself for it!" she exclaimed, the words passing beyond her lips and her self-control: "as it is, I despise you for tempting me to it!"

As Christ drove the money-changers out of the temple, so she cast even the shadow of a sordid thought out of the holy sanctuary of her perfect love and faith.

If she had struck Tom in the face, he would have flinched less than he did at that one word, while the

color could have sprung no more hotly to his cheeks.
He set his teeth as he answered her: —

"I have finished: I shall try no further. You have
made your own decision, and must abide the result.
Hitherto," he went on with dogged desperation, "I
have been able to pray from the depths of my heart
that you might live and die in blessed blindness; and
you cannot tempt me to wish that light may burst
upon you in all its dreadful power, compelling you
to see what I see now. But, Christie," — and, un-
clasping those tightly-locked hands for the first time,
he put them upon her shoulders, and held her firm
while he spoke his last sentence, — "as surely as we
stand here, you will learn the truth. I demand that
you shall then remember this hour, and do me tardy
justice; at least, in your own heart. I appeal from
this judgment-day to that; and I can afford to await
the verdict."

And, without another word, he left her.

Almost maddened by the blow she had struck him,
nearly savage with pain, and sense of wrong, he
was still conscious of an absolute enthusiasm for the
woman who could be so unworldly; who could feel
such indignation, and spurn from her that which she
imagined to be meanness, as though it were vile con-
tamination. Blinded and mistaken, she was, nevertheless, right by a higher law than earthly wisdom;

she held to a truth which was better than fact; and Tom's aching heart throbbed with a love for her, a high, pure pride in her, which had never before filled it. As soon as the first wild thrill from her stroke had passed from his frame, he more than forgave her; he gloried in her for having dealt it. She had enshrined herself in a more exalted place in his thoughts; and he bowed in humbler, more reverent worship than ever. This almost divine folly of trusting youth, this injustice of blessed ignorance, seemed to him priceless, as guaranteeing the truth and honor of a heart that might never be his.

He was experiencing what Corinne meant when she said, "I would far rather lose my love than my admiration;" which is the cry of all natures in which conscience and intellect hold indestructible places. To respect, to admire, to adore freely and utterly, is the dearest joy of which they are capable. That which they worship must be pure and spotless, or their devotion vanishes, and secret pity, if not contempt, takes its place. If they find their idol in the dust, or discover earth-stains upon it, the real chain which bound them breaks, though their hearts break with it. They love with their souls; and their souls must be satisfied.

Christie and Tom were one day to learn how akin they were in this matter; that the love of each must

be fed from a higher source than mere animal gratification, sentiment, even emotion, or it dies. This is,
to such natures, the real death: the physical dissolution which follows sooner or later is to them of little
consequence. I hold Tom Archer, bereft of all hope
and joy, to have been a thrice fortunate and happy
being, in that he could absolutely respect the person
he loved.

He himself realized this so thoroughly, that he
could meet Christie an hour or two after with no
bitterness in his sore heart, or in his grave, quiet manner. Dark days were to roll over Christie's head, and
a weary road was to be traversed, before she could
comprehend him as he comprehended her; before she
could attain such clearness of sight. At present, she
did him all the passionate injustice of an undisci-
plined heart and an inexperienced brain.

As soon as he left her, she ran swiftly up stairs,
and, locking herself in her room, threw herself upon
the bed in a burst of weeping, which arose partly
from nervous re-action, but still more from the pain
of the first shock her faith had ever received. That
Tom should fail her, and fall so far below what she
thought him, — if that could be, what else might not
give way at any moment? In her temporary depression, she felt as though every thing were slipping
from her grasp. It was her first lesson in distrust;

and she found it very, very hard. Utter doubt of God and man was the creed she was destined to learn with terrible thoroughness, and then, thank Heaven! to unlearn forever.

She lay there, sad and half sick, until she suddenly remembered Reginald would soon come, and that she must go down to meet him.

She started up hastily to bathe her eyes and to wash away the traces of her tears. The thought that Reginald might demand the cause of her emotion, and in some way gain a hint of the subject of the conversation between Tom and herself, made her blush with shame. She shrank from having the idea of money suggested between them, even as the thought of another. She wished to save Reginald from the knowledge that his brother had stooped so far, as well as to shield their love from even the shadow of a mercenary consideration.

So she bathed and perfumed and powdered her face, with an industry and earnestness which were piteously amusing when one considered their object.

She succeeded quite well in her purpose, but not so thoroughly as to deceive the acute eyes of either brother when the three met at the dinner-table. Tom did not need any explanation of what he saw before him: he well knew what had produced this effect, and a certain quiet change in her manner towards him. He had counted on its coming, and was neither surprised nor outwardly discomposed at its appearance. As for Reginald, having an infinite disgust for scenes except of a certain sort, and perceiving very soon that her emotion, whatever might be its cause, did not refer to him or endanger his chances of her fortune, he systematically took no notice, and sedulously avoided the bore of an explanation. The tender anxiety and jealous scrutiny of a true lover Christie had not greatly to fear, though she had taken such vast pains to blind them.

A somewhat keener insight into human nature might have spared her exertion, both in these days and those which immediately followed them.

CHAPTER XI.

LLOYD TRUXTON dined with the Archers that evening; and the final arrangements for the wedding were discussed and decided upon.

In consideration of Christie's mourning, it was to be a quiet affair. Only a few old friends were invited to the wedding-breakfast; after which the bride and groom were to go off on a tour of sufficient length to give time for furnishing the magnificent residence which Reginald had secured as their future home. Ellen and Lloyd were to act as bridesmaid and groomsman, greatly to the satisfaction of each; and the planning of the small details of the occasion kept all those personally interested occupied and eager, full of business and conversation, for hours.

Tom sat silently by, apparently listening, but really thinking his own weary thoughts. The work of the past week was very evident upon the face thus left open for scrutiny. Accidentally glancing towards him, Christie recognized for the first time how worn and haggard was his appearance. She had no idea of the real cause : but she felt that the outbreak of the afternoon must have additionally depressed an anxious, troubled man ; and she repented having added a burden he was evidently ill able to bear. Looking at him again and again, her womanly heart softened and melted. He had sorely disappointed her. In her childish ignorance of life and of his motives, she imagined that he had fallen forever in her estimation ; but she was sorry she had hurt him. From the spirit of what she had said, she did not waver in the least ; she had no shadow of regret on that point : there was but one course open to her in the matter, and she had taken it. But she wished now that she had put her meaning into less vehement words ; that she had been less violent and personal in her reply. While he was eagerly urging his proposition, she thought only of resisting it by any and all means : now she witnessed their effect with pain, and began to wish for some method of reconciliation.

The arrangements had apparently been completed, when a thought struck Maria.

"By the way, who is to give away the bride ? We haven't decided that yet."

"Why, Tom, of course," answered Lloyd. "He is so entirely the proper person, that I never thought of questioning it."

At the words, three of his hearers made sudden movements.

Tom awoke, as it were, and gave a quick, vehement gesture of dissent.

Reginald turned towards him with a curious expression of countenance, but, for the moment, said nothing. He never wantonly hurt Tom, — the only person in the world he hesitated to trample upon for his slightest convenience. His sentiment towards his brother, though one of purely mental appreciation, was evidently his nearest approach to an emotion. His acuteness was such, that, heartless himself, he comprehended perfectly what the situation must be to a man who possessed a heart. He had taken the woman Tom loved from him because he held her necessary to himself; but he had no wish to do his brother any petty injury, or to aggravate the misery of his position if he could well afford to avoid it. Consequently, Reginald remained silent, and did not immediately throw his influence in the scale against Tom.

Christie had also turned eagerly, and now spoke out earnestly in reply to the negative gesture.

"O Tom! I am sure you will do it for us," she exclaimed, coming up to him, delighted to have a chance to speak kindly, to make friends with him again. "There is no one in the world I should like so well to do that service for me. I have none of my own blood to call upon, and not a friend in the city outside of this house," she added rather piteously.

"Why, Tom, I can't imagine how you can hesitate in the matter!" said Maria almost impatiently.

"I am not accustomed to making public appearances; I should probably spoil the artistic effect of your arrangements," he answered with rather a bitter smile. "You had better have some one more used to such things.   Reginald has plenty of fine friends, with commanding figures and sonorous voices, who would be glad to serve him on the occasion."

"How can you talk so?" exclaimed Maria. "They are not Christie's friends, and would be entirely out of place. It is your proper position; and it will look very singular if you do not fill it."

"Tom, I am sure you won't refuse," Christie broke in again, "when you recollect that it is the last request I shall make of you."

The blood flushed up into the man's face at the words and the pleading tone in which they were uttered. He wavered visibly.

"I am afraid you will have to oblige us in this matter," said Reginald at last. "The family honor requires it, and you will have to lay another sacrifice upon the altar of duty." He laughed slightly as he spoke, but, nevertheless, watched his brother closely.

"Well," said Tom hastily, "I suppose it must be so." And then he gave that slight movement with his hand which he so often used to prevent further discussion of a subject.

"They thus understood it; for after Christie had said pleasantly, "Thank you, Tom; we are both very much obliged to you," they returned to their old places and previous conversation.

The wedding-presents which Reginald Archer received within the two days preceding his marriage were a sight to witness. They were so numerous and magnificent, that even that self-complacent gentleman was astonished. Each person felt called upon to send something in proportion, not to Reginald's past *status*, but to his coming splendor. On such occasions, the gifts seem to be graded in exact inverse ratio to the needs of the recipient. The fashionable world is far too pious not to follow the biblical example of giving, to him who has ten talents, ten other talents; and of taking, from him who has none, even that which he has. Reginald had passed from the latter position to the former, and was receiving appropriately-different treatment. If his kind friends had presented him with the equivalent cash, he might have lived upon it in luxury for a long period.

Except that the wedding-ceremony seemed the only key to the coffers of his acquaintances, he might have made friendship, instead of matrimony, his means of support. The magnetism of his coming wealth, and the force of fashion, had drawn gold from pockets which would have been very securely fastened against all other extractive powers.

There is nothing in which the inherent snobbishness of human nature is more fully exemplified than in this matter of wedding-presents. On other occasions, the same principle is, no doubt, equally active ; but it does not equally prank itself up, and attract attention by assuming airs and graces. Ordinarily, it puts on its apron, as it were, and does its dirty work at home ; but on such holiday-times it arrays itself in gorgeous apparel, and seems to cry, " Come and look at me as I go through my genuflexions and offer my prayers and my gifts at the altar of Mammon!" Few weddings, indeed, take place, at which a sermon might not be preached, and a satire spoken, over the presents.

Reginald perceived the satire, if not the sermon, in his own case.

An offering of unusual magnificence had been brought in, and, after much girlish admiration, had been carried off to be put among the other gifts. Reginald watched the departing present with the queer smile which so often found place in his eyes. Glancing, a moment after, towards Tom, the only other occupant of the room, he saw the shadow of his own thought in his brother's face.

Reginald broke out into delighted laughter, charmed, as he always was, at their mutual recognition of the humor of any situation. He declared Tom was the only person he could securely count upon to see the fun of any thing. He saved his brightest sayings for him, and, if he fell into a good thing in talking to any one else, felt that it had not fulfilled its mission until he had repeated it to Tom, had seen his mouth twitch with appreciation, and received his dry comment in reply.

"Tom," he said after a moment, "do you remember that instructive little incident in the history of Job, — how, after he had fought through all his poverty and troubles, and become richer and more prosperous than ever, then, and not until then, his friends and relations came to see him, and brought each man of them a piece of money and an ear-ring of gold? I have always regarded it as one of the finest touches of truth to human nature in all literature. It really is remarkable to perceive, not only how little humanity has altered, but how perfectly this charming custom has been preserved to the present day."

And he went off into soft inward laughter, as

though rolling his amusement like a sweet morsel under his tongue.

"Yes," answered Tom rather grimly, "I can un-understand your appreciation of Job's feelings on that occasion."

"Precisely," returned the other. "Why, the very man who sent that present slipped out of the club not a month ago to avoid meeting me, for fear I should ask him to lend me money!—which was so much unnecessary exertion on his part; for you know, Tom,"—and here Reginald's eyes twinkled, and his voice broke again into laughter,—"that I almost always gave you the preference on such occasions, and seldom hurt your feelings by turning to strangers."

"No," responded his brother somewhat sardonically: "it must be admitted, that, in that matter at least, you have faithfully stood by your family."

"Well, never mind, old fellow! all that will be over when I am married," Reginald exclaimed carelessly.

The change that came over Tom's face, though faint, was so expressive of the throb at his heart, that even this selfish, self-absorbed man recognized it, and hesitated before it. He quickly returned to the subject they had been discussing.

"Would you believe it?—one of those silver

pitchers came from a person, who, not a long while since, got up and left the room because I trod on his moral toes! I thought that right enough, if he did not like my way of thinking and talking; but it strikes me as a little peculiar that he should recognize so suddenly my merits and my claims. It is a pleasant, consistent world we live in," he wound up with radiant good temper and charmed sense of humor over that which would have caused a deeper-natured man to sigh, or to smile bitterly.

"If I had known the extent to which my friends' purses were at my service, it would scarcely have been necessary for me to marry as a provision in life," he was about to exclaim in gay mockery; but, suddenly remembering to whom he was speaking, he caught himself in time not to thrust his marriage and its mercenary motive again in Tom's face, and so let the subject drop.

CHAPTER XII.

MARIA, Ellen, and Arnold had each given Christie gifts, bought, of course, with Tom's money, and, at his express private injunction, as handsome as could be procured.

But, as yet, he had given her nothing in his own name.

The night before the marriage, he entered the parlor with a small box, held almost hidden in the palm of his hand. Maria, Ellen, and Lloyd Truxton, were leaning upon the piano, upon which some newly-arrived presents had been placed ; while upon a sofa, at a little distance, sat Christie and Reginald.

The girl was looking up at her lover with a pure, tender adoration in the sweet eyes, that a man with a heart and a conscience might willingly have spent a lifetime in striving to deserve. As it was, the person to whom it was directed received it with outward tranquillity. Numberless eyes had looked what they called love into his : hot glances and long burning gazes he had drunk in like fiery wine ; but their heat and brilliancy were caught from a far different flame, — from hell-fire, rather than heaven's light. He remembered them as he sat there, and drew the comparison for himself; and, doing so, calmly and deliberately decided that he preferred the lurid glare to the soft sunshine then being shed upon him.

" Fresh air is certainly not my native atmosphere, and I must have something to drink with a little more taste in it than pure water," he thought, acknowledging to himself his entire unfitness for any wholesome, natural life.

" This *nurseriness* is certainly very pretty, and I suppose there are persons who would find it agreeable; but really it is too much, or rather too little, for me." And he mentally yawned in unutterable weariness.

But, with practical good sense, he fell to regarding the material compensations of his marriage, and took comfort. Thus doing, he looked down at the girl so near him with an ineffable expression, which left her nothing to wish for on this side of heaven.

Tom entered, and saw them before him.

He had need to be the strong man he was to enable him to walk quietly up to them, and speak in his usual straightforward manner. His brother's presence suited him, as that which he had to say was intended as pointedly for the man as for the girl;

and he wished both to remember his words and his meaning.

They looked up as he stood before them.

"Christie," he said, "I have brought you a little gift. I want you to wear it, and, when you look at it, to remember me, and my promise to be your true brother under all circumstances."

As he finished speaking, his glance left Christie; and he and his brother looked straight at each other.

"Recollect, this girl, alone and friendless as she seems, has one head and hand enlisted for ever in her service; and, for your acts towards her, you will have to reckon with them," was what Tom's look said, as plainly as words could have put it.

An almost imperceptible movement of Reginald's eyes seemed to sign the contract; to answer,—

"I am aware of the fact, and I accept the condition."

"I do not require the presence of any gift to keep me in mind of all your kindness, Tom," Christie exclaimed quickly, unconscious of look or meaning other than appeared on the surface.

Then she sprang up, and came under the chandelier to see what the small parcel contained. The rest gathered eagerly around her, curious to know what Tom had brought.

As she lifted the top of the box, the light flashed upon a diamond cross, of such size and beauty that the whole party broke out in one half-inarticulate exclamation of surprise and admiration. Even Reginald was startled out of his tranquil toleration of things in general.

"It is perfectly beautiful!" he said. "Upon my word, Tom, you give *en prince*. But you always did that," he added with magnificent but somewhat cheap gratitude, considering their past monetary relations.

"Tom, I never saw any thing so lovely in my life!" cried Christie, with eyes as brilliant as the jewels from which she looked up. "I don't know how to thank you."

She made a slight step forward, as though with some idea of expressing by a kiss that which she did not know how to put into words: but Tom turned slightly from her, as though unconscious of her intention; and she fell back with the same sense of repulse she had experienced several times during the preceding week.

"I am glad you are pleased," he rejoined with that weary quietude which had become his habitual manner. "I like diamonds, not only because they are so bright and clear, but because nothing can render them otherwise; because no contact with impurity can make them impure. I sometimes wonder, when I look at persons," — he added slowly, as though he were speaking more to himself than to them, and looking at Christie, in spite of himself, with the wistful questioning of an infinite sadness and tenderness, which must have given the girl some hint of his secret, had she not been wrapped in an enchanted dream, — "whether they are like snow, which is merely fair and white until soil touches it, and amalgamates with it; or whether they are like diamonds, which nothing can really contaminate. This is the one dreadful doubt in life, and seems to me the great, essential difference between persons."

And this time he turned quickly and entirely away with what would have been a shuddering sigh, had he not stopped it almost before it had birth.

"They remind me of dewdrops," said Ellen, taking them in her hand, and looking very prettily sentimental over them; while she was thinking in her secret heart how devoutly she hoped Tom would see fit to present her with something equally splendid when she came to be married, or sooner, if he thought proper.

"I am glad he has given her such a handsome present; for now he can't do less, and he will probably do more, for his own sister," she meditated.

Ellen's mind was of an eminently practical cast,

and enabled her to escape unpleasant pangs of jealousy by a fine, far-reaching perception of her own interest.

" They remind me of tears, — a cross of tears," said Maria softly, almost under her breath.

" Maria, hush ! " exclaimed Tom, as though she hurt him, " or you will make me regard my gift as an evil omen, and wish to take it back."

" No," said Christie earnestly, — and this time she put out her hand steadily to Tom, — " I shall wear it without any fear, dear Tom ; for it will always have the association you have given it : it will mean to me a purity which can dread no assimilation with evil, because it has nothing in common with evil."

Gazing at the girl's face with its radiant courage of perfect innocence, but, alas ! of perfect ignorance also, the fear at Tom's heart passed away for a moment. But he had learned the awful power of companionship ; and the dread of what she must almost inevitably become, through breathing Reginald's moral atmosphere, soon resumed its dominion over him. It held its sway ; when he answered with a grave sadness, —

" If it retain that meaning for you, Christie, I shall indeed think I have given you a good gift ; but, if the talisman lose its power, I warn you I shall know it even sooner than you do," he added suddenly, so

7 *

full of his own thoughts, that he forgot she could not follow them nor his intention.

The girl's puzzled look of astonishment brought him back to himself.

"I did not mean to frighten you, my dear," he said, the red blood coming into his face as he saw Christie's slight shrinking and Reginald's glance of comprehension; "but I shall be very glad if my cross will bring back a recollection of me and as many good thoughts as can come with it. Good-night!" he concluded, in comprehensive adieu to the party, and left the room.

The rest soon followed, leaving Reginald and Christie together to take their last parting before they twain should be one flesh.

"I shall say good-night to you now, darling; for you must go to sleep very soon, as you will have a fatiguing day to-morrow, and will need all your strength," Reginald said in a very few minutes, in apparent tender consideration for her, and in real consideration for himself.

He was weary with acting, with keeping up appearances before her: moreover, he wanted to go down to the club and meet some friends.

"It is the last time we shall have to part, dearest," he whispered as he took her in his arms; and the face upon his breast crimsoned with happy blushes.

" By to-morrow night you will be my precious little wife, and we need never separate."

" The tone, and quick, passionate pressure as he spoke, were triumphs of dramatic instinct ; of a certain intellectual fidelity which led him to omit no point he considered in character. He satisfied his own taste and critical judgment, and mentally furnished his own applause, doing his work with the enthusiasm of a true artist.

" Reginald," said Christie a moment after, raising her head in her impetuous fashion, and speaking with a hurried breathlessness which showed her embarrassment and difficulty in putting her meaning into words, " I am afraid, that, when I am your wife, you will be miserably disappointed in me. You are so utterly beyond me in every thing, so noble and grand and good, that I can never be like you. But I will try very hard : and oh ! my darling, be patient with me ; for I love you so dearly, so dearly ! "

The trust and faith, the almost divine aspiration, that was in the uplifted face, silenced even Reginald Archer. He saw, like a revelation, just what her coming life must be : he comprehended just what he seemed to her now, and how his real character and past life would strike her when she saw them in their true light. Such was his perception, that he understood a situation and a nature with neither of which he had any thing in common ; and, doing so, there came over him the nearest approach to the emotion of pity of which he was capable.

That the virtue of the woman before him was radical, that no temptation could shake it, he did not think, believing it true of no woman under the sun ; but he saw that she was as yet utterly ignorant of evil, and he knew that the tremendous shock of being brought into personal contact with sin in any being she loved would inevitably come upon her. As Tom had said, years before, he was " to give his wife her first lesson in actual evil." He recognized the fact, that her sudden, close introduction to the world, the flesh, and the devil, incarnated in him, would be a trying ordeal, a revolution in all her preconceived ideas. That she would settle down to circumstances, and, incited by his past and present example, learn to join hands with that trinity in pleasant good-fellowship, he had no doubt ; but he was quite sorry for what she must first go through, regretting the necessity as he did that of all disturbing occurrences. This conviction, that her shock and scruples would soon pass away, and her life and character rapidly approximate to a comfortable level with his own, almost instantly re-assured him : so with a kiss, and the sweetest tranquillity of mind and manner, he answered, —

" My little pet will not try my patience, I am sure. I am not at all alarmed on the subject."

" It is no use to open any discussion in the matter," he thought, " even if I could mention such things to her, and if I could afford to tell her the truth. She would comprehend it too little to prepare her for the realization which must come; and, indeed, I cannot afford the risk, as it is quite possible she might refuse to marry me even now. There is really no measuring the folly of what they call good women; and, ignorance being bliss in this as in most cases, I certainly shall not deprive her of the blessing sooner than is necessary."

He fell back upon mute caresses as the safest mode of communication under the circumstances; and finally, with a kiss and a few appropriately sweet words of adieu, left her.

The girl went to her chamber to offer up pure, loving prayers for him before she fell into her childlike slumber; and he, lighting a cigar, walked slowly down to his club, thinking coolly and philosophically of the scene he had just left.

" Upon my word," he calmly considered, " it *is* a rather hard case when a woman supposes she is marrying a saint, and discovers afterwards that he is a sinner; when she imagines she is allying herself with one man, and finds herself tied for life to an entirely different person. It never struck me before; for most of the women I have known have had too much experimental knowledge to be capable of any delusions on the subject. But, for any one as ignorant of ordinary existence as this girl, the enlightenment which such a marriage brings must be rather overwhelming," he went on with that interest and impartial justice with which he viewed any fresh problem. "If a man were to make the same discovery, I suppose he would feel called upon to shoot her or himself: if he found out that she had taken even one step upon the path I have always trodden, he would have the whole world sympathizing with his wounded honor, and justifying him in any degree of abhorrence and vengeance. He would probably send her to the right-about, as though contaminating his name and station, even though he had committed the same sin himself countless times; whereas, if this poor child complains of my past life, and allows it to affect her conduct towards me, she will be laughed at for her pains, and considered a morbidly sentimental young person. What a farce it all is!" and the soft, sweet laughter, which was one of Reginald Archer's chief charms, stirred the quiet night. "Both the girl and the man would, according to my way of thinking, be fools to expect any thing but what they found, or to care particularly on the subject; but I really can't see what greater right of complaint one has than the other."

And then he smoked his cigar quietly for some time, in a state of gentle resignation at his inability to square his perceptions with generally-accepted social tenets.

Like most selfish men, he disliked the sight of pain, as unpleasant to himself; and the fact that his wife, whom he must see more or less, would, for a time, be miserable, and show it, gave him an un-doubted sense of discomfort.

"This marriage of mine is absurdly incongruous," he thought, with mingled amusement and faint annoyance. "It is a pity I could not let Tom have her; or that I could not afford, pecuniarily or socially, to marry a woman on my own moral level. Gertrude would really have suited me much better, for she could have taken care of herself; and there was no special contrast between our lives and characters," he went on, alluding to his mistress of the year before, — a woman who had spent her life on hire at so much a month, for the sake of a finer dress, a better dinner, a softer bed, and an idler existence, than she could have gained by any honest alliance in her own low station.

"We certainly had far more in common, both in

taste and experience, than Christie and I can have for a long time to come; but I suppose society would have held up its hands in horror at my legal connection with such a woman, though it winked comfortably at my illegal one. However, I have no idea of suffering martyrdom for women here, whatever may come hereafter: so I marry money and position, and let the future take care of itself. Christie will soon get over her inexperience, and console herself like other women; especially as I shall be neither so selfish nor so unfair as to prevent her from enjoying any of the privileges or pleasures I have claimed for myself, and found so agreeable."

With this reflection, and the calm satisfaction of the just, he went up the steps of the club-house, and disappeared within, to spend the last hours of the evening with his intimate associates.

CHAPTER XIII.

CHRISTIE MACALASTER'S wedding-day rose
as fair and unclouded as her outward beauty
and inward happiness. The golden sunshine of the
morning bathed all things in glory, and roused all
nature to life and joy. The birds sang; the summer breezes stole through the trees, whose leafy tops
swayed towards each other, and seemed to murmur
love songs and secrets in their soft cadences. All
tokens were in keeping with the appearance of this
marriage, which youth, beauty, wealth, health, and
hope united to render brilliant. It seemed an ideally
perfect union: what it was, time would show.

The world, at least, appeared to consider the match
a most suitable one, and smiled upon and congratulated the fortunate pair, in whom all the elements
of happiness were conjoined.

One man alone seemed to remember that purity
and honor could not sit at this wedding-feast; that a
sinful past must hold place there, casting its shadow
not merely over the present, but far into the future.

That chastity and truth were lacking; that the broken law of God brings its own consequence with absolute inevitability; that as we sow, thus we must reap, — all this apparently troubled no one except the person whose burden and sorrow were heavy enough, God knows, without it.

Of the hundreds of women who were that morning eagerly discussing Reginald Archer's marriage, there were not many who would have refused to change places with Christie, though knowing, but far from realizing, what Reginald's life had been, and what it had necessarily made him. Women marry men with apparent disregard for their lack of purity, — sometimes because they know too little, and sometimes because they know too much. With one class, it is the seeming indifference of ignorance; with the other, it is the real carelessness of experimental knowledge and natural taste. With both orders men like Reginald Archer are particularly successful, though in different ways. And there were many foolish, blinded, but not impure hearts, among those who looked kindly upon that groom, and envied the bride her place at his side, — women who would have realized the misery of a granted prayer, had their wish been given them. Seeing only what is elegant and attractive in a successful *roué*, they cannot believe such beautiful sin to be very sinful; or that, as is inevitably the case, it is a radical part of the nature. They build an ideal from outward appearances, and worship it, only to have their dream dissipated, and to learn that evil is the one utterly hideous, cruel fact in the universe.

A curious variety of beings awoke that morning with this marriage as their first thought. Men who admired and imitated him, — who had followed his example to the ruin of soul, body, and estate ; women who had adored him, or who adored him still ; others whom he had inspired with passion, or a sentiment of flattered vanity, or any of the numerous emotions which are classed under the generic term of " love ; " numbers of other persons whom curiosity, his reputation, and the wealth of his bride, interested in the matter, — each and all remembered in their waking moment that this was Reginald's wedding - day. Sore hearts and light ones, passionate feeling and trivial interest, smothered revengeful anger, and smiling good will and good wishes, the highest blood and fashion of the land, and members of the *demi-monde*, — all these found room in the crowd which assembled in the solemn old church in which Reginald Archer and Christie Macalaster were to be made man and wife. It was the social event of the season ; and consequently the unbidden guests were almost numberless : but a strange variety of emotions were hidden under the obedience to fashion which apparently brought them thither.

An equal difference displayed itself in the feelings and actions of those more closely connected with the marriage.

Reginald rose calmly, at his usual late hour, giving himself his ordinary time to dress and to breakfast with extreme comfort. He never allowed himself to be either hurried or delayed in these important operations.

" Reginald, you remind me of Goethe's expression, ' Never hasting, never resting, like a star,' " said Tom one day, when he had watched his brother enjoying his meal with tranquillity under rather trying circumstances.

" Which means, my dear boy," answered the other, " that I have learned the true science of living, and the really important point in life. I never allow my comfort to be interfered with. I see persons occasionally who are anxious about their souls ; but I spend my care and pains upon my body, and I find myself repaid more visibly and immediately."

" Upon my word, I think you are right," exclaimed Tom ; " for I believe you have nothing else."

" Exactly ! " Reginald responded with the utmost pleasantness. " My physical frame is all that I am at all sure of : so I treat it well, and gain as much as possible from it." And he certainly had the merit of living up to his doctrine.

He had so perfected his routine, that, even upon his wedding - morning, it admitted of no improvement; and not the slightest agitation marred it or his manner. He surveyed himself leisurely and critically in the glass; and, without vanity, decided that he had never looked better. His costume he knew to be faultless; and so all shade of anxiety left his mind.

Experience seems to show that handsome men are far less vain than ugly ones. They become accustomed to their own beauty and its effect, and gradually forget both. Having the tranquillity of certainty, their minds are not led back to the subject by doubt; and it is a fact, that Reginald Archer thought less of his own appearance that morning than did any one of the hundreds of persons who looked at him.

Ellen was the only other individual in that household who breakfasted at just her usual hour, and with her usual appetite. Then she retreated to the sacred shades of her own room in company with a hairdresser and a maid, and was not seen again until the bridal party assembled before starting for the church; when she appeared in a costume which it had taken her dressmaker days and days to manufacture, and herself hours to assume. But the result was worth the trouble; for it rendered her beautiful. She passed the same verdict upon herself as she scanned the effect of her labors, and hoped to read fresh evidence of the fact in Lloyd Truxton's eyes. It was for his final subjugation, in addition to her desire for general admiration, that she had worked; not knowing that he had made up his mind to ask her to marry him upon far more solid grounds than any passing phase of her beauty. But she had her wish in exciting his admiration; for he met her not only with a gallant compliment, but with a look which said much more than the words, and gave them their value.

As for Maria, neither she nor any one else knew whether she took any breakfast that morning. After giving general household directions for the comfort of every one else, she hurriedly dressed for the wedding, and dismissed herself entirely from her own mind. She knew she appeared as a lady should; and that was all for which she really cared. She might have been aware, also, that she was a very fine-looking woman, strikingly like Tom, with his waving hair and bright dark eyes, and so could afford to dispense with anxiety in the matter. Then she went to Christie's room to devote the rest of the time to her.

" 'Happy is the bride the sun shines on,' Christie dear," was her salutation as she took the half-dressed girl in her arms and kissed her very tenderly.

The sunbeams were streaming through the vine-shaded windows, and dancing upon the floor; and all things within and without were radiant with the brightness of the summer weather: but it was the light in Christie's face which seemed to illumine her.

" Child, you look so happy, you scare me ! " exclaimed Maria involuntarily.

Christie gave her a slightly-startled glance, a shade coming over her face.

" No, no ! I didn't mean what I said," the other suddenly retracted, as she saw and regretted the effect of her words. " Be as happy as you can, my darling; and I pray God you may always be so. And now let us see if we can make you look any lovelier than you do now," she added gayly to change the conversation; and was soon engrossed in that momentous question.

Maria had had her own doubts concerning this marriage, which, like Tom, she had kept to herself, from a hopelessness of doing any good by expressing them. As is almost always the case with men's female relatives, she was ignorant of the active criminality of Reginald's life; but, of the inner character formed by that life, each day gave her evidence in some almost unconscious word, look, or tone. She had the family acuteness of perception, and not only saw that her brother was utterly selfish, but felt, rather than knew, that he was a bad man in more ways than one. This consciousness had secretly overcast her joy at Christie's becoming her sister, and made her regard the girl from time to time with an indefinable sentiment of pity and anxiety.

"It is like a day that is too bright to last. I am afraid the clouds will come before noon, — certainly before night. I fear trouble must come to Reginald's wife, let her be what she will; and how is this poor child to bear it?" the woman was thinking, in her kind, honest heart, as she turned her kind, honest face, with its brightest smile, towards the girl she was arraying.

The tender beauty of the young face, the perfect purity and gladness which shone from it like a halo, touched this good woman inexpressibly. With not many years dividing them, a wide difference of experience and character made her feel towards the orphan-girl almost as her own mother might have done. An infinite desire to protect and shelter and aid her filled Maria; but it was with a consciousness of entire helplessness. It is in such moments of need and weakness that women carry those they love to the strong arms of the great Father; that they appeal to the only love which is mightier than theirs. In the midst of all this happiness and prosperity, Maria's instinct told her of past sin and coming sorrow: it vaguely forewarned her of danger and disaster which as yet were not. An impulse she could neither control nor explain, but upon which she looked back with astonishment before another year had rolled round, prompted her next act.

Christie's toilet was nearly complete, and Maria was giving it a few last touches, when she said to one of the servants,—

"Go down stairs and tell Mr. Reginald that we will be with him in a few moments;" and, turning to the other attendants, dismissed them upon trivial pretexts.

Going quietly to the door, she closed it, and, returning, met the girl entirely ready, about to descend.

"Stop a moment, Christie," she said nervously, her face flushing, the tears coming into her eyes, and her tone deepening ·with the smothered earnestness with which she spoke. "Say a prayer, my child, before you go: say 'Our Father;' say 'Lead us not into temptation, but deliver us from evil;' and 'Forgive us our trespasses as we forgive those who trespass against us.'" And the woman's voice broke utterly with the last word.

The appeal went straight from one heart to the other. The girl's face flushed and her lips quivered as the elder woman's had done. The next moment, without a word, she knelt down in her flowing bridal robe, with the white veil covering her beauty like mist, and the sweet, fresh blossoms falling about her dress. Thinking of it afterwards, and of that up-lifted, innocent face, Maria remembered that other wedding-garment of which Christ speaks as worn by those who were bidden to the marriage of the king's son, and which those must wear who enter the kingdom of heaven. At Maria's knee, as in her childish days at that of her old nurse, she repeated the words· which had been upon her baby-lips, and which came to her now as the highest ever uttered on earth. Together those low, quivering voices went through that prayer, so solemn, so tender, and yet so awfully searching, that it leaves no re-cess of the human heart untouched, uncleansed, or unfilled.

Then Christie rose, and the two left the room in silence.

"Whatever fate she is going forth to meet, I have given her the best preparation for it," thought the pious, loving woman. "If life is to be a battle to her, I have put her strongest, truest weapon in her hand: whatever comes, or whatever goes, whether she meet the temptations of pain or of pleasure, so long as she can hold the spirit of that prayer within her, she is safe."

That firm, triumphant faith which comes from an immovable belief in the ultimate security of right-doing, from an unshakable trust in the infinite power and love above us, sprang up within her; and she followed Christie with a more hopeful heart than she could have believed possible a few moments before.

When Tom Archer awoke that morning, it was with the same dull aching which had been in his breast ever since that night, when, meeting his brother in the hall, he had seen his triumph in his face, and heard it from his lips. From that time to the present, he had had a sensation of living under a species of nightmare, with which he struggled in vain, but which he hoped to cast off when this marriage was over and he should be left in peace. The heavy weight upon him had brought with it a numbness to all his sensations; and his chief feeling on that morning was a consciousness that the next few hours contained for him a task he must accomplish, a trial he must undergo, and that, too, without giving evidence that his office was aught but a pleasure and a pride.

The man's strong, reticent nature prepared itself for the effort.

"If I can only go through it without letting Reginald see what it is to me, if I can only avoid getting up a little dramatic entertainment for his private benefit, it is all I ask," Tom thought, with a dull, heavy anger, no less against himself than his brother. "As for Christie, no matter what I might do, she would not notice it. She does not care enough for me to be conscious of my existence when her radiant lover is present; and, unless I drop dead at her side, I am quite safe from exciting her observation or comprehension," he added with bitter truth.

He did not care to try his strength by meeting Reginald before it was necessary, and so did not leave his room until it was about time to set out for the church. Then he went steadily down stairs to the parlor, where the whole party awaited his coming.

Reginald turned with apparent carelessness as he heard his brother's step, and gave an almost imperceptible glance towards him.

"He'll do," was his comment of entire satisfaction. "It's just the same old Tom; the same plucky fellow he always is," he added, with delighted relish for the courage and the effort he perfectly understood: and he had an almost irresistible impulse to go up to his brother, and make him a magnificent bow, as doing homage before a stronger, braver man than himself. Tom was fated to afford his brother entertainment, let him do what he would.

But he cared little for Reginald or his criticisms just then : he was looking at Christie.

The girl stood silent at her lover's side, with her dark eyes raised towards him, yet seeming to be gazing inward rather than outward.

Her pure white bridal draperies, and the expression upon her face, which was the reflection of those words she had just spoken upon her knees, and the thought of those coming words so soon to be uttered before the altar, — these seemed suddenly to have changed the nature of her beauty to a mystic, sacramental holiness, which placed her apart from him, and far above him.

"She is like one of the angels in heaven," he thought, with that tender, adoring reverence which had always found place in his love. " How dare I profane her, even in thought, with my passion and suffering ! "

He seemed to leave earthly pain, with other earthly feelings, behind him, as he came within the influence of this absolute purity. Some of its eternal calm passed into his nature, stilling the throbbings of his sore heart, and lifting him, for the time, above his personal sorrow, into a region where it did not venture to intrude. A different man stood before her from the one who had entered the room but a few seconds before. He did not speak to her : he did not feel worthy to break in upon the thought and feeling which were in her face.

" Reginald," he said quietly after a moment or two, " if you are ready, we will go."

" Yes," returned the other : " we shall be just in time."

And the whole party entered the carriages, and drove rapidly to the not-distant church.

As he sat opposite her during that brief drive, Tom disturbed Christie by no word; but he gazed at her with that hungry despair with which we watch those we love when death is coming nearer and nearer each moment to take them from us. We make no vain struggle; but our awful dumb protest speaks in that last, long look.

And she ?

Rapt in a dream of tender love and holy aspiration, she was as unconscious of his agony as though she had been indeed one of those angels to whom he had likened her.

Arriving, alighting, and forming the bridal procession, they left the glowing sunlight without, and entered the shaded aisle of the dim old church.

That strangely-mixed throng turned with boundless curiosity to see Reginald Archer's bride, — the girl of whose face, fortune, and family they had heard so much. There were eyes among them which looked even more earnestly at Reginald himself, — eyes which, had he been any other than the man he was, he would not have cared to meet. It would be hard to say how many in that assemblage had loved him, or how many he had professed to love.

In one of the front pews sat a woman, who, though belonging to neither class, turned, and watched with curious intentness the magnificent man and lovely girl approaching her, — a woman who was destined to influence the life of one and the death of the other. One of Marian Lester's few beauties was a rather pretty little hand, which she was then, as always, conspicuously airing. But beyond a dull envy and ill will towards both, and a natural malice, and love of mischief, she had as little reason as they to suppose that her hand was to be the instrument to bring down retribution upon Reginald Archer's stately head. Yet thus it was to be.

"A pretty fool, and a mere child! I knew how it would be," she whispered, with a hard, cackling little laugh to the lady next her, — handsome Mrs. Conrad, her bosom-friend, in whom the worst form of fashionable life had not burnt out a constitutional, slipshod good nature. " Just Reginald Archer's wonderful good luck and good sense, — to get a great fortune, and no one with it who will be able to interfere with him ! "

" Yes," returned the other gayly : " that mite will have a very small chance if she should attempt to set up any opposition to him, or try to control him. A good many women have made that effort, and failed," she added, speaking a general truth, but not without some personal reference to her dear friend at her side, — a kindly attention which the other laid by for future repayment, as she always did such things.

Each hit the other when she could without injury to their outward alliance, which was built upon the firm foundation of mutual convenience and advantage. Having thrown her little stone, and struck the mark, Mrs. Conrad felt a comfortable elation of spirits, though she knew that her missive would shortly be sent back to her. But they had played this game too long for either to fear mortal wounds.

" She'll look at her brilliant match somewhat differently six months from now, unless she has a great deal more sense than I give her credit for," Mrs. Lester coolly remarked, ignoring for the present her friend's side-stroke.

"She is a pretty woman," Mrs. Conrad exclaimed as Christie passed by her to the foot of the altar; "and Reginald Archer certainly is the handsomest man that ever lived," she added enthusiastically as he went forward and took his place at the girl's side.

As Tom passed up the church with Christie on his arm, he rigidly held back, as though it had been a physical foe, his intense consciousness of what this ceremony might have meant to him under other circumstances, — of the place he might have held in this bridal train. Aware, to his finest fibre, of all her beauty, of the sweep of her garments against him, of the touch of her hand upon his arm, he walked on to the altar, and there gave place to his brother.

The organ, which had pealed out its joyous wedding-march at their entrance, ceased its music, and the glad sounds died away. There came the momentary hush of expectation over the whole audience and edifice; and then the clergyman's voice rose sonorously above the stillness: —

"Dearly beloved, we are gathered together here, in the sight of God and in the face of this company, to join together this man and this woman in holy matrimony; which is commended by St. Paul to be honorable among all men, and therefore is not by

any to be entered into unadvisedly or lightly, but
reverently, discreetly, advisedly, soberly, and in the
fear of God.   Into this holy estate these two persons present come now to be joined. If any man
can show just cause why they may not lawfully be
joined together, let him speak now, or else hereafter forever hold his peace."

" The face of this company " was very curious to
contemplate as it leaned forward in eager interest.
The dreadful satire of those ceremonial words, in
this case, was clear to numbers of those spectators;
and smile, sneer, sorrow, and savage anger, passed like
a wave over that sea of countenances.

In the momentary pause which followed that
appeal to any man to show just cause of impediment,
how many beating hearts under dumb lips throbbed
fearful protest ! how many asserted their claim upon
" this man " to be stronger and truer in the sight of
God and Nature than that of the woman at his side !
But the Prayer-Book, perhaps discreetly, restricts its
demands to the masculine sex, and does not ask the
testimony or the opinion of women.

The service went on, undisturbed by any sound,
let the unspoken emotion be what it might.

Before the awful charge, calling upon them to
"answer as at the dreadful day of judgment, when
the secret of all hearts shall be disclosed," Reginald

Archer's steady nerves and empty emotional nature quailed as little as did the pure, devout one beside him. Then each soul took upon it that holiest vow of perfect love and constancy, — a vow which was to bear so lightly upon one, and with such terrible weight upon the other.

"Who giveth this woman to be married to this man?" the minister's voice demanded. And Tom Archer performed his part of giving away, instead of taking to himself, the woman he loved then and forever. He scarcely heard the rest of the ceremony; until, the benediction over, Reginald and Christie Archer arose man and wife. Then he, with the bridal party, passed rapidly out of the church into the carriages, and thus home.

The wedding-party and the few invited guests were in such gay spirits, that the breakfast passed quickly off in a little whirl of excitement. Tom had not much to say or do beyond a quiet general direction of the affair.

"If the whole thing were but over! if they would only go, and leave me in peace!" was his one sentiment; and finally he had his wish.

In order to reach the train, which left the city at an early hour in the afternoon, they were obliged to cut short both their merry-making and their farewells.

Christie, in her pretty travelling-dress, was no

longer the separated, almost mystical being she had seemed in her white wedding-garments: she was again the sweet, lovable woman, whom a man might long to take to his heart and to his arms. As such, Tom did not dare to trust himself to give her the affectionate farewell the others were bestowing upon her, and receiving in return. He was, apparently by chance, a little out of the way whenever it would have been his turn to bid her adieu. He seemed engrossed in giving orders for their comfort and convenience. She had entered the carriage, and Reginald was about to follow, before she noticed the omission.

"Good-by, dear Tom!" she exclaimed eagerly, and put out her hand through the window.

"Good-by!" he responded pleasantly, and held her palm for a second, but without leaning forward to kiss her, as she had intended, and as he might easily have done.

Again, in the height of her joy and gayety, Christie felt that curious little sense of repulse; but even the memory was swallowed up, a moment after, in the perfection of her happiness. Reginald saw the whole scene, and, with his foot upon the carriage-step, could not resist the temptation to turn back for a final word with his brother. The man's pluck, self-control, and rigid sense of right, had an absolute fascination for Reginald, from which he could scarcely tear himself away.

"Tom," he said, half under his breath, and without the slightest preface, "you believe in a moral arithmetic. When all this is balanced, somewhere and at some time, your account may show rather differently than at present."

"Good-by!" Tom answered doggedly, not even looking up at him. He wanted none of this man's condolence, sympathy, or comprehension. He did not wish even to touch his hand: he revolted from him soul and body. All he asked was, that the other should take himself away where he would never be called upon to see or speak to him again.

"Farewell!" returned Reginald pleasantly, understanding his brother's feeling, without in the least degree resenting it; and in another moment the carriage rolled off, and Tom re-entered his own door.

Changing his dress hastily, and escaping from the few lingering guests and the air of past festivities which pervaded the house, he went down to his place of business, and shut himself up in his private counting-room. He did not appear again until night.

He had been looking over his books, he said to the clerk who came in at last to hint politely that he should like to close the warehouse and take his departure.

He had spent those hours with ledgers open before him; but how they had been really occupied, he alone, if indeed he, could have told.

CHAPTER XIV.

TOM had believed, that when the marriage was over, and all evidence of it removed from his sight, he should find life more endurable; he should even attain a certain rest and peace: but he discovered that he had been mistaken. Up to this time, he had had occupation for thought: he could at least look forward to what he supposed would put a definite period to his pain. Now there stretched before him an unlimited vista of dull, ceaseless, hopeless torture. The monotony and apparent endlessness of his suffering made it absolutely intolerable. Looking back upon these days in after-life, he sincerely wondered that he had not taken to hard drinking or to opium-eating to deaden his pain; or, indeed, that he had not put an end to it and to himself by suicide. With his terrible capacity for feeling and suffering, he had need to be a brave man not to seek such ready refuge: it required all his strong uprightness to enable him to stand in his lot.

His desolation, his unutterable loneliness, seemed

more than he could endure. It was the one great
effort and desire of his proud, sensitive character,
to cover his emotion; and it would have been like
death to him to think that those around him recognized and watched his struggle. And yet, with the
strange inconsistency of the human heart, it gave his
suffering its last exquisite touch to find that those
who professed to love him, whom he had spent his
life in serving, did not regard him sufficiently to be
conscious of his grief or his need of their succor.

Maria, noticing his worn appearance, asked him
affectionately, on one or two occasions, whether he
were ill; and, receiving a negative reply, said she
supposed it was the effect of the warm weather; that
he ought to take take care of himself, and, above
all, leave town for a summer trip, as the rest of the
family intended to do. He answered, that business
would prevent him; and the subject dropped.

He had been conscious for some time past that
Arnold hung about him, and followed his movements,
more like an affectionate dog than ever. He had
derived a vague sense of comfort from the fact and
from this unobtrusive companionship; but that his
brother had the least comprehension of his situation
did not occur to him. That where Maria's strong
sense and womanly kindness had failed to apprehend
the truth, where Reginald's acuteness had merely

shown him the outside facts of the case, this "divine idiot," as his handsome brother had once called him, should, by the subtile wisdom of love, enter into the secret recesses of his heart, was what Tom little expected or imagined: still less did he dream that Arnold's unskilled hand would be the only one found sufficiently delicate to touch his sore nature without agonizing it; that his brother alone would know the comforting and strengthening he needed, and bring them to him.

That awful uncertainty which steals over us from time to time, whether, after all, virtue be more than a name; whether the worship of Mammon be not wiser than the worship of God; whether we are not sacrificing all the real good of life to the merest dream and idea, — this deadliest of doubts had held Tom in its cruel, paralyzing power for days past. After all, might not his life and its whole principle be a mistake and a delusion? Might not Reginald be the truly prudent man, and he the miserable fool who was casting from him all that was really worth possessing in existence? Why not give up his struggle with his lower nature, and get some good out of this world, which was, perhaps, all he should ever know? His striving to hold to his own standard, his self-denial and self-discipline, might be sheer idiocy, for which shrewder men very properly laughed at and despised him. His life-long devotion to another rule had only brought him to his present lonely wretchedness: why not try the law of the world, the flesh, and the Devil, and see how that worked?

He was not a romantic man; he had no idea of passing for a hero; not the least intention of doing or saying fine things, or putting them into well-sounding sentences: but as he walked doggedly up the street, with his head down and his hat half over his eyes, bitterly arguing the case with himself, he was fighting upon the most terrible of all battle-grounds, — that on which we contend with invisible forces; that on which souls, not bodies, are slain.

This conflict comes to the noblest and truest as surely as to the feeble and degenerate; and we learn from it that virtue means literally manhood, — the power to fight, to struggle, and even to die, rather than weakly and basely surrender our natures to foes without and foes within. According to the measure of our defeat or victory, we stand before our consciences and our God: we know that we are cowards and weaklings, or brave, true men and women. There is no reversing this decision to ourselves or to others: it stands fatally recorded against us.

Tom Archer was a strong man, struggling with the

subtlest of temptations as he walked on, through the summer afternoon, through the streets in which the hum of business was beginning to be hushed. The surroundings were strangely incongruous for such a grim closing-in with a man's inner self; but the decisions of one's life have little regard for time or place. The busy porters brushed against him as they closed their warehouses; draymen and clerks nearly ran over him in their eagerness to get away to their homes; and merchants nodded to him as they left their counting-rooms for more agreeable regions.

He was so absorbed in his own thoughts, that he supposed it to be one of these latter who came behind him and spoke. Looking wearily around, he saw that it was his brother Arnold.

"It is well you were not walking very rapidly, Tom," the other said, "or I could not have caught up with you. I went down to the office to come home with you: but they told me you had just gone; so I followed." And the long, awkward figure took its place at his side.

"Thank you," answered Tom. "It was very kind in you to think of it." And then, really unable to carry on a conversation, he lapsed again into his own thoughts.

Arnold hooked his brother's arm into his own, and brought his thin legs to keep step with the other's steady pace. Thus they moved on in silence for perhaps half an hour; gradually leaving the crowded, commercial parts of the city, and coming to the broader, quieter streets nearer their home. But Tom seemed as little disposed for conversation then as before.

Arnold had from time to time been looking down into his brother's face, in his near-sighted, half-blind way, with a singular expression of countenance. Presently he said quietly, though with a curious tone in his voice, which arrested even his brother's wandering attention, and brought back his far-distant thoughts, —

"Tom, I went to church with Maria on Sunday morning."

"Did you?" returned the other, still rather absently; striving, as he always did, to interest himself in what interested Arnold, but vaguely wondering why his brother put such emphasis upon such a trivial occurrence.

"The psalm for the day was that beautiful one about a good man's steps being ordered by the Lord. There was one verse which struck me as never before in my life; and I have been thinking of it ever since: 'Keep innocency, and take heed unto the thing that is right; for that shall bring a man peace at last.'"

Tom glanced quickly up at his brother.

The love, the high faith and earnestness, which vibrated through the voice, were shining clear and bright in the face usually so dreamy, doubtful, and shadowy in expression. The glory and wisdom which are not of this world were in those purblind eyes, making them beautiful and benign; the majesty of eternal truth covered that gaunt, slouching figure, ennobling it to strength and decision, to power and dignity. It seemed to Tom as though some strong, pure angel had entered that feeble form, and come to his rescue. He stood still for a moment, and gazed at Arnold, but without a word adequate to express the feeling that rushed over him.

Then again the two walked on in silence.

There was a great lump in Tom's throat, which kept him speechless. The unbearable weight of his burden seemed lightened; his sense of utter loneliness and desolation passed away. There was at least one being in the world who loved him enough to comprehend him, and suffer with him; who sufficiently shared his needs and nature to bring him tenderest, highest help in his sorest peril. The very weakness of the hand gave it ability to soothe: the lack of worldly skill in his comforter made it possible to accept his comforting.

There are times when we learn that the feeble

have their peculiar powers and privileges as surely as the strong; that there are places they may enter, whose gates are barred against the able and successful of this earth. We accept with infinite thankfulness and melting hearts the companionship and sympathy of the one class; while we steel ourselves against the other, as towards intolerable intrusion. We fear the critical judgment and after-thought of strong-brained persons, however kindly disposed. To most of us there come moments when we absolutely require a fool for a friend, and, in default of him, take to the affection of dumb beasts. At that moment, this "divine idiot" was, by his very worldly incompetency, that which no other man alive could have been to Tom. The elder man's gentle consideration and unselfish care for his brother were recompensed then and there.

"If I have ever loved him, and tried to make his life peaceful and happy, he has repaid me now a thousand-fold," was Tom's thought, with a tender glow at his frozen, sickened heart, as the two went homeward through the summer evening air; was the emotion that filled his mind for weeks and months that followed.

Neither by look nor word was further explanation entered into between them; and the subject, which was never really absent from the consciousness of either, was not again alluded to: but the bond and comprehension were no less strong because tacit. Honor and right required that the matter should not be discussed, and that Tom's trouble should be kept to himself, and fought out by himself. Christie was now another man's wife, and must not be profaned by any word of his, — by any thought, if he could prevent it: so between the two there remained only a deep, tender silence.

They fell into constant association. It was curious how little they said, and yet what a sense of companionship they supplied to each other. It almost seemed that their previous relations were reversed, and that it was Arnold who kept watch and ward over his strong, resolute brother; tending him spiritually and physically with something between the devotion of a mother to her sick child, and the unreasoning, unquestioning faithfulness of a loving animal. His quiet, contented presence never disturbed Tom, let him be ever so much occupied, outwardly or inwardly.

"Don't I interrupt you sometimes, Tom? I am afraid I am often in your way," Arnold once penitently and anxiously inquired.

"Dear boy, you are never in my way. It always rests and comforts me to look at you," Tom answered, laying his hand on the other's shoulder, with

a tone and manner which set that matter at rest for
ever.

And thus, upheld by the weakest arm he had ever
himself strengthened, Tom lived through these dark,
weary days, until his tried nature grew somewhat
accustomed to the strain life had laid upon it, — until
he learned endurance, if not resignation.

CHRISTIE'S honeymoon was over. She had returned from her long wedding-tour, and was settled as the mistress of the beautiful home which Reginald's taste and her means had provided. Nothing had been omitted to render the house perfect; all that art could devise, culture suggest, and wealth procure, was there; and Reginald Archer presided over it with quiet but supreme satisfaction. At last, he had obtained unlimited command of money, and a position and residence which he felt he occupied with perfect grace. He knew that he and his surroundings were in admirably artistic keeping, and experienced the calm ease and comfort which that consciousness engenders.

"The right man in the right place," he thought, and felt that his real life had but just commenced.

The *ennui* of his honeymoon would have been almost insupportable but for the constant change of scene and association, and the pleasant titillation of his vanity, caused by the impression his appearance everywhere created.

His manner towards Christie was formed upon a finely-graduated scale, — from the lover he had necessarily appeared, to the cool, courteous, and absolutely unrestrained husband he intended to be. The change was so adroitly managed, that Christie, feeling the effect in every fibre of her being, could scarcely define or analyze the cause. It was like an almost imperceptible but constant lowering of the temperature, that deadened the warm springs of life within her; it was like a nightmare stealing over her, against whose invisible power she vainly and vaguely struggled. Utterly ignorant of evil, of falsity, of the world and its tenets, of every thing but her own pure nature, and necessarily judging all things by it, she had to work through these barriers to a recognition of facts which an experienced woman would have seen and understood at a glance. She had to discover society-life, and some of its worst phases, as truly as Pascal discovered geometry for himself, ages after it had been known to all the world. The education of most persons, on this point, begins at too early an age, and their teachers are too numer-ous and skilful, to leave much room for the personal finding-out of many things. Still, life comes to all as an unsolved problem; and to those who attempt it

without rule, training, or tutelage, the solution is difficult and delayed. In this matter, Christie had literally to do her own work; and circumstances and characters around her held her painfully and ceaselessly
to the labor.

Col. Macalaster had bequeathed to his daughter, not merely his large fortune, but the shrewd
brain which had accumulated it; above all, that capacity for original thought, that necessity to form
and act upon his own judgment, regardless of the
opinions of others, which had been the real cause
of his success. Like her father, Christie was compelled to think for herself, to believe for herself;
to look at things with her own eyes, and weigh them
in her own balance. Hitherto an infant in experience, and living wholly in her large, passionate af-
fections, her intellect had had no food to stimulate
it, no opportunity to act. The brain like the soul
of the woman might as yet be called unborn; but
the travail of both had begun. Even her delusions
had been essentially her own; and her perceptions of
truth, when in the fulness of time they arrived,
would be her own also.

Her growing, sickening doubt of Reginald's love
for her did not at first affect her opinion of him: it
only filled her with infinite pain and sorrow. Her
fear that she could not be a fitting wife to her hero,

could not satisfy a nature so lofty, so utterly beyond her own, seemed realized. In the perfection of her faith, nothing affected it; and Reginald's interest in every other woman with whom he came in contact only filled her with sore-hearted shame at her inability to be all and in all to him.

Reginald himself thought he acted extremely well; and in one point he did, setting an example to better men. Never, then nor to the very end, did he omit the smallest point of courtesy to his wife when in her presence. Pride (which was his nearest approach to principle), taste, and the instinct of good breeding, did not permit him to fail in this matter. Mrs. Reginald Archer was, *ex officio*, a person towards whom all outward ceremonies must be fulfilled by himself and others: their omission towards his wife was an insult to him. If with love, as with the law, it were not the letter which killeth, and the spirit which maketh alive, Christie would, apparently, have had little of which to complain. If one could live on husks, if forms could feed a woman's soul, then the fading-away of hope and light and happiness in her nature would, up to this time, have been causeless.

A look was gathering in her face which no happy wife can wear. The difference between the child of the past and the woman of the present was very curious to analyze, it was at once so small, and yet so great. It seemed chiefly in her eyes. From them spoke out the deep disappointment, the trouble and sorrow, she kept otherwise within herself. Dark shadows had come into their depths, and sudden changeful lights upon their surface : their wonderful latent power of expression was rousing into life, and giving token of a nature capable of boundless emotion. No one could now look into them, and make any mistake as to her age ; could ever doubt her ability to suffer, to love, and even to hate. She had not then learned to govern the expression of her eyes ; would probably never learn to do so completely : but her power of repression in other ways was, considering her past habits, nature, and circumstances, something amazing. That wonderful heritage of outward self-control, into the possession of which women come at the call of pride, honor, or delicacy, Christie gained, almost unconsciously, the moment she needed it. She held her clasped hands, as it were, over her throbbing heart, to still its visible beatings.

She gave small evidence of her pain to any one, — to Reginald least of all.

To have shown him her heart, by word or look, would have been like crying to him for mercy ; and that she could not do. She could not ask his help if he did not care sufficiently to see her need. She could go on looking up to him and loving him ; but she could not sue for his love in return : there was a deep, strong pride in the woman, which could not stoop to that ; which made her strive to hide her pain from him like a shame.

Yet Reginald saw her gradual awakening to the truth, and, as far as was in him, comprehended the effect clearly. He was well satisfied with the result, and could not sufficiently congratulate himself and her upon what he called " her extreme good sense " in quietly accepting the inevitable, and settling down to the situation without any foolish resistance. He was genuinely thankful to her for sparing him certain scenes he had vaguely dreaded, — the form of discomfort he most disliked.

" It is a strong little face and a brave little spirit," he thought, as he critically surveyed her with the mental justice he did all things. " She has far more force and intellect than I gave her credit for. She needs time and experience to develop her; but I should not be surprised if she turned out something extraordinary. At any rate, it is a blessing that I did not marry a little fool, who would have annoyed me with complaints and tears."

And Reginald sung a hymn of rejoicing to himself at the prospect of having his matrimonial paths made so smooth, and was more punctiliously courteous to

Christie than ever; that is, when he was with her, — when he was not being more than courteous to some one else.

But deeper shadows than ever come into a pure sorrow were stealing into Christie's sky even before their return; before they were settled in their new home-life.

The faint disturbance of a false faith is the beginning of the end. When the tide of righteous distrust is kept back by merely artificial barriers, it is, after the first crumbling, only a question of time as to when the sea of doubt will rush in. Even a faith which has a foundation is like a magic spell, — every thing or nothing, — and, once injured, can never regain its pristine perfection. In losing her belief in Reginald's love for her, she had lost more than that: she had parted forever with her capacity for blind belief in any thing., Doubt had entered in as a slave where he would soon reign as a sovereign. Having once been fearfully mistaken, and, as she supposed, self-deluded, in giving credence to that which seemed as secure as her own identity, she was forced to suspect and examine every other belief she possessed. 'Life's necessary scepticism (in the original sense of the word) had been born within her, — with what agony and struggle, she alone knew; and henceforth she must look at all things with the eyes and the reason God had given her. If what had seemed granite rock under her feet had given way, might not any thing else in heaven or earth prove an illusion? Her day of fond delusions was over: she was compelled to give her intellect, as well as her heart, a place in her existence.

She had no longer the power to accept blindly even the character of the man she adored, and for whom she would gladly have died. In spite of herself, without realizing the truth concerning him for either past or present, she vaguely grew to feel that the person she had married was not the person she supposed him to be. Actual, personal sin was to her so horrible a thing, that she did not dream of imputing it to him; she would as soon have connected him with any crime against the law of the land : but, shut it out as she might, the knowledge would steal in upon her that their standards of right and wrong differed widely, if not fatally. She held with a death-grasp to her old boundless loyalty and admiration; but the power of truth baffled her efforts. As it were, she had erected a noble temple within her heart fo his homage : she still maintained the splendid edifice; she chanted the service, and kept the sacred fire burning, with more than devoted care ; but the whole structure was undermined to its fall, though she was unconscious of the fact.

Without being aware of it, Reginald, like all men, displayed his real character in every word, look, and act, to eyes keen and clear enough for the seeing. The change was not in him, but in Christie's mental vision, which was surely but slowly developing to its native power and acuteness. The torture of the process might be measured by her passionate resistance to it. Reginald did not willingly assist her clear-sightedness. He no longer affected the devotion of a lover; but he preserved the silence, the decent respect, which he always maintained before what are called good women. Reginald Archer was a thoroughly bad man; but he was also a thoroughly well-bred one. He would calmly ruin a woman for time and eternity; but he was incapable of offering one what he would have considered an unnecessary insult. He would no more have spoken to Christie of any of the women with whom he had sinned than he would have introduced them to her personally; he would no more have alluded to one of them in her presence than he would have struck her full in the face; holding one act as possible in a gentleman as the other. In the distant days, when that which was now the dreadful future had become the dreadful past, and Christie looked back upon her married life as upon a frightful dream, at least she had not this insult to remember forever.

In this early time, she had only that impalpable some-thing which seems to exhale from the whole nature of a person to guide her newly-awakened perception ; but it was sufficient to bring her far nearer the truth than she knew or comprehended.

This was the state of feeling and of mind in which, after two months of travel, she returned to the city. No event had happened that she could define, no mis-fortune that she could explain, no grievance that she could put into words ; yet to her all life was changed, and the merry girl who had left her friends upon that bright bridal morning came back to them no more. In her place they found an indefinably altered woman, with whom they had a singular consciousness of mak-ing a new acquaintance.

CHAPTER XVI

"TOM," said Maria slowly and hesitatingly, and then sat silently looking at him for a moment.

It was the morning after Reginald's return : she had been at his house to welcome him upon his arrival, and to make it seem to Christie really like coming home. She had dined and spent the evening with them ; and was now, at the breakfast-table, giving Tom an account of every thing connected with her visit. She had told with spirit all that had been said and done, adding the many particulars interesting to herself and to her brother.

But there was one point upon which she had not touched, and upon which he could not question her. Had Christie brought back her pure, happy heart, her blissful blindness? If the truth had begun to break upon her, she would hardly allow the evidence of it to be perceptible even to Maria's kind eyes. Still he waited, he scarcely knew for what, — for some chance word or information from which he could draw his own conclusions. The others had left the table ; but he sat lingering over his breakfast, though it was past his usual hour for going down to his office.

"Tom," she said again ; and something in the tone and the perplexed expression in her face forewarned him that what he desired was coming.

He looked up quickly at her.

" Perhaps it is merely my imagination, and perhaps it may not strike you in the same light when you see her; but Christie seems to me to be changed."

" In what way ? " he asked, a catch in his breath making his sentence short.

" My God ! " he thought, " has it come so soon ? And what is it ? Is it only sorrow, the beginning of a long heart-breaking ? or has the poison of his moral nature contaminated her already ? "

" I hardly know how to explain it to you," Maria went on doubtfully. " She was quicker and brighter than ever; talked more and better than I ever knew her to do : yet she did not seem as really gay as she used to at this table. I could not help thinking she was under a kind of constraint, for which I could see no reason," she continued, looking earnestly at her brother; for she truly loved the girl, and had likewise boundless faith in Tom's perception, and powers of succor. " Besides, she seemed to have gained a hard side to her character."

"Most things have a hard side, which are not analogous to mush," he answered, with an irritation which was really soreness of heart. He could not bear criticism upon her, let his own judgment be what it might.

"But you know she used always to think that every one acted from the highest motives; and last night, from several things she said, I could not help believing that she had changed that opinion. Then she isn't half as affectionate as she used to be; and, when I kissed her several times at parting, she gave me a curious, questioning little look, which I could not help thinking of all the way home. I can't bear to believe that Christie is growing cold and worldly already; but it really seems so," this good, kind woman went on, with the injustice of ignorance.

"Tom," she exclaimed a second after, speaking hurriedly, and as though ashamed to give voice to her doubt, "there is no use in our trying to conceal from each other that Reginald is a very selfish man. Do you think it possible that he could have ill treated her, or made her unhappy?"

"If you mean," bitterly exclaimed Tom, who had been sitting looking straight before him, with his mouth held firmly shut, "that he has either struck her or starved her, I can answer, No. Further than that I can't guarantee. But whatever may be the

matter, Maria," he added, "you and I can do nothing, and ought to say nothing." And he rose wearily,
and went off to the daily treadmill of his work,
which at least afforded the relief of partial occupation of his thoughts.

But the effect of Maria's words went with him.
The pain and doubt they had re-awakened were busy
at his heart as he sat in his counting-room, bending
down his faculties to important business-letters and
mercantile plans. His chief clerk, who came in to
bring him the latest gold-quotations and to receive
his orders concerning certain importations, listened
with admiration to the clear instructions and shrewd
reasons Tom gave him for acting in some cases, and
refraining in others.

"What a cool, steady, money - making fellow
he is!" thought the man, looking enthusiastically at
the head of the house; "and what a splendid capacity he has for knowing his own mind, and holding to
it! I suppose he has no nerves, and nothing disturbs
him. He's like steel, he's so keen and hard and
true," he added, with that loyalty and absolute
confidence which Tom inspired in all his subor-
dinates.

To have suspected his chief of heartache, of weary
doubt of himself and others, would have struck him
as a magnificent joke.

" He isn't very sentimental, to be sure ; and he can speak pretty sharply when there's any shirking around him : but give him time, and he will be worth his millions ; and that's what he cares most for, I suppose," was the man's somewhat natural thought as he went off to execute his orders ; and Tom turned again to his writing-desk.

It was noon before he was again interrupted.

The door opened, and Reginald entered, just as he had done at about that hour for nearly every day in the past five years.

" How do you do, Tom ? " he asked in his most charming and charmed manner.   " I am really delighted to see you ! " and he spoke the exact truth.

" I am very well," answered Tom quietly, neither rising, nor offering his hand, nor welcoming his brother in any way.   He had no pleasure in seeing him there ; and he would make no pretence of it.

Reginald sank back into his usual seat, which he had long since ascertained to be the most agreeable in the room, and by his peculiar faculty looked more at his ease under these somewhat repressing circumstances than any one else could have done under the most favorable surroundings.

" My dear boy," he said airily, " I spare you the trouble of likening me to the bad shilling in the proverb, which was sure to come back ; though the comparison is so in keeping with the general monetary atmosphere of this place, that I cannot help making it. I am perfectly aware that you had much rather I had staid away; but I have made my first visit in town to you, because I really wanted to see you. The fact is, old boy, I have missed you, as I always do."

Tom looked at his brother.

The other's liking for him, and persistent clinging to him, were, perhaps, nothing more than refined self-ishness, and love of entertainment; but, so far as they went, they were certainly genuine: and that strange tie of blood, which lasts so long, and bears unbroken so many strains, faintly stirred again at Tom's heart. Let him be what he might, the man was his brother: he could not utterly divorce himself from him: he must, in a certain degree, accept him, as he did the rest of his lot in life. If he could not distract him from some of his evil purposes, at least he might be able to ward off from innocent heads the conse-quences of the sin and sorrow he foresaw. If he utterly threw him off, as his instinct dictated; if he shut his doors against him to save himself from the pain and disgust caused even by his presence, — might he not repent it in after-days? Above all, if the time ever came for him to fulfil his promise to Christie, might he not be putting it out of his power to redeem his pledge? He would not disguise or compromise any honest opinion, there or thereafter: but he would control the evidence of his personal revolting; he would try to put aside his individual share in the situation, and let the outward bond of their relationship and association remain intact. He thought, or rather felt, all this out in the moment he sat silently gazing at his brother.

Reginald caught the change in Tom's eyes, and, interpreting it, acted upon it instantly.

"I came in this morning to ask a special favor of you, Tom," he said, — "not any of the old kind," he exclaimed a second after, with a laugh, as his own form of expression struck him. "It really gives me a delightfully novel sensation.to come into this room without breaking the tenth commandment, — without coveting my neighbor's goods in the shape of checks and bank-notes."

As Reginald mentioned the tenth commandment, there flashed upon both men a consciousness of how often one of them broke it outside of that apartment by coveting his neighbor's wife, and what a tremendous temptation was now upon the other to do likewise. But neither cared to show his own thought, nor to recognize that of the other; and Reginald continued, without change in voice or manner, to give proof of what was in his mind.

"I want you to come and dine with me to-morrow."

Tom's refusal was written so plainly in his face, that his brother answered it without giving him a chance to put it into words.

"Oh! you must come; the family honor demands it," he exclaimed, touching a string which he knew would respond. "It is to be a little house-warming for our intimate friends; and it would be absolutely disreputable for the head of the family to be absent. I can't let you off on my own account, or yours either."

Had it been any other man whom he wished to secure for his own purposes, and whom he knew to have a tenderness for his wife, he would have coolly used her name and influence to gain him; but he understood his brother far too well to bring Christie into the discussion.

Yet it was the thought of her, though not in the way Reginald would have supposed, which was really drawing, almost compelling, Tom to give an affirmative answer. Maria's words in the morning were upon him again in their full force.

"I must see for myself how much there was in them. I cannot bear the suspense of doubting her; and, if the worst is coming, I had better know it, and face it beforehand. I shall probably do no more than speak to her: but, if I can watch her for a little while, I think I can get at the truth; I can tell whether she is beginning to lower to his level."

His brother's argument as to what was decorous for the family respectability certainly had its weight; but it was a far deeper feeling which made him give a partial promise to be present.

"You know I am not much of a society-man, and I had much rather be left out, Reginald," he demurred.

"But you can't be left out; because who would entertain me?" the other answered, giving his real reason; "or play god-father to our first-born party?" he added, neatly bringing in a somewhat less selfish plea, and transferring the argument to safer grounds.

"Well, I will think about it," said Tom. But Reginald felt that he had won the day.

"You might as well come to it at once; for I give you fair warning that I will not let you off."

And then, elated by having gained his wish and a difficult victory, he expended his entire force of fascination upon his brother for a full hour; enjoying himself inexpressibly, and literally compelling the other to share his pleasure in some degree.

The old sorrowful, hopeless, generous admiration came over Tom as he looked and listened; softened his heart, and almost stayed his judgment for the moment.

" Good-by ! " said Reginald at last ; and, with an imperceptible glance at his brother's face to see if it would be safe to do so, he put out his hand to him.

Tom hesitated visibly ; and then, with a weary sense that it was useless for him to struggle against the tie which connected them, took the other's palm in friendly farewell, as he had supposed he should never do again. And Reginald departed radiant with satisfaction.

" We are all to dine with Reginald to-morrow, you know," Maria said as they sat round the dinner-table.

" He called at my counting-room and invited me this morning," was Tom's inconclusive reply.

" He sent me a special invitation," remarked Arnold ; " but I hardly think I shall go." And, as he spoke, he seemed to have more than his usual difficulty in disposing of his long limbs. " Are you going, Tom ? " he asked a little wistfully.

" Yes, and I am going to take you with me ; for you will certainly enjoy yourself after you get there," Tom answered pleasantly.

And thus it was that the next night saw the whole party, with Lloyd Truxton added as Ellen's escort, enter Reginald's house. They were rather late, and the company had assembled. Tom had scarcely more than a moment, before the announcement of dinner, in which to make his salutations to Christie and his swift observation of her.

She was standing at the head of the room, looking fair and lovely in her bright evening-dress, from which, at Reginald's express desire, all signs of mourning had been discarded. She was smilingly receiving her friends, and gayly talking to those around her; but Tom had not reached her before he saw and realized the change of which Maria had spoken.

"She looks two inches taller and five years older than she did when she went away," he thought in astonishment, "and has more society air and style than I supposed she would ever possess."

Reginald's prophecy, that Christie would become a very stylish woman, was even then being fulfilled: indeed, he had diligently striven during his short married life to bring about that result.

Tom had entered the room with a heavy beating at his heart, which made him faint and sick. He had prepared himself for the meeting: but it was no light effort which enabled him to go up that room with the composure of a well-bred gentleman; to keep his tone and look merely that of pleasant, appropriate cordiality. The alteration in her, however, came to his aid. It was possible to greet conventionally the somewhat conventional lady who stood smiling before him, as she had done before a dozen others; whose poise was such as scarcely to permit its absence in any one else.

Again, with the curious adaptability of women, this inexperienced girl filled an unaccustomed *rôle* with perfect ease and fitness. This was hardly his Christie, the loving, childlike creature, the thought of whom had never left his waking and scarcely his sleeping moments since their parting; and he found it within his power to address her with perfect steadiness.

"I am very glad to welcome you home, Christie," he said as he held her hand for a moment.

"And I am very glad to be welcomed," she answered, with a smile she might have given any one; and then he stood aside to allow some one else to speak to her.

He had no time to study her face more closely, for dinner was announced; and he found that Reginald had secured him at his end of the table, with the next best talker within speaking-distance. The meal was an affair of state, and occupied hours; and sustaining his part in the conversation, and apparently engrossed in the topics broached, Tom found much time and opportunity for quiet observation of the fair young face presiding at the other end of the table. She was brightly entertaining those near her; and he watched the varied expressions which passed over her countenance. But whether it were made brilliant by smiles, or whether it sank suddenly and apparently unconsciously into a strange, weary gravity, from which it emerged just as abruptly, there was always in it that curious new something which it had acquired since their parting, — something which the face of old could never have expressed, which the heart of old could never have experienced. It was no less plain through gayety of lip, and glitter of eye; it was no more clear when pre-occupied blankness stood in their place.

"She has acquired the knowledge of good and evil; but is it bitter, or sweet, to her?" was the question which kept rising in his mind. "Her eyes are as bright and clear as ever; but they are not as frank as they used to be. They have acquired the power to look, yet refuse to be looked into: she has learned merely to see, instead of thinking, feeling, and speaking with them, as she once did. She has gained the ability to keep back part of the price; but what is it she is guarding so carefully? Is it bitter disappointment that is already graven into her face? By this time, she must know something of Reginald's real nature, however little she may know of his life; and that strange change in her face looks to me like the dawning knowledge that there is no love on his side, and, worse still, that there can be no respect on hers I wonder how much she knows of the truth."

And thinking of what that truth was, and gazing at the woman he loved, with its shadow resting upon her even then, his old loathing for his brother rushed over him with such force, that the very food upon his lips sickened him.

" I despise myself for coming here and hobnobbing with him, for eating his salt, knowing what I know, and thinking what I think."

" Tom, you must be having a ' revery of a bachelor,' laughed his opposite neighbor, having previously spoken to him without gaining an answer.

" Not at all," said Tom, smiling, and joining in the general conversation.

But his thoughts flowed on in their previous channel, the deep undercurrent holding its own beneath the tide of light talk.

" Starved and hungry-hearted already ! And is she trying to satisfy her nature by tasting the impure food Reginald lives on ? He will never stop her ; as indeed, in common justice, he has no right to do, being what he is. But is she beginning to think that it is better and happier and wiser to make the best of her bad bargain by following his example, and accepting his standard ? "

At that moment, with this horrible dread contracting his heart, Tom Archer, the shrewd, calculating, unromantic trader of the shrewd, calculating, unromantic nineteenth century, realized what the old Roman must have felt when he slew with his own hand the being he loved best, rather than let her live dishonored.

"Better in her grave, better that those bridal flowers should be her burial wreath, than that a day which may be coming should ever dawn," he thought literally and sincerely. "She has passed the critical turning in her moral life; but has she taken the upward, or the downward road?" And he could give no certain answer.

The doubt haunted him like an evil spirit, standing between his inward thought and his consciousness of the outward world, whispering suspicions between his own careless sentences and quick retorts, and ceaselessly repeating his sad forebodings like the sorrowful refrain of a gay song.

Tom had noticed at the first moment that Christie wore her diamond cross at her white throat.

"I wonder if she wears it because it happens to be costly and becoming, or whether it still has any of the associations I tried to connect with it?" he questioned. "If I could find out that, it would give me the clew I want."

But divided by the length of that splendid table, with its burden of fruits and flowers, its glittering glass and shining silver, and its circle of gay guests, he saw little chance to gain his object,— even to speak light words to her, far less serious ones. It seemed to him like a dreadful fantasy or demon-dance to see the whole gorgeous effect; to hear the sweet laughter and merry words, and to know what they covered. Reginald slightly flushed with wine, looking like a radiant demi-god, and talking in the tones of an enchanter, yet being what he was, with such a past at his back; Christie shining like a star, and beaming as brightly, but with a present crushing her nature, and a future darkly gathering in the distance; himself with his heart bleeding, and his brain torturing itself with doubts and fears, yet talking as though life were an endless, merry feast, sending out quick sentences which seemed to scintillate with their own keen brilliancy, — the whole scene gave him an impulse to cry out wildly, as though that might break some terrible spell which was upon them.

" Are we all acting our parts in some mad comedy? and have we all brought our private demons with us to torture us? " he thought as he glanced round him with a sense of unreality ; persons and things becoming almost phantasmagorial before his eyes.

There are times, when, compelled to maintain an inner and outer character, to feel and act in direct contradiction, our conviction of our own identity wavers. We have a curious sense of duality ; and this slight unsettling of the fundamental point, that we are unchangeably ourselves, gives the most singular feeling of insecurity and incertitude with regard to all else. We fall into a state in which strange fancies and imaginations take hold upon us with a power, which, in ordinary moments, would seem absurd. Our customary natures fail to influence us; and we are revelations to ourselves of our possibilities of vagary. Practical, clear-headed Tom Archer was the last man to be susceptible to such fantasies; but the sensation was none the less strongly upon him: and when, at last, the dinner was over, and he came out into the drawing-room, it was with a feeling of awakening from a bad dream.

It was late; and, to Tom's great relief, the company soon departed. One by one they left, until only the family remained.

Reginald, who had been uncommonly gracious to Arnold that evening, partly from whim, and partly because he knew it would please Tom, had taken him, with Lloyd Truxton, to an adjoining room, to show him a new picture. Ellen and Maria had gone up stairs to put on their wrappings; and thus Tom and Christie were left momentarily alone. He was standing in the cool, softly-lighted hall, when the pretty figure, with its flowing evening draperies, came to the drawing-room door, and, seeing him, joined him.

"Alone, Tom!" she said brightly, but with the manner she had had all the evening. "I thought you had gone with Reginald to see his last pet purchase."

"No," he answered: "I preferred staying here, as it was cooler."

"Then I'll compensate you for your loss by showing you a statue, which was his pet purchase before the last. This is the dethroned princess, whose reign was uncommonly long, for she amused him almost a week!" she exclaimed, turning to a lovely marble at her side, and speaking with a gay mockery, which was very graceful and charming, but through which a faint tone of bitter earnestness jarred like smothered discord.

Tom made no corresponding movement, and paid little heed to her words, though the tone thrilled through him. His chance had come; and he seized it, like the resolute man that he was.

"Christie," he exclaimed, and his voice, more than his words, spoke his meaning to the woman, "you still wear my cross! Is it still the talisman I told you I meant it to be?"

The woman gave him one swift glance, so intense that it seemed to read his very soul; the glance which, alas! she now gave every thing, — that of weighing and testing it to the uttermost before daring to trust it. With his strong, true eyes, Tom Archer faced her look as he would have faced the highest of all tribunals.

In another second she had changed as though by magic. All her restrained, acquired manner had dropped from her like a garment; and she was standing before him with hands tightly clasped, as though to keep back a flood of emotion which would have swept her away, with tears filling the eyes which were raised with such passionate earnestness to his.

"Tom, dear Tom," said the low, quivering voice, which hardly dared to trust itself, "I thank you for your gift, as I was too ignorant to know how to do when we parted. I have learned its worth and its need; and I bless and thank you for it; I"— The voice failed, and the head drooped down upon the breast.

All Tom's mighty love and infinite pity rushed over him, until he shook from head to foot. He put out his arms with a wild desire to take her to his heart, and lavish its pent-up devotion upon her. She did not see the gesture; and before she raised her head, and partially regained her self-control, he, too, had remembered himself and what was his hard duty. When the sad, sweet eyes looked up at him, they met a glance as sad, but as pure, as her own; and the strength of a man who has fought a good fight, and conquered, was in them.

"Good-by!" he said gently. "We may not see each other very often in future; but whether we meet, or whether we part, remember my promise if you ever need me. Nothing can alter that. And, Christie, so long as you can wear the cross, and carry its lesson in your heart, I shall have no fear for you, let come what will."

"Tom!" cried Reginald's voice, "where are you? I thought you were coming with us." And he and Arnold and Lloyd came out into the hall also.

Christie turned to speak to Maria, who was descending the stairway; and Tom made some commonplace excuse to his brother for his desertion; while Reginald began again to talk to him, with the gay eagerness of perfect health and spirits, in a way to lead any one to suppose that he had not spoken during the evening, and was making up for lost time.

As Lloyd Truxton assisted the ladies into the carriage, Tom turned at the front-door; looking back into the superb hall to see his far more superb brother standing there in all his pride and glory, and the lovely woman's face beside him gazing forward with sad, wistful eyes.

"Good-by!" he said, and crossed the threshold; never to recross it until the tragedy of their lives had been lived out, and one of them lay dying. For Tom Archer had learned a deep lesson as he stood

for those few moments at Christie's side; had found
that he could not see her suffer, and make no sign
of his love; had convinced himself that he must put
distance between them if he hoped to keep the
thought always before him that she was another
man's wife.

CHAPTER XVII.

O F course, with Christie's return, and entrance into society, it became "everybody's" duty to call upon her, — a duty performed with extreme alacrity. Fashion, interest, and curiosity, all tended in the same direction, and produced the same result. Her life gradually became a round of receiving visits, and returning them; and, as the winter season began, of issuing invitations, and accepting others.

Reginald's determination that his house should be popular was fully carried out; and such constant and brilliant entertainment was to be found there, that his friends began to have an impression that a sort of social millennial period had set in. Persons who sincerely hated each other; who had disliked Reginald in his poverty, and now envied him in his prosperity, — these eagerly met around his festive board, unable to resist its fascinations.

"It is quite a case of the lion lying down with the lamb," Reginald answered, as Mrs. Lester laughingly pointed out to him several intimate enemies taking wine with each other at his table. "Good heavens! what won't society men and women do for a good dinner and a good time! and right enough they are," he added with a sort of delighted contempt.

The fact that the remark was supremely true of the person addressed, merely gave it a pleasant piquancy; for he was aware that she acted upon the advice of Dr. Watts, and "never let her angry passions rise" when it was against her interest to do so. When there was any thing to be gained by Christian forbearance, Mrs. Lester was impervious to any insult short of a blow; and even that she would have ignored if she could have kept the occurrence quiet, or could have told her own version of the story effectively to society. Reginald could have made no speech to her for which she would have given up the advantages of his house, the fine dinners and fine company she met there, and the occasional convenience of his carriages. He was not afraid that Mrs. Lester would make a personal application of his words, though sure she would carry them to the individuals commented upon at the earliest opportunity; but he feared them equally little for exactly the same reasons.

This style of life Reginald enjoyed to the full. It was the flower of what he had tasted in the bud: he was master where he had previously been guest; and he liked the position much better.

He had resumed his old habits and connections, but had thrown a sufficient veil over them to prevent their coming to Christie's ears, as he wished to save both himself and her the annoyance of public scandal. Reginald never outwardly offended against good taste, as the re-action jarred upon his nerves, and disgusted him with himself. He spent but a small portion of his time within his own doors; but Christie knew too little of him or of the world for the fact to excite any suspicion on her part. It only showed her sadly that he cared nothing for his home unless it were made brilliant by other persons. She had learned that her marriage was a dreadful mistake, though she still dreamed that it had been an unwitting one on his part as on hers. She knew that his character was set to a far lower standard than she had imagined; but she still loved him passionately, with the enthusiastic admiration which his charm of person and manner hourly called forth. That he had deliberately married her for her money was a thought she had never taken in, with which she would not have insulted the man she even yet believed him to be. His coming step still made her thrill with joy; but she was so conscious that he did not share her emotion, that his presence brought pain as well as pleasure.

She also found that her own time was very much
occupied; that she had become a part of a social machine which carried her on in spite of herself. She
recognized the fact that society has its bond-slaves,
and holds them to task-work; that in her case there
had been substituted for the quiet domestic life she
loved the laborious public existence she disliked but
could not throw off. In this way, Reginald contrived,
without apparent plan, that their lives should be
passed chiefly apart; leaving him room for the liberty
of action he desired for himself, and which he was
perfectly willing to grant to her. Christie's dream
of hope and happiness had disappeared as completely
as though it had never been. In all the outward
splendor of her life, she walked through her routine
of duties a hungry-hearted woman; doubting all
around her, but still more doubting herself.

The women she met, who were so lavish of compliment and apparent kindness, were so unlike any
thing she had ever known, that, by turns, they
charmed, shocked, and bewildered her. Most of
them rather liked her, as she was sweet-tempered
and perfectly generous; entering into no rivalries,
and offering them favors instead of offences. At first,
they had the instinctive shame to put a bridle upon
their tongues and restraint upon their actions in her
presence; to let only that part of their natures ap-

pear which was least unlike her own: but, after a little while, the effort was too great. To keep up a part was more than they could afford to do for any one's comfort; and gradually they disregarded her, and fell back into their old ways.

This was the case with the worst portion; and from them she shrank as completely as circumstances would permit. She was too innocently ignorant to comprehend half that was said before her; but she understood enough to fill her with shame and disgust. However, living in the same circle, she was necessarily thrown with them; especially as they had no scruple in pushing themselves upon her, and in using her and her establishment as far as Reginald would allow it.

The kinder class of these women compromised the matter with themselves by keeping away from Christie, except on state occasions; not wishing to annoy " the foolish child," as they considered her, and still less being willing to bore themselves by appearing other than they were. It was a case of oil and water; and they both felt it. Each was a restraint upon the other, and they were better apart. Those who spoke kindly but half-pityingly of her behind her back were just those of whom she saw least. Consequently, with Christie's many acquaintances, she had no friends, and, in the midst of her constant mingling with the gay world, was as curiously alone as though a magic circle had been drawn around her. She was conscious at all times that not incessant intercourse and nearness of association lessened in any degree the distance between those who called themselves her friends, but who, in many cases, were more truly her enemies; for they gradually grew to dislike her with that singular intolerance with which we regard those who make us mentally, physically, and morally uncomfortable.

To those who had once been what she was now she brought back the memory of pure, innocent days, which seemed like a ghost come to haunt them; and they hated the unconscious cause of their pain. Others resented the contrast she made with themselves. Dingy white, and even the paler shades of gray, may look quite fair and pure in certain judiciously-managed lights; but let immaculate snow be brought near them, and they can no longer hope to be mistaken for any thing but what they are. The eye can become so accustomed to a large deviation from the perpendicular, that it may seem almost straight; but let the plummet be laid to it, and even self-deception becomes impossible.

It was this office which Christie unconsciously performed for the set of women Reginald had drawn around her, and for which they could not forgive her. As soon as they found that they could not make her in spirit as well as in form one of themselves, they instinctively turned upon her passively, if not actively. "He that is not with me is against me," was their necessary motto.

"No, we none of us love Mrs. Reginald Archer," said Mrs. Lester one day among a set of her intimates when Christie's name was mentioned with some half-sneering remark. "She never hurt me particularly: but it sickens me to see any one set up for such a saint; and I have no faith in people who profess to be so much better than their neighbors. Then she is such a little fool, I lose all patience with her. I believe she thinks that magnificent husband of hers has been as idiotically saintly all his life as she has been, or as they say that rich brother of his professes to be. I should not be surprised if she thought Reginald Archer came out of a sort of moral monastery to marry her. I wonder what she would say if some one were to enlighten her a little as to her handsome husband's past life and her predecessors."

Mrs. Lester cackled as usual; and the way in which the rest laughed showed that she had expressed the sentiment of the company.

Her final sentence rested in her own memory, and was probably the first suggestion of her future action. It was upon this, her own hint, that she took her first step in that course of interference with the life and affairs of Reginald and Christie Archer which was to bring dread disaster upon so many heads, laying them in the dust, and some of them under the sod. With sin putting terrible weapons into her hands, she wrought such sorrow, that, by position rather than character, she demands a more minute description than she has hitherto received.

Marian Lester, let us hope, was an exceptional woman: at least, any society composed of even a large proportion of such persons would soon bring itself to a close ; would end by self-destruction or spontaneous combustion. A small, ugly, clever woman, with a coarse nature, whose force seemed divided into animal passion, a craving for admiration, and a malicious love of mischief, she spread trouble and moral contagion wherever she came. Vain and ambitious, with a sharp eye, a sharp tongue, and a hard, clear perception of her own interest, she had begun life with a determination to succeed ; and that she had not done so was certainly not owing to lack of effort.

To have filled any one of three *rôles* in life, she would have given what small soul she possessed ; but she soon found they were entirely beyond her. First, she longed to be a leader of society ; but she

had neither the requisite position nor wealth, nor
the rare executive genius which takes the place of
both : second, a great belle ; but she needed the
necessary beauty : third, a distinguished literary
woman ; but the entire lack of the essential talent
and imagination put an end to any aspirations in
that direction. She not only envied all who held
these positions, but had a dislike and resentment
against them as though they had robbed her of them.
Looking round her with shrewd calculation, she instinctively felt where her strong point lay, and estab-
lished her line of policy.

To this woman and her class, success means a certain number of men really or apparently attached to
their train ; and any power which controls the largest
proportion is by them cultivated and used to the
uttermost.   Attractions of various kinds attract
various persons ; but a dexterous ability to rouse
the masculine passions by glance and gesture as well
as by word ; to put men entirely at their ease, and
keep them constantly surprised and amused by an
audacious freedom of speech, whose unexpectedness
gives it the effect of wit ; to flatter them by ceaseless,
boundless, and indiscriminating devotion and attention until their backs are turned, and then with fine
mercantile tact to use them for the entertainment
and flattery of the next male comer, — this seems to

strike almost all heads ; and there are few indeed who cannot be reduced to a momentary allegiance by these means. It is amazing how far a little wit will go when thus used, and what a very large business can be done on a very small capital. It is a clear case of mathematics ; and shrewd women act accordingly.

"But you lose men's respect," said a good, refined lady to her in her youth, — that is, if Marian Lester ever had a youth, and was not born with the spirit of a wicked old woman within her, — "and you must confess that you gain no permanent hold upon them."

"My dear," returned the other with an unspeakable sneer, "as far as my observation goes, respect is a very mild sentiment in men ; and I have rarely seen a man who was sufficiently influenced by it to make it worth the having. As far as I can see, they chiefly show their respect for such women as you by keeping at a respectful distance. You are quite welcome to the sentiment, I am sure : I prefer something a little more powerful, and universal in its effect. I agree with the man who said, ' Be virtuous, and you will be happy ; but you won't have a good time.' Why, look at it for yourself ! Who are the women men run after ; upon whom they spend their time, their money, their admiration, and what they call their love ? They are those who have either given up all pretence of chastity, and live serenely in open sin; or they are those who imitate these as nearly as they can without losing their position in society. No, my dear : you have made a mistake as far as this world is concerned. I hope you may get something in the next; for you are not using the tools to gain this one."

And having made her friend exceedingly uncomfortable, and slightly confused her moral perceptions, Mrs. Lester went away in a delightful frame of mind to pursue her accustomed occupation.

In classifying the fascinations a woman may possess, it seems necessary to place at the head of the list, before beauty or brilliancy, a genuine love of men. We ordinarily do that well which we do *con amore;* and the woman to whom a man of any kind is a boon and a blessing, preferable as a companion to the most charming female alive, is inevitably the one who will be agreeable and entertaining to the largest number of the opposite sex. No masculine stupidity bores her; nothing in male habiliments comes amiss : she is at least gratified by his presence until something more desirable can be obtained. Consequently, she is in danger of hurting no man's vanity beyond forgiveness by being wearied, and allowing him to suspect it. It surrounds a man, as it were, with circumambient flattery, which, like atmospheric pressure, he feels everywhere, without resisting or defining.

This was the chief dower Nature had bestowed upon Mrs. Lester, — apparently not a large fortune, but one which she spent lavishly, and which had the singular advantage of increasing with expenditure. She had probably never committed what is called actual sin : first, because she was too shrewd, and valued the loaves and fishes of this life too highly to risk their loss by detection, even for the gratification of her passions ; and, second, because she was a coward at heart, and still retained some wholesome fear of hell-fire.

For Mrs. Lester, like so many of her kind, was a rigid church-woman, and fancied she bought exemption from the spirit of the law of God by over-emphasizing its letter. She put a curious degree of trust in forms and ceremonies, considering how little faith she had in any thing else. She served the Devil laboriously for nearly eleven months of the year, and then imagined that she restored her spiritual allegiance to its proper balance by ostentatiously serving the Lord during the forty days of Lent. To speak in the language of the turf, she made her book in life by putting most of her money upon the powers below, and then hedging in the opposite direction, so as not to be left out in any contingency. She was mighty at fairs and fashionable charities (which strike one sometimes as the modern form of buying indulgences), regarding them as a neat combination of the advantages of this world and the next. She held to the value of days and periods; apparently believing that the Lord is more clear-sighted at one time than another, or that the moral law is intermittent in its operation.

"Mrs. Lester's idea of religion seems to me to be the exact reverse of that of St. Paul," said Christie, after she had learned to know the woman thoroughly; "for he said, 'Of the times and seasons, brethren, write I not unto you:' and they seem all she has any regard for."

"Yes," Reginald had replied, laughing. "I think her idea is to get all she can here below, and to enjoy herself as much as possible; then, in the nick of time, and at the last moment, to repent, and 'read her title clear to mansions in the skies.' Nothing less luxurious would content her. I imagine she aspires to be that one sinner that repenteth, over whom there is to be so much joy in heaven. She wishes to be an eminent and interesting person in both spheres, and to drive the best possible bargain here and hereafter; and, if the thing is practicable, she is a wise woman," he added impartially.

Then, too, she was a woman of sentiment: they

always are. She professed a devotion to the purely
ideal, of which she had about as much conception
as she had of the emotions of an archangel. She ob-
jected to realistic novels, as being too much like life,
and as not supplying her need of association with
beings higher and nobler than those of this world.
She adored Bulwer and Byron, without sufficient
humor or truth herself to perceive the absurdity and
falsity of either.

It was chiefly through her lack of these qualities
that she bored Reginald.

" For a clever woman, Mrs. Lester is the least bear-
able person I know, because she is essentially second-
rate," he had said long before. " I could forgive her
ugliness : but she doesn't know humbug when she
sees it ; and that is fatal in a person who must be entertaining, or nothing. She has wit ; but she has no
real humor : she has plenty of hard common sense ;
but it is all hard, and all common," he wound up,
uttering an epigram which was repeated against her
for many a day, and for which she never forgave him.

He had hurt her vanity ; and, though she accepted
every favor she could extract from him, she would
have been charmed, at any moment, to bring trouble
upon him.

Really, though, Reginald could not plume himself
upon this as a distinction, as she pursued the same

policy, and cherished the same benevolent sentiment, towards most of her acquaintances. Her happiness required the additional element of the unhappiness of some one else. Physically idle, and yet active-minded, she found an occupation in perpetually making others uncomfortable; which afforded her the excitement, without the fatigue, which hunting and fishing give to lovers of those sports.

She had found her natural malice rather a boon, as it added zest to her life, and point to her wit; and now that she was growing old, and losing the hope of being admired, she expected it to assist her in building up that defence against insignificance in which she intended to take refuge in her old age, — the hope of being feared.

She was not wealthy, and so was compelled to supply the luxuries she would not deny herself by genteel blackmail, by broadest hints, or audacious demands, for what she wanted. Another system she practised, which seems largely in vogue with her class, — she would make trivial presents, chiefly her own handiwork, to gentlemen, and expect costly gifts in return, of whose solid value in cash no one was a better judge.

A complaisant husband is essential to such a woman and such a career; and this blessing Mrs. Lester possessed. Not being able to make an ornamental marriage, she had made a useful one ; and her husband was a slow, quiet man, admirably fitted to do her bidding, — to be a sort of watch-dog for her. In return, she relieved him of all trouble of thinking on any subject by doing it for him.

Upon the whole, her theory of life seemed analogous to that of the coachman, who urged as his greatest recommendation his ability to drive nearer than any one else to a precipice without actually going over it.

It was into the companionship of this woman that Christie's destiny brought her.

At first, their intercourse had been sufficiently pleasant ; for Mrs. Lester confined the conversation to the discussion of sentiment, in which she believed herself to shine ; and, as a difference in taste is by no means vital, they simply disagreed amicably. But the *rôle* of decorum soon bored Mrs. Lester ; and her reticence cracked and melted like thin ice. Then she began talking of subjects which the younger woman had never heard mentioned, and which she did not know were ever brought into the conversation of decent people. Then the innate, immeasurable difference between them appeared : each took her own side, and fought under her own colors. There could be no compromise here ; for the poles are not more sundered than were their thoughts and beliefs, their hopes and fears, both for heaven and for earth.

Mrs. Lester was deeply read in the history of courtesanship in every form: she was learned in the lives of all the famous wicked women of her own times and past ages. She gloated over such books, and delighted to give extracts from their spicy contents; to retail maxims and anecdotes sandwiched between appropriate original remarks. It was to such conversation Christie listened, at first with horror and protest, and then with shrinking disgust. Hitherto Mrs. Lester had had a genuine contempt for Christie, as being too weak and stupid to use the advantages of beauty, wealth, and position, which fate had put into her hand; to utilize her opportunities for winning admiration and social success. As soon as she saw with what scorn and loathing Christie regarded such triumphs as she prided herself upon achieving, she added hatred to her previous feeling. Thus Christie secured an enemy, for whose handling no weapon was too mean and low, no scratch too contemptible, and no blow too unscrupulous.

The younger woman tried to keep away from her as much as possible; but she was of too much use to Mrs. Lester for the latter to think of giving her up. She enjoyed shocking, and making her uncomfortable, under the guise of extreme intimacy and friendly interest.

She liked to come in earlier than ordinary visitors,

and amuse herself with Christie ; partly because she had nothing to do, and partly for the chance of manœuvring herself into a seat in the other's carriage for a ride down town. She would talk until the younger woman would grow sick and bewildered with a dreadful wonder as to whether this were the true picture of life and society, and whether the men and women around her were all alike, and Mrs. Lester merely more frank than the rest. Her growing distrust of all things was never so strong upon her as in Mrs. Lester's presence, whose existence seemed to justify any degree of suspicion.

It was upon one of these morning-visits in the early winter, that Mrs. Lester, having tried in the cheeriest manner several ways of making Christie uncomfortable without adequate success, suddenly recollected her own suggestion of enlightening Mrs. Archer as to her husband's past, giving her a hint of his real character.

"‘ I have piped unto you, and you have not danced ; I have mourned unto you, and you have not lamented : ’ now I will try another sort of treatment," she sneered to herself.

They were sitting in the drawing-room ; and, glancing around the apartment for some point from which to start her intended remarks, she caught sight of a picture hanging just above Christie's head, which gave her exactly the hint she wanted.

It was a small painting of a woman's face ; but its rich, voluptuous beauty, its golden hair and rosy tinting, made it shine from its shaded recess like a living countenance.   Her plan was formed in a second, without reference to any thing but the fitness of the accidental weapon for the work she intended it to perform.   She began the conversation, vaguely trusting her own dexterity to bring in the point she desired to make.

Chance favored her.

"That is a beautiful face, Mrs. Archer," she said by way of commencment.

"Yes," Christie responded: "it is very handsome."

"Did you choose the picture?" was the next remark.

"No: it is Reginald's taste.   He saw it the other day, and was so struck with it, that he bought it immediately."

"Ah," laughed Mrs. Lester, with a world of meaning in her look and tone which was almost lost upon the inexperienced woman before her, "very naturally! I could not understand why the face seemed so familiar to me ; but I see it all now."

Christie looked at her inquiringly, wondering what she was talking about, and why she glanced at her with such a curious leer.

"Of course you don't perceive the resemblance, as

you have been in this part of the world such a short time; but if you had ever lived here, and watched the *demi-monde* driving in the Park, you would see that this picture is almost the portrait of one of them," Mrs. Lester went on in her apparently off-hand way, but glancing covertly at Christie to see if the falsehood she was concocting were having the desired effect.

But Mrs. Archer was merely gazing at the picture, with a shadow of disgust upon her face which was entirely impersonal; and the elder woman saw that she must speak very plainly if she wished to accomplish her object.

To do Reginald justice, he was utterly incapable of putting any picture of his mistress where his wife could possibly become conscious of its existence. He had absolutely no moral nature and no heart; but the mere blood in his veins would have saved him from such an act of coarse insult, as it would have preserved him from personal cowardice and petty larceny. Besides this, he was perfectly clear-headed, and so had none of that strange, blind vanity which enables a man to feel complimented by the devotion of a woman to whom complaisance is a profession, and whose support requires her to smile upon some other man if not upon him: he could not feel flattered by favors which had been granted to some one before him in consideration of hard cash. No: Mrs. Lester's falsehood was a libel even against such a man. At least he possessed brain and breeding ; and the accusation was an insult to both.

"I don't know what has become of this woman; for I have not seen her for a year or two. I heard she went to another city to live. Mr. Archer can probably tell you more about her and her picture, though other people have forgotten her by this time ; but, when she was your husband's mistress, everybody knew her by sight," she wound up airily, as though saying the most natural thing possible, and one from which her preceding words and looks had taken away all abruptness.

Gazing quietly at the picture, with her profile within Mrs. Lester's range of vision, Christie heard that final sentence. Still looking upward, without sound or motion, she remained during the full moment of silence which followed the speech. If a pistol-shot had gone through her heart, she could have had no more frightful pang, no greater sense of sudden death. With that wonderful self-control which comes to women in dire need, she did what so many women before her have done, — spiritually died, and gave no sign.

Not an eyelash quivered to show Mrs. Lester how her bolt had sped ; and that lady, after waiting a minute, found herself obliged to resume the burden of the conversation.

" Of course, my dear," she said with her customary cackle, " it is not telling tales out of school to mention such a thing to you; for you must have known something of your husband's life before you married him. It is impossible to have heard Reginald Archer's name without some little history attached to it; and of course you are too sensible to mind such bachelor escapades," she continued genially. " Men will be men, you know; and the only objection I find to it is, that, by the same rule, they don't allow women to be women. I can't see the justice of confining the privilege of sowing wild oats to the masculine gender; and Mr. Archer is one of the few men who have sense and fairness enough to agree with me. And then your husband has always been such a handsome sinner, that nobody could condemn him," she went on, tiding herself over the inconvenient silence by a flow of words, and literally talking for two.

" Mrs. Lester," said Christie, after the stillness had been unbroken for several seconds, "I cannot possibly discuss my husband and his affairs with you or any one else."

The voice was low, though perfectly steady; but there was a curiously-deadened sound through it, to

which Mrs. Lester listened with curiosity and satisfaction.

"Certainly, my dear child," she replied, thinking
of the tone, and answering the words; "quite right!
You are a model wife and a modern Griselda, I
may say, — just the person for Reginald Archer to
marry, taking all things into consideration," she
sneered with the most cordial manner.

Christie made no answer. She was looking down
now, with her face still somewhat averted from the
speaker, who could not exactly determine the damage
she had done.

"Perhaps she is not such a fool after all, and
doesn't care more than the rest of us would under
the same circumstances. She certainly does not
seem very much startled or overcome, and probably
it is no great news to her after all; but she must
have been annoyed at my speaking to her of it, because her voice sounded queerly," the kindly creature
thought within herself.

"Are you going down town this morning?" she
asked affectionately, finding she could get nothing
further out of the subject.

"No," was the monosyllable which exhausted
Christie's powers of speech.

"I am sorry; for I thought we might go together,
as I have some shopping to do: but, if you are not
going, I shall have to bid you good-morning."

Christie turned round and bowed her adieux ; and Mrs. Lester took herself out of the room and out of the house with a strong sense of injustice upon her, in that Christie had afforded her neither the certainty of having cut her to the heart, nor a good story to tell around town, nor even the foundation for a neat dramatic fiction ; and she walked down the street with a discontented sense of having fallen below her customary standard.

Left alone, Christie quietly reseated herself upon the sofa ; and there, silent and still, with no outward sign but the closely-locked hands, she fought out the great battle of her life ; with what shedding of heart's blood, women like her, and their God, alone know.

Let a man put himself in her place ; let him imagine the truth suddenly coming upon him, that the being he had loved and held pure and honorable, the person whose existence was irrevocably inter-locked with his own, was foul and tainted, the rightful property of those who had gone before him ; let him dream of himself as absolutely upright ; and then let him faintly conceive the loathing, the scorn, the horror and anguish, which were tearing this woman's heart, which were vibrating through every atom of her flesh and blood.

Differing in all else, Christie and Reginald Archer

had one thing in common, — their necessity to look at facts for themselves. The clear intellects of each entirely refused to accept two standards of right and wrong, or to hold that there can be any sex in sin. Infinitely different as were the laws in which they believed and on which they acted, they both possessed the fairness and justice to lay the level alike to all. The absolute scrupulousness of one, and unscrupulousness of the other, had brought them to the same clear perception, unclouded by earthly creed or custom. Christie measured her husband and his act by the same immutable law of God which would have been applied to her had she been the criminal; which she would have used had their positions been reversed, — she being the man, and he the woman. No drop of bitterness, which, in like circumstances, would have filled a man's cup to overflowing, was lacking in hers. The fear of being the laughing-stock of a community, which seems to be the most powerful emotion in most masculine minds in similar cases, was, in some degree, spared her; but, on the other hand, what good man even can measure the agony of a delicate woman's shrinking from unchastity and impurity? Her whole body was one hot blush of shame. She felt scorched by the breath of sin, humiliated and contaminated by her involuntary contact with it. She had a sensation of self-loathing and self-contempt, as though name and fame and person had been soiled by disgrace, — as most men would have felt under like circumstances, although they had long lost the right of so feeling.

It never occurred to her to doubt Mrs. Lester's words, which were accurate enough as to the main fact they announced, though not as to the supposititious likeness they pointed out: their truth came upon her with utter conviction. It seemed the suddenly-discovered key to all that had been so strange and bewildering since her marriage; the clew to the dreadful difference between the ideal Reginald she had loved and the real Reginald she had married. The foundation of her faith had crumbled away to its last support; and, when that was touched, the whole edifice fell in an instant.

Her feeling towards her husband was one unutterable, boundless sense of revolt and repulsion. What could a love and caresses be to her which had been previously offered to a professional woman not sufficiently above an animal to believe even in any obligation of chastity? It was not only such dreadful sin, but such low sin; and the woman shivered from head to foot with disgust.

A man, with all this maddening him, would have broken the restraints which bound him, — would have committed some wild act, — and the world would have pitied and justified him. What the braver, truer woman did was to stand in her lot, fighting the mad passion at her heart as though for her soul's salvation. Above the wild tumult in her nature, the fundamental conviction of her life began to assert itself, — that, in all this conflict of wrongs, somewhere her duty lay clear and fixed; and that it greatly behooved her to find it and to do it. Long hours had gone by before the blood in her veins had stilled sufficiently to allow her to think, — to permit her to be capable of any thing beyond unspeakable sensation. The morning had passed into evening; and still she sat hidden in that shadowy recess, with her soul in deadly combat with the fate that had come upon it. Gradually conscience and intellect regained their constitutional sovereignty within her, and spoke out in tones to which she was compelled to listen : —

" Duty is like death : it comes to you, and to you alone. Its claim is absolute and indestructible, let others do as they will. Their failure can give you no release; for your allegiance is not to them, but to yourself and to your God. You have taken upon yourself a vow to love, honor, and obey this man; and your struggle must now be to keep it to the utmost possibility. You cannot afford to look back, with the present claiming you for its own. Your one great duty in life is to be a good wife; and you cannot go behind that."

Ah! it was bitter, bitter hard for that woman to sit there, and feel the truth evolved from the depths of her nature; to hear it slowly enunciated as by some terrible relentless power apart from herself. But when the night came, and the darkness fell upon the face of the earth, which was no blacker than that which had been upon her soul at noonday, a light had come unto her steps, and a lamp unto her feet, which could never lead astray; for it was the light of heaven.

She had heard herself inquired for from time to time, but without responding, or, indeed, thinking of the flight of the hours: but the servants lighting up the house recalled her to the fact that the dinner-hour was at hand, and that she must make ready to meet the man towards whom her whole emotional nature had changed; that she must prepare to take the first step in the life of duty she had laid out for herself.

She rose, and stood for a moment before going out of the room, with a sensation of having returned to earthly existence. Years seemed to have passed over her head; a great gulf divided her from her old, loving, believing self; and she knew that an utterly different woman would pass out of that apartment from the one who had entered it that morning; and night and morning are not more unlike than the heart she had brought hither and the heart she would take away.

"God help me! God help me!" was the passionate cry of that nature, which could turn nowhere else for comfort.

This was a sorrow and a suffering of which she could speak to no living being. She must fight this battle alone, without human aid; and she knew it, and applied her brave, steadfast nature to the conflict.

She went up stairs and dressed for dinner, and, descending, entered the dining-room as quietly as though all life had not changed for her since she left it. She found Reginald awaiting her, there being no company that day. He was standing very much as she had first seen him, — with the chandelier illumining his splendid beauty; with the light shining on that white brow, upon which heaven and earth seemed to smile; with the blue eyes and the glittering teeth rivalling each other in their brilliancy.

But the glamour of his loveliness for the first time had no power over her: she had caught sight of his real character, and it seemed to look out at her now as from behind an exquisite mask. She gave herself no time to hesitate: she came forward, and said "Good-evening" in as nearly her ordinary, pleasant tones as she could compel her voice to sound.

"Good-evening," Reginald returned, glancing at her carelessly. But the next moment he looked again with more attention, caught by something in her manner and appearance which he could not quite define.

"She looks stronger, and more of a woman, than ever before," he thought, "and, by the way, handsomer too."

This last consideration occasioned his next movement.

"What's the matter, Christie?" he asked. "You don't look quite like yourself this evening. You can't be sick, though, with that color in your cheeks, and light in your eyes." And, as he spoke, he put his arm around her, and, stooping idly, kissed her.

If she had been turned into stone, she could not have been more absolutely motionless than she was while his touch was upon her. No muscle recoiled, no fibre stirred, not even the eyelashes trembled; but, if ever that woman prayed, she prayed then. Standing silent, with every nerve held rigid, if she had cast herself upon her knees, and cried aloud to Heaven for help, no more agonized, passionate entreaty for strength to keep the spirit as well as the letter of her vow could have gone up to the throne of God.

Some answer must have been vouchsafed; for when,

a moment after, Reginald moved away, she passed to her place ; and, when he began talking upon ordinary subjects, she replied gently, even smilingly, though at no very great length.

"Something has certainly happened to change Christie," Reginald thought more than once as he noticed a fixed look around her mouth and an unnatural brilliancy in her dark eyes. "I wonder what it is."

But being by no means vitally interested in her emotions, and well aware that his wife might have many causes for inward discomfort which it would be wiser for him to ignore as long as possible, he took no outward notice, but ate his dinner, and chatted pleasantly, with great personal satisfaction.

When the meal was concluded, he announced that he had an engagement down town, and calmly left his wife to seek companionship in her own thoughts, or consolation from any one who might chance to come in.

CHAPTER XVIII.

DURING the weeks and months which followed that day, Christie walked her appointed course; lived the life which seemed so brilliant, and was so inexpressibly lonely. Through all its trials and temptations, she struggled to hold that inner consciousness of right-doing which to her was life, and more than life. To be an honest, loving wife, to stand clear before her own conscience, was the one passionate desire of her whole being. Had Reginald Archer possessed a heart and a conscience, however warped, their existence might still have been peaceful and happy. Her love would have struggled back into a semblance of its early self had he fostered and fed it; had he given her the great joy of being able to respect him at any time and in any way. A true love dies hard; and, when duty and devotion go together, they maintain their vitality even when it seems crushed out of them. That blessedness which arises from perfect forgiveness, from taking the spirit of Christ into the very heart, would have come to

Christie, had Reginald had the soul of a man; had he been any thing but a beautiful, intellectual animal.

But he was perfectly satisfied with his marital relations. He saw his wife's awakening to his real character, and, perceiving her struggle with herself, regretted it.

"I owe her a debt of gratitude for accommodating herself so quietly to circumstances; but it is a great pity the poor child gives herself so much unnecessary trouble. She had much better amuse herself with some one else," he thought, in his heartless good humor and impartial fairness. "If I supposed she would understand me, I would give her a hint to that effect; but she is such a little goose, I shall have to let her make her own discoveries, and be happy, or unhappy, after her own fashion. So long as she does not interfere with me, or annoy me with public scandals, I don't care what she does," he wound up with perfect sincerity.

Thus Christie was left to fight her hard battle alone, with only her God to whom to cry for help. This was her one refuge; and she sought it ceaselessly. Through brilliant scenes and varied gayeties, through witty, sometimes shameless companionship, and through solitary hours, her life was one long passionate prayer.

I sometimes wonder that women ever cease praying. To me there is no truer touch of genius in that inimitable story of "The Newcomes" than where the author speaks of Laura Pendennis as "engaged where pious women ever betake themselves in moments of doubt, of grief, of pain, of separation, of joy even, or whatsoever other trial. They have but to will, and, as it were, an invisible temple rises around them: their hearts can kneel down there, and they can have an audience with the great, the merciful, the untiring Counsellor and Consoler."

But for this relief, Christie would have died as these days went on; for she began to feel that what Reginald's life had been in the past it was in the present. Without fixed data to go upon, without testimony which she could offer to reason, much less to law, she believed that the veil of decorum covered the same hideous facts now as before. The last remnant of her love died then and there. She ceased her terrible effort to keep breath in its body: she buried the corpse, and hushed down her bitter wail over its grave. She made no pretence of an affection she could never feel again: she scorned to act a lie, as she would have scorned to speak one. She had neither the power nor visible right to leave her husband; but, in her own eyes, she was utterly divorced from the man who stood in that legal relation to her, and yet whom she suspected of daily breaking the tie which bound them.

She did nothing, said nothing; for she was too clear-sighted not to perceive her own helplessness. She fulfilled each day's duties as they arose: she was the courteous wife of a courteous husband; the elegant mistress of an elegant home; the gay, agreeable acquaintance of many gay, agreeable persons. But there was growing within her a wild desire for escape from an intolerable position. An inexpressible longing to die seized hold upon her. An utter sense of being inadequate to life, as it had come to her, crushed her soul and body. So lonely and so unlike all around her, equally unable to change her nature and standard of right or to alter theirs, she felt that all that was left to her was to go away forever and be at rest.

This craving for death, and the peace she hoped it would bring, was so intense, that it spoke out in her face. That longing look was in her eyes whenever she was unconscious of observation; whenever it was not dismissed by an effort of will. Mrs. Lester seldom saw it, as Christie was always on her guard in her presence; but others perceived it, and put their own widely-differing interpretations upon it.

Shallow, good-natured Mrs. Conrad, finding Mrs. Archer alone one day, with an inexpressible weariness of life upon her face, took up the burden of prophecy on this wise : —

"Mrs. Archer, you are evidently growing moped, and are running down."

She spoke kindly; and Christie smiled as she replied that she did not feel very well, and consequently was not very bright and gay.

"You need amusement and excitement more than medicine," the elder lady went on.

"I can scarcely want excitement in the constant round of gayeties in which we both live," was the reply.

Her needs were too deep to be discussed with any one, — least of all with the woman before her.

Mrs. Conrad sat looking at her for a moment or two, with a curious expression growing in her face. It was like the faint shadow of some long-gone pain, now only to be recalled by an effort of memory or some strong outside influence.

"My dear," she suddenly exclaimed, "it's no use : you can't do what you are trying to do. Little as you would think it, I made the attempt once myself; and I can tell you that it won't answer."

Christie looked at her in astonishment. Accustomed as she was to the lady's inconsequent style of expression and apparent obtuseness of perception, she could not take in her meaning, nor believe that she was recklessly entering the innermost recesses of her life and nature.

"It's no use trying to be absolutely devoted to your husband," she went on eagerly and disjointedly; "because no man is worth it, and no man gives you the same thing in return. Strange as it sounds now, I married for love; and for six months I did not remember that another man existed besides my husband. But dear me! child, I soon found I was having my trouble for my pains; that I was simply making a fool of myself for nothing. I saw he was amusing himself with other women; and so all that was left for me was to amuse myself with other men. It was not a very pleasant experience at first;" and, as the woman spoke, the shadow on her face deepened, and the trivial carelessness, and hard, worldly lines, faded out for the second: "but I soon got over that; and now nobody has a better time than I have," she resumed, with almost her accustomed laugh.

"Mrs. Conrad," said Christie, standing before her with her eyes beginning to glow and her voice to vibrate, "as what you call a good time would have to be purchased with all I hold sacred, I cannot afford to pay the price nor enjoy the profit."

This was neither a saint nor an angel: it was only a miserable, sore-hearted, tortured woman, striving desperately, above pain and temptation, to hold to that which was right. ‚She was not merely resisting and answering the woman before her : she was fighting her own nature, which made the same subtle suggestions to her, like the whisperings of an evil spirit.

“ In fairness and justice,” it said, “ why should you feel called upon to give your husband more than he gives you ? His failure in any part of the contract releases you from your corresponding obligation ; and it is silly and senseless in you not to use your just right.”

The temptation was upon her daily, fanning the flame of anger, pride, and revenge, — of all the stormy lower passions. With her increased knowledge of life had come a sickening clear-sightedness as to persons around her ; and she saw with shrinking disgust that there were numbers of men about her whom it needed but a change of expression in her eyes, but the faintest answering look of comprehension or invitation, to bring to her side in a base homage whose degree and result would be for her decision. She saw women every day doing this thing with apparently untroubled spirits and consciences ; certainly with uninjured positions. She knew exactly what Mrs. Conrad’s advice meant ; and, in replying to her, she was replying to herself, to the world without, and the flesh and the devil within.

“ My dear child, don’t get excited,” Mrs. Conrad answered good-humoredly. “ I meant no harm. I only intended to give you a little good advice from my own experience. It is no use striving to be unlike other people : if you live in this world, you must be like it, unless you want to be miserable. Devotion, and all that sort of thing, is very well for a little while : and even now I think it would be better worth marrying for than any thing else, if it would only last ; but it never does, and that makes the utter folly of love-matches. Men are all alike : they break whatever heart a woman has. I hadn't much," she continued with a careless laugh : "so I got off easily. But I am afraid you are taking it rather hard. I don't set up for a wit, as Marian Lester does : but I have learnt one thing in life ; and that is, that, to be happy, you must like a great many persons a little, and not care too much for any one except yourself. Since I have acquired that secret, I have been a contented woman," she announced with perfect sincerity, and without the least idea of sarcasm.

" Did you find the lesson very difficult to learn, Mrs. Conrad ? " Christie almost involuntarily inquired with smothered bitterness.

" Not very," the other replied cheerfully ; " but I am fortunately constituted in being able to make the best of every thing. You see, when I found that love was nothing but a young dream, I had still my house and carriage and all the solid results of my marriage to fall back upon, besides the amusements of society. That is the great advantage of a rich match, — you have something of permanent existence and value after the illusions fade away. My daughter shall marry money, even if she imagines she is going to break her heart for some poor man ; because I know, that, ten years after, she will be ready to thank me on her knees for what I have done. And I give you the advice now that I shall give her then, — amuse yourself, and make the best of life as you find it."

"Mrs. Conrad," Christie returned slowly, "your ideas of making the best of life and mine differ so entirely, that we can never agree on the subject."

"Very well, my dear," she responded, with unruffled, careless good nature, her temporary interest in the matter dying out: "just as you please. I didn't mean to offend you or hurt you; for I really like you; which is more than many of your professed friends do," she went on with heedless truth. "There's Marian Lester, who is always talking against you behind your back; though, to be sure, she does that to everybody," she added, partly to exalt herself by contrast, and partly upon her general principle of hitting her dear friend whenever she could.

"By the way, I ought to be at home now," she exclaimed as she looked at her watch, "as I expect company to dinner. Good-by!" And the volatile

lady went off, and, ten minutes after, had forgotten
that the conversation had ever taken place.

Christie sat and wondered whether this woman and
those around her could be right in their estimate of
life and humanity. They had certainly worked out
the problem further than she had done : they seemed
to have the force of logic and fact on their side ; and,
differing in disposition, they all agreed as to the result
of their experience. To their weight of argument
she could only silently oppose her passionate inward
conviction that love and truth are the only great last-
ing blessings here as hereafter ; that faith and honor
must exist in other hearts besides her own ; that, let
come what would in this world or the next, purity,
devotion, self-abnegation, and forgiveness are un-
speakably, infinitely better than all the satisfactions,
pleasures, and animal gratifications this earth can
offer ; and that they, and they alone, are to be pursued as the true life of both soul and body.

When this belief, born in every fibre of the woman's
original being, was crushed out, her moral nature
would die a natural death, and she would become, like
her husband, a well-bred animal, gratifying her instincts with as little sense of sin as now troubled
him. Utterly alone in spirit, with the paths of evil
made straight before her, it was simply a question
between her own soul and herself. She could listen

to the " still small voice " within her, leading her over a weary, desolate road ; or, following the example and teachings of those around her, she could drift with the current over shining seas and through flowery banks. No hand was put out to help her ; no love in her heart, or in another's for her, made right-doing the glory and happiness of existence. The hard, bare choice, uninfluenced by love or fear, was laid before her, and she made it : but it was not strange that with that choice came an unutterable longing to pass away and be at peace ; to share the rest prepared for the people of God.

Maria, also, had surprised this look in Christie's countenance, and had been perplexed and saddened by it.

" You must grow very lonely in this great house sometimes, when you are by yourself, Christie," she could not forbear saying.

" Yes, sometimes," was the indefinite reply ; " but it is generally so full of company, that I am seldom alone for any length of time."

" Christie," exclaimed Maria abruptly, " it will be a great blessing to you when you have children to occupy your heart and mind."

" Do you think so ?" was the quiet response ; but a subtile something in the tone and manner made Maria pause, and then change the subject.

Christie could not tell the other woman, that, if she thanked God for nothing else, she thanked him from the bottom of her heart that it was not probable that she would bring any child into the world to sin as its father had sinned, or to suffer as she had suffered.

It was only those who caught glimpses of her inner life who were dimly aware of her real feeling. To the world she became every day more brilliant and agreeable, and consequently more admired. She was gaining a keen, arrowy wit, and a power of expression, which the aggressive members of her set soon learned to respect and avoid. She tried hard to carry Christianity into word as well as deed; to forgive both speech and act: but she found that self-preservation is the first law of nature; that she was forced to defend herself, and to teach others to forego the amusement of tormenting her.

"Upon my word," exclaimed Reginald in delighted surprise, "my wife is growing to be the wittiest woman I know! While she and Tom are alive, I can never lack amusement." And he had a genuine sentiment of gratitude to Providence, or whatever power had thus provided for his entertainment.

He liked nothing better than to have a chat with her over the breakfast-table; and ceased, in consequence, to take that meal in his dressing-room. He would discuss the persons they had met the night before, and listen to her shrewd comments and fine perceptions of character with the same interest that a good play or a well-written novel afforded him.

"You gave Mrs. Lester a Roland for her Oliver last night," he laughed one morning.

Christie flushed slightly, with a pained look in her face.

"I could not help it," she answered. "She forced me to teach her that she must let me live in peace."

"I think you drew sufficient blood to prevent her from trying such a passage of arms with you again," he replied gayly.

"Mrs. Lester's mistake in life is, that she does not understand human nature well enough to play the game she attempts," Christie said slowly.

"That is the silliest of all blunders!" exclaimed Reginald.

"She always reminds me," she answered, "of a story papa used to tell, because she does not know just what its hero found out. A friend of papa's kicked a man down stairs for cheating at cards, and, five years after, happened to see the same man performing the same operation upon another person. 'Why, how is this, my friend? where did you get courage to kick anybody after letting me do it to you?'—'Ah! my dear sir,' the man answered with the most charming smile, 'you and I know whom to kick.' Mrs. Lester is just the reverse of this : she doesn't know whom to kick. She tries it upon everybody ; but sometimes she finds herself mistaken as to the proper individual."

"Precisely !" returned Reginald with peals of soft laughter. " That story contains the whole practical philosophy of life."

And he soon after went off to his club to repeat it again and again.

Thus day by day Christie was compelled to fight, forced to use weapons she hated. She seemed to herself slipping away from all her old ideals, her old aspirations ; and the wit and keenness which others admired were a shame and a sorrow to the woman who possessed them, and who used them in self-defence. If a lamb were thrown among wolves, and lived long enough among them without being devoured, it would certainly develop teeth and talons, and exercise them after the wolf fashion, from absolute necessity. " Lead us not into temptation ; but deliver us from evil." Ah ! the Divine Wisdom and Love well knew how needful was that petition to each frail mortal who walks this sinful, sorrowful earth.

The woman who prayed it then, prayed also for deliverance from life and its intolerable burden.

CHAPTER XIX.

LLOYD TRUXTON'S wooing had sped famous-ly; and he and Ellen had been for some time past engaged to be married.

As yet, Tom knew nothing of the matter. Lloyd had not courage to approach him on the subject, feeling instinctively that he would meet with opposition, and wishing, above all things, to conciliate his future brother-in-law, upon whom he hoped to lean for support. He soon felt that Ellen would be a much more successful advocate than himself; and to her he confided the difficult task of gaining Tom's consent.

For such a silly little creature she accomplished it adroitly, working upon her brother's nature with instinctive dexterity.

She waited for him one night when he came in rather late. Noticing a light in the drawing-room after the usual hour, he looked in to see who was there, supposing it might be Arnold sitting up for him.

"You here, Ellen?" he exclaimed. "Why, how is this, little woman? You will lose your roses if you sit up so late."

"I waited to see you, Tom. I wanted to say something to you."

He had spoken carelessly, though kindly; but, as the girl answered, he glanced at her face, and saw that she was in earnest, and that what was coming was important, — at least to her.

"What is it, my dear?" he asked pleasantly as he sat down before her.

Still the girl hesitated, with a flush upon her face; and Tom saw that it must be something even more serious than he had imagined.

"Ellen, you are not afraid of me. Whatever you have to say, say it, my dear."

"Tom," she broke out suddenly, "I am engaged to Lloyd Truxton, and I want you to let me marry him."

Tom started visibly. He opened his lips as though to make some energetic exclamation; then slowly closed them, and, sitting back in his chair, looked at her with a weary, pained sadness in his eyes, which would have deeply touched a deeper-natured woman. The girl before him had neither heart nor brain to comprehend his feeling; but she had the instinctive good sense to say nothing, and to let him speak first.

"Ellen," he said slowly, "I must tell you that Lloyd Truxton is the last person to whom I would wish to see you married; and I am not at all sure that I ought to give my consent. He is a bad man, and has led a bad life; and I do not see how any good woman could be happy with him. If I could tell you the whole truth, you would shrink away in disgust from him, instead of wishing to be bound to him forever."

"He is good enough to be Reginald's intimate friend. I have never heard him say any thing against Lloyd," she answered, with a sullen resentment of his words.

Again Tom hesitated painfully. To lower his brother in his sister's eyes, to exhibit him to her, even partially, in his real light, was what he could scarcely bring himself to do.

"Unfortunately, Ellen," he said very gravely, "Reginald has no friend whom I would choose as a husband for you; none, indeed, whom I would select as an acquaintance for myself. I am sorry to say that his standard is not that which any pure man or woman could hold."

"He can't be so very bad, when he is received and welcomed by the best society, by the finest ladies in the city," Ellen replied, planting herself upon the solid ground of hard fact.

"I know it," exclaimed Tom bitterly: "so much

the worse for them! But if you either square your
conscience or choose your husband by the rules of
what is called 'good society,' I am sorry for you."

"Tom," she suddenly cried out, abandoning all
other ground, and using her one unanswerable argument, "I love him!"

A singular change came over the man's face as he
heard the words. With however little comprehension of their deep meaning the girl was speaking
them, to him they meant all that was real and last-
ing in the universe. She had struck his vulnerable
point both by nature and circumstances. He unconsciously measured the depth of her feeling by his own,
and imagined her suffering would be what his had
been in the loss of the being he loved. Poor Tom!—
he had not the heart to inflict this torture upon any
one,—least of all upon his weak little sister.

"My dear," he said very tenderly, "if that really
be the case, I have nothing more to say, except to
warn you as to Lloyd's true character, and leave you
to come to your own decision. But, for God's sake!
don't deceive yourself on either point, and make
yourself wretched for life."

"I have considered the matter well," Ellen answered; "I have thought of nothing else since last
summer; and I have determined to marry Lloyd
Truxton."

"Then," said Tom wearily, "there is nothing left for me to say or do. Your being my sister affords me no control over you; but it gives me a deep interest in your welfare, and a love for you which can never change, Ellen, as you know without my saying it."

"I know it, Tom," she replied softly, and, going up to him, kissed him.

They were not a demonstratively affectionate family; and the somewhat unaccustomed action touched Tom's sore, hungry heart. He took the little creature in his arms very lovingly.

"If he makes you happy, I will try to forgive him his past life; but I can't see my little sister miserable, either without him or with him," he said as he returned her kiss.

"But, my child," he exclaimed a few moments after, "how does Lloyd expect to take care of you? I have never heard of his being in any business. Has he any thing to support you on?"

"Ah, Tom!" she replied, clinging more closely to him, "we thought you would take care of that."

A curious chill struck through the man; and his warm, affectionate clasp loosened suddenly into a formal embrace.

"Ah! that's it, is it?" he thought bitterly. "It is money, after all, that this unusual tenderness means. That is why she asks my consent, instead of coolly acting without it. I am expected to bestow a yearly income upon the young people with my blessing. Well," he continued to himself, with a sinking sense of disappointment in every thing human and material, " my money might as well go in that way as in any other. It has certainly given me very little happiness; and, if it can bring it to others, why should I withhold it?"

" Ellen," he said quietly after a pause, during which the girl had waited eagerly for the effect of her words, " it is not my duty to support an idle man, nor do I think it best for Lloyd that I should do so; but, if he is willing to work, I will see that he is very well paid. You are my sister, and have an inalienable, natural claim upon me; and, if you determine to marry him, I will do what I can for you and your husband. You can tell Lloyd what I say, and let him act as he chooses."

" Thank you, dear Tom!" replied Ellen, radiant at having secured this much thus easily, and trusting herself and time to make it much more: " you are always as kind as you can be."

" Good-night, my dear!" was his only answer; and then he went out of the room and up stairs to bed.

He did not give her a farewell kiss, nor allow her a chance of thus bidding him adieu. He could not accept tokens of affection, for which he, at least partially, paid in dollars and cents. He was capable of any Quixotic generosity; he would have given her all he possessed uncalculatingly, almost unthinkingly, had she really needed it: but this cool balancing of emotion and gold, this deliberate mixing of love and money, sickened him to the heart. If they wanted his cash, let them take it; but he preferred not accepting the offered payment in return.

"I am a sort of walking porte-monnaie or checkbook; I believe that is all I am to anybody," he thought, with a disgust equally divided between himself and those who had systematically traded upon his family feeling.

Thus thinking, he passed Arnold's chamber. The door was ajar; and he remembered that such was always the case when he came in late. He entered the apartment, led on by his hunger and thirst for even the sight of something upon whose disinterested truth and love he could absolutely depend. Arnold was lying upon a lounge, fast asleep; and his brother went up to the couch, and stood looking down upon him. Long, ugly, and ungainly, in any thing but a graceful attitude, he was more lovely in Tom's eyes than the most radiant physical beauty could have made him. He had the strongest impulse to stoop and kiss him, as he might have done to a woman:

as it was, he drew the hair back from the temples with the softest loving touch.

"He really loves me: he would be the same if I had nothing to give him." And he seemed to rest his world-weary heart and tired eyes by even looking at him.

"Wake up, my dear boy!" he said presently: "you'll take cold if you lie here."

Arnold shook himself, and rose; a pleasant light coming into his dull eyes as he saw who was arousing him.

"Waiting for me as usual, Arnold?" Tom asked, with a laugh that had a curious thrill through it.

"I did not keep very good watch," returned the other; "but I fell asleep while I was reading."

"Why do you always sit up for me, you foolish fellow?" said Tom, with the same vibration in his tone.

"Oh! I don't know," answered the other, half laughing, and coloring slightly; "but I have a feeling that I can rest better when I know that you are safely and peacefully asleep."

Tom laid his hand on his brother's shoulder, and the two men looked at each other with inexpressible tenderness. Then, with inherent Anglo-Saxon reticence, Tom turned quietly away, without a word to give voice to his feeling.

"You can go to your bed now," he said after a moment, "with nothing on your mind; for I am going to mine. Good-night!" he added, and went off.

It was the farewell word he had spoken to his sister but a few moments before; but what a different meaning it now bore! The tone was a caress and a blessing; and it came from a heart whose bitterness and chill had vanished before the warmth and light of love.

Tom's consent to his marriage, and promise of assistance, being announced to Lloyd, he felt that he had a provision for life. Thus re-enforced, he went to Reginald, and told him his plans and intentions. That gentleman was rather surprised, but acquiesced calmly in the arrangements, as he did in every thing which did not personally incommode him.

"So Ellen worked Tom up into saying yes, and in agreeing to help to support you both? She's a sharper little thing than I gave her credit for being," Reginald said when Lloyd told him all the circumstances. "You are certainly not a very great match for her; but, after all, it is better than having a stranger coming into the family and making things disagreeable. So the marriage suits me well enough; and I promise you I will do as much for you and Ellen as Tom does," he wound up, magnificently disposing of Christie's money as he had done with that of some one all his life.

And again Lloyd Truxton thanked his lucky star which had led him to ally himself with the Archers.

Reginald announced the news to Christie that day at dinner. She did not seem as much astonished as he expected.

" I imagined something of the kind was going on last summer ; but, as nothing seemed to come of it, I hoped I was mistaken," she said slowly, with a troubled look in her face.

" Why did you hope you were mistaken ? What is your objection to the match ? " he asked.

" Oh ! I don't know," she answered evasively, "except that I don't think he is the sort of man to make a woman happy."

Reginald knew perfectly what she meant ; but, not caring to discuss the subject, it dropped.

The next morning, Christie went to Ellen's home, apparently to congratulate her upon her engagement, but really with a different purpose.

" I cannot let her take such a step in utter blindness, as I did," she was thinking as she walked towards the house. " She will neither understand nor believe me, I suppose : but I cannot have it upon my conscience not to give her some idea of the character of the man she wants to marry ; some reminder of the truth, and its inevitable consequences. It cannot be that she knows what she is doing; and, in the barest justice, some one ought to tell her before it is too late."

Entering the house, she found Ellen and Maria together. She went through some of the forms and phrases customary on such occasions; all of which Ellen received with a cool serenity wonderful to behold. Maria was much the more agitated of the two; for she was capable of hopes and fears which could not be satisfied by the certainty of a future material support and a matrimonial position. She had a brain to think, and a heart to feel; and both took a wider range than could have been filled by money and gratified vanity. Lloyd Truxton was no favorite of hers, though she had only heard vaguely of his course of life. She had very little pleasure in this marriage; though, like Tom, she thought it useless to oppose that which Ellen was determined upon. But she was so generous in her love for her sister, that she showed her interest, and not her anxiety; and talked cheerfully of an engagement upon which, in her own heart, she sat in sorrowful judgment.

Thus they talked of Ellen's plans, until Christie began to fear that she would have no opportunity of carrying out her real purpose. She was about to relinquish her intention, and take her leave, when Maria was called out of the room; and her chance for speaking unexpectedly came to her.

"Ellen," she said hurriedly, "when I heard last night of your engagement, I prayed God you might be happy; but I thought some one ought to tell you the character of the person you have promised to marry, as you must be ignorant of it. I can't see you, unwarned, link yourself to a man who has led an impure life, and who has no idea of honor as regards women. You may hate me for telling you the truth; but I can't stand by and see you unconsciously make yourself wretched."

In her passionate earnestness, Christie had risen to her feet, and was standing before Ellen, with her voice and her lips quivering, and the tears springing into her eyes.

The girl looked up coolly at her.

"Lloyd is Reginald's constant companion, and I suppose is no worse than he is; yet you found my brother good enough, not only to engage yourself to, but to marry," she returned quietly.

The color rushed into Christie's face; and she turned away quickly, almost as though Ellen had struck her. She could not give the answer which sprung to her lips: —

"If I had known even the shadow of the truth,

I would have bitten out my tongue before it should have said yes; and I judged you by myself."

She shut her teeth to prevent the words from escaping in spite of her will.

"Lloyd is just about what men ordinarily are," Ellen went on calmly; "and most married women seem to get on very well."

Christie looked silently at her in weary hopelessness, and with a contempt which wavered strangely between herself and the girl before her.

"It would be as well to talk to a blind man of color, or to a deaf man of sound, as to appeal to purity, honor, delicacy, and truth, in a person devoid of moral sense and fine instinct. I am an idiot for my pains," she thought hotly.

And then came the old subtle doubt, whether, after all, Ellen were not the wiser woman of the two, in taking the best of life that she could get without troubling herself with any higher considerations than daily pleasure and daily food. She and Reginald were certainly the most contented persons Christie knew; and they were surely those who lived most entirely without a care or a thought beyond animal comfort and gratification. The moral of the story might be instructive; but it did not tend to strengthen aspiration. Her striving towards a great invisible standard and a more elevated life had only brought her sorrow and anguish of spirit; and it was scarcely strange, that, at the moment, she hardly knew which to despise, the girl or herself.

Maria's re-entrance cut short the conversation; and, soon after, Christie went back to her splendid home, more heart-sick and weary of life than ever.

Lloyd Truxton determined to secure his promised pecuniary advantages as soon as possible, and so pressed for an immediate marriage. As Ellen was easily persuaded, he gained his object; and the preparations went speedily forward. Every one lent a helping hand; even Christie and Tom facilitating that which they could not prevent. Tom offered his sister a very handsome wedding, or the money it would cost invested for her benefit; and, with unexpected good sense, she chose the latter.

Consequently, the end of the month of her engagement saw her quietly married; saw her made Mrs. Lloyd Truxton, greatly to her own satisfaction, if to that of no one else.

One fact, at least, concerning this wedding, must not pass unnoticed; for, in Ellen's eyes, it was a most important item: the diamond cross which Tom presented her was even larger and handsomer than the one he had given Christie.

Could mortal bliss demand more!

CHAPTER XX.

"WAS the ball brilliant last night?" asked Reginald carelessly, as he and Christie sat at the breakfast-table one morning several weeks after Ellen's marriage.

He had accompanied his wife and sister to the entertainment, but had soon excused himself and gone off in another direction, leaving them both under Lloyd's care.

"Yes," she replied, — "about what such things usually are. But you missed the chief sensation of the evening; for the new beauty, Mrs. Van Arsdale, came in after you left."

"Ah, indeed!" exclaimed Reginald, awakening into sudden interest. "I am sorry I did not see her; for they have been talking about her at the club for a week. All the men are raving about her singular red-gold hair and her black eyes. Is she still so very handsome?"

"Remarkable looking, and extremely, strikingly pretty. She would be beautiful, if she had either sense or soul in her face," Christie replied.

" That is just as I remember her," answered Reginald.

" Why, I did not know you had ever seen her."

" Oh, yes! I was introduced to her when she was here five years ago on her bridal trip; but she was too nearly an unformed girl in those days to show her beauty to advantage. I hear her social education, and knowledge of how to use her charms, have progressed amazingly since then," he added with a laugh.

" She said she had come to the city to live permanently; and she seemed very glad of it."

" I can imagine so," he exclaimed. " ' No pent-up Utica ' for her any longer."

" Shall I call on her ? " asked Christie indifferently. " Every one is doing so."

Reginald paused for a moment before answering ; and a curious expression came into his eyes.

" Just as you please," he said quietly ; " but, unless you wish to go, I think I would stay away. She is not at all your style ; and I am sure, that, the more you knew her, the less you would like her."

The moment Mrs. Van Arsdale's residence in the city was announced, Reginald had foreseen possibilities of connection between himself and her (as indeed he did with every beautiful or distinguished woman with whom he seemed likely to be thrown), which would render it best that she should be cut off from intercourse with his wife : so he prudently provided against contingencies, as it were on speculation, and discouraged the acquaintanceship, as generally undesirable.

" Leave her to such women as Mrs. Lester and Mrs. Conrad ; they will suit her much better," he added.

" She seemed to have left herself to them last night," said Christie, smiling. " They appeared to have fallen into a sort of spiritual triangular embrace, from what I saw."

" I understand exactly," laughed Reginald : " they will agree capitally for a little while, — until she happens to offend one of them, or stand in her way. Then let her look out ; for they will make her wish she had never seen them. I have watched that game too often not to know it by this time ; and I advise you to keep out of the whole affair."

Talking in his grand, debonair manner, and gracefully patronizing the whole social system, Reginald Archer little realized what truth there was in his own words : far less did he dream how terribly it would behoove him to follow his own advice.

" I am sure I have no desire to know her more intimately, and should be quite satisfied if I were never to hear her name again," Christie answered indifferently.

She would repeat those final careless words again and again in her heart with a strangely-altered feeling; for the days, even the years, were rapidly approaching, when a wild desire never again to have Lucretia Van Arsdale brought back to her consciousness would be the great, agonized longing of her life.

"Very well, then; don't put her down on your visiting-list," Reginald said as he left the room; and the matter was settled.

Years ago, I stood looking at a picture by Leonardo da Vinci, with an admiration which was mingled with a curious sense of astonishment. The subject was Herodias' daughter. The hideous, swarthy executioner stood there, offering to Salome the charger upon which lay the pale, bleeding head of the prophet. Over the girl's shoulder peers the handsome, old, revengeful face of Herodias, with its smile of cruel and complete satisfaction. Passionate triumph over her fallen enemy, the fire of wounded pride, all the emotions of the strong, wicked nature, are in the strong, wicked face. But it is Salome herself who rouses surprise, and rivets attention, by the strange contrast between her trivial slightness and the intensity and strength of the others. Not as she is usually painted — an imperious, hot-blooded, superb woman, sharing her mother's nature, and executing her will because it is also her own — had the great master represented her, but as a delicately, felinely beautiful creature, with a shadow of cold, hard cruelty in the almost meagre lines of face and figure. A slight young girl, radiant with the sheen of red-gold tresses, the dark gleam of drooping, almond-shaped eyes, and the color of scarlet lips drawn some-what closely over glittering teeth, but, withal, a senseless, soulless being, who shocks you, even in that scene, like a monstrosity; a court-dancer, will-ingly doing her mother's bidding, through sheer indifference to any thing beyond her own comfort and pleasure; destroying a great prophet as gayly as she would have killed a fly, from lack of sufficient brain to comprehend the difference between them, from want of sufficient heart to consider others for a single moment, — this, and nothing more.

She stands extending her lovely arms to receive the charger with its ghastly burden; her only recog-nition of its horror being, that she slightly turns away her head to save herself the physical annoyance of gazing at any thing disagreeable. The shine in her eyes and the smile upon her lips are those she has brought from dancing before the king; and the in-toxication of gratified vanity is so strongly upon her, that she seems swaying, almost swooning, with sen-suous delight. The plaudits of king and court are

still ringing in her ears; and the death-moans of her
victim do not even suggest themselves to her remotest
consciousness. The shallow, pleasure-adoring nature
has only room for self-love and physical gratification :
the necessary space for remorse, or suffering for sin,
is not in it. The old painter had studied, not merely
the deep mysteries of his art, but those of humanity ;
he had reached the subtlest truths of each; and I
learned afresh from his wondrous hand that the most
dangerous of created beings are those soulless sinners
who will not know what they do, and who are too
absolutely fitted to their lives and occupations ever
to turn from them, or to feel degradation in dreadful
act or lowest life. Passion fades out, hate relents,
revenge sometimes sheathes its weapon ; all the mad,
evil impulses of the human heart die a natural death
in course of time, or waver before obstacles : but
what can ever change vanity, ignorance, and utter
levity ? and before what will they stop or stay their
course ? Let come what will ; let the prophet of the
Lord perish ; let truth and right be trampled in the
streets ; let blood flow, and sin and shame follow, —
Salome will be glad and gay so long as she can dance
and be applauded ; so long as she can read admiration in the eyes of a goodly Jew or gallant Roman.

My first sight of Lucretia Van Arsdale gave me
so strong a sensation of having seen her before, that

I could scarcely believe such was not the case. Yet we had never met; and for a long time I searched in vain for a reason for the strange familiarity of her aspect. Suddenly the recollection of Leonardo da Vinci's picture flashed upon me, and made all clear. The faces and figures were almost identical; and I lived to know that the characters were no less so.

This was the woman who was now to cross Reginald Archer's path; who was to bring sorrow and destruction alike to the innocent and the guilty.

She had been born in one of the smaller Western cities; and there her husband had married her, — a beautiful but unformed girl. There, too, she had lived until she had matured into her present appearance and style.

Mr. Van Arsdale had adored his wife; still admired her extravagantly; and, indeed, loved her as much as it was possible to love such a trivial being after long association. He was a quiet, gray-eyed man, who toiled at his legal profession for money, which his wife had the pleasure of spending. Morally, he was no better and no worse than the majority of men, and led very much their life. He had but two striking characteristics, — a capacity for hard work, and for still, concentrated passion. Both temper and heart combined to give him the power to love and to hate with unmeasured intensity. He was a

13

curiously undemonstrative person ; but it would have
been difficult for a keen observer to look at him without seeing that it would be as well to allow him to
remain so.   What little culture she would take, and
what social style she had acquired, were chiefly owing to his endeavor; but she had long since passed
beyond his control.

"Van Arsdale has built up his wife," Reginald
once laughed ; "but I declare he would have to get
on a scaffolding now to reach her, the little lady
carries her head so high."   And he stated the case
very correctly.

It was the night after his talk with Christie upon
the new social star that Reginald entered a ball-room
with curiosity and interest roused by the prospect of
seeing the much-discussed beauty.   He was not disappointed.   He recognized her, standing near the
host, surrounded by a *cordon* of admirers, the centre
of observation.   Moving up the room with Christie,
he surveyed Mrs. Van Arsdale at his leisure.

She was one of those women whose radiant coloring requires none in their dress ; whose tinting becomes a vivid glory when contrasted against a dead
background.   She wore this night a dress of rich
black lace, with some striking arrangement in her
red-gold hair, which gave her the effect of a Spanish
beauty.   Her slender neck and arms and snowy

shoulders shone like alabaster against their slight shading; and skin and lips and eyes had a clear brilliancy of color which was almost magical. Without flower or jewel, she seemed the most splendidly-dressed woman in the room.

She was evidently enjoying her position to the full; giving a look to one, a side-glance to another, and a smile to a third; making each think his favor best worth having, with a cool dexterity which showed she had practised the art long and well. As Reginald approached that end of the room to make his salutation to his entertainer, she glanced at him, and then looked again, with the thought that had been in so many women's minds, — that he was the handsomest man she had ever seen.

She remembered him in a moment, and, as Mr. and Mrs. Archer turned from the lady of the house, smiled the sweetest smile upon the wife to attract the attention of the husband.

"I remember Mrs. Van Arsdale so well, that I presume to hope she has not entirely forgotten me," said Reginald, as he made his superb bow before her; and she returned it with equal grace and *empressement*.

As he raised his head, their eyes met; and that strange, slight look of mutual recognition and understanding, which always flashes between such a man and woman, passed swiftly between them, and the beginning of the end had come. That curious glance, and the smile in the depths of the eyes, notifies each instantly of the past life and present character of the other. It is as though the devil in each silently looks out, and salutes his fellow in the other. There is no need of further explanation : each knows the old familiar ground, and exactly how any word or act will be received, — just the old game ; and the players have the confidence of certainty and long practice.

Standing quietly by, Christie caught the expression, as she had done so often before. A man seldom makes eyes over his wife's head without her becoming aware of the fact, whether he be moved by criminal intent or mere shallow vanity ; and there is scarcely a woman alive whose love will bear such attrition, or who will not learn with startling rapidity the lesson thus conveyed and the art thus taught. Once making up her mind to benefit by the instruction, and practise upon her own account, she soon surpasses her teacher in skill, dexterity, and ardor in the pursuit. Unless, like Reginald Archer, a man be absolutely regardless of his wife's love, attention, or honor, unless he be perfectly willing for her to go to any length that may please her, he is paying a hazardous price in setting her such an example ; in making her feel, that, let come what will, the initiatory responsibility rests with him.

But Reginald had long since divorced himself from such weakness and unfairness concerning his wife, and enjoyed himself without fear.

Christie, like all innocent but original, clear-sighted women, from seeing nothing, had come to see every thing. Nothing escaped her silent observation, nor her terribly truthful interpretation ; and, as she stood talking to the gentleman in front of her, she was quietly watching the by-play between Mrs. Van Arsdale and her husband, with the sensation with which such scenes always filled her. He had no longer any place in her heart, and consequently could not make that heart ache and bleed : she had none of the ordinary feeling of jealousy, as that necessitates some remnant of affection. But when a man or woman has had a great magnanimous faith in another, and has seen it pass away forever, there sometimes grows, out of very sorrow and shame, a dreadful sense of bitter humor. To look unshrinkingly at the thing we have worshipped, and see it in its naked outline and natural colors ; to watch it in its blind vanity displaying itself in all its lights, exhibiting more and more with every movement its weakness and coarseness, if not its mean falsity ; holding up to view its shallowness, its triviality, its pitiful susceptibility to flattery from any and every source, — to do this sometimes stirs a laughter which is more terrible than burning tears. Love can co-exist with almost every sensation except absolute contempt : that kills it once and forever. The devotion which would be strong and steadfast to resist poverty, temptation, the powers of earth and hell combined for its destruction, will wither like Jonah's gourd at the breath of this subtile sentiment. If it once dimly enters a woman's heart in connection with the man she loves, let him look to it speedily ; for his power over her is going, and going fast. Nothing is so effective nor so permanent in healing heart-wounds : when the full heat of that iron has gone over them, they are indeed cicatrized.

It was this cruel cure which had come to Christie, enabling her to stand and watch the scene before her with such a terrible perversion of the grief, anger, and shame, which would have naturally filled her heart at the sight. She had long since parted with personal feeling in regard to her husband's conduct ; and its absence told its own wretched tale.

Special resentment towards Mrs. Van Arsdale did not occur to her. She knew that, if not she, it would only have been some other of the thousand and one bold, if not bad women, which such men meet ready to their hands at every turn. Talking wittily to those around her, her physical frame was thrilling with disgust : her soul was filled with the old wild longing to escape by some means from the evil which surrounded her like a tainted atmosphere. That startling difference between a woman's feeling and seeming was seldom greater than then, as Christie's eyes and words both grew brighter, though the glitter of each was that of steel rather than of sunshine.

Mrs. Van Arsdale was undeniably the great success of the evening. She had, as it were, the whole company pursuing her ; but Reginald held his own gallantly, keeping the head of the course like a splendid racer. He soon found she was below mediocrity in intellect, and did not comprehend half the beautifully-turned compliments he paid her ; but it gave for a little while a piquant spice to the situation to see her turn up her splendid eyes and show her pearly teeth at appropriate moments, as though by instinct, in reply to sentences she did not and could not comprehend. Handsome as she was, he might have tired of this, but that two-thirds of the men in the room were dying to be in his place ; and that sustained the excitement. He had openly entered the lists ; and his reputation did not suffer him to leave or to remain, except as winner. Incapable of love at any time, coolly critical of the woman before him, and conscious of her absolute worthless-

ness except as a fine animal, he and his intimates well
knew the work for the next few months which this
night was carving out.

But Reginald seldom cheapened himself by bestowing too large a portion of his time and attention
upon any one, and, before the evening was over,
left Mrs. Van Arsdale, and came to that part of the
room where his wife, Mrs. Lester, and several other
ladies, formed a gay group. Making himself supremely fascinating to the party, he showed Mrs.
Van Arsdale his value among other women.

But that lady was of a most practical turn of
mind, and never wasted her time in even momentary
regrets over any one man, let him be what he might.
So, turning to the next comer, she lavished upon him
the same smiles and meaning glances she had given
his predecessor.

He happened to be a rich young fool, whose money
gave him a certain importance in society, which par-
doned his stupidity and homeliness in consideration
of his prodigality. He was accustomed to the deference he was receiving, and to keeping better men at
bay. Except that he was the ugliest, instead of the
handsomest man in the room, Mrs. Van Arsdale
found him quite as agreeable a companion as the
witty, cultivated gentleman who had given place to
him ; indeed, understanding his conversation much

better, she answered it with much more comfort to herself.

The group around Reginald looked on with an amusement which he perfectly shared. Reginald's vanity had the rare peculiarity of never injuring his sense of humor, as his vices did not affect his perception nor his sense of justice, — traits which place him alone in my memory. The situation tickled his fancy; and he smiled over it more genuinely, perhaps, than any one present. But even the millionnaire was not allowed to retain his place very long : he was soon crowded away by a set of old society beaux, who had been waiting their opportunity, and who each received the same prodigal welcome.

"It's all fish that comes to Mrs. Van Arsdale's net," laughed one of the gentlemen who stood by Christie.

"Did you ever see such a woman!" exclaimed Mrs. Lester, who was beginning to lose her temper at this entire monopoly of the general attention. "Why, she would make eyes at the archangel Gabriel!"

The tinge of virtuous indignation with which she spoke was, coming from such a source, almost too much for the self-control of the party. Many of them bit their lips to keep down their laughter.

"Reminds one of the old saying about the pot

calling the kettle black," whispered the first speaker to Reginald, evidently having a habit of saving himself the wear and tear of original expression by putting his thoughts into proverbs.

"I think Gabriel would be quite safe from Mrs. Van Arsdale's attentions," said Christie quietly. "I imagine she directs them to human rather than to angelic attractions. But I fancy, that, like some other persons I have known, she acts upon Burns's broad general principle, that ' a man's a man for a' that.'"

There was a laugh, apparently at Mrs. Van Arsdale's expense; but it was Mrs. Lester who really paid for the epigram, as she was well aware. Not a few of those who stood round her, who had suffered from her evil tongue, rejoiced in their hearts at the double hit; and Christie's quotation from Burns was repeated in connection with the elder lady for many a day.

At his wife's final words Reginald turned around, radiant with delight. Humor and wit charmed him at all times; and to be the legitimate possessor of the wittiest woman present was always a sweet morsel which he rolled under his tongue.

"Of course you have said the best thing which has been said this evening, Christie; you always do," he whispered laughingly. "But the idea of Marian Lester objecting to an equal and universal distribution of favors! It's too funny! Angelic characters are not in much danger from either lady, I imagine."

"And yet I can fancy Mrs. Lester discoursing sentimentally to St. Paul concerning his thorn in the flesh," Christie replied under her breath, "and attempting to build up a flirtation upon that slender foundation."

Reginald went off into soft, smothered laughter; and those around him vainly begged to know the cause of his amusement.

He appreciated the delicate flattery of the fact that his wife was never so brilliant as when alone with him. She talked from genuine interest in her subject, and not to astonish society with mental fireworks; and consequently was most responsive to the listener who best comprehended her. He had acquired, in some degree, that mental belief in and admiration for his wife which he had so long possessed for his brother Tom. But, alas! his feeling was as powerless in one case as in the other to restrain him from evil, or to control him for good. Not half an hour after, he was again at Mrs. Van Arsdale's side, with that meaning look and touch of the hand at parting, which were a portion of as cool and deliberate a plan for his self-gratification as the ordering of his carriage or the eating of his dinner.

CHAPTER XXI.

SINCE the night when Tom had stood under his brother's roof and seen Christie's head droop with grief, he had scrupulously avoided meeting her. He had tested his strength, or rather his weakness, in regard to her; and he did not dare to let any strain come upon his self-control. They met occasionally at his own house; but he made these encounters as few, short, and quiet as possible.

Yet, such as they were, he did not recover from them for days after. They quickened the dull pain at his heart, set his nerves quivering and his blood throbbing. What slight mastery he had gained over his passionate love he could not afford to imperil, and consequently put a safe distance between them.

Yet he watched her from afar, sedulously and ceaselessly, always with one great dread of what he might read in her face.

"Is it possible to touch pitch, and not be defiled?" was the thought ever in his mind. She seemed to him to be undergoing the old ordeal of walking over hot iron; but would she be unscathed? She was perpetually in his thoughts; and he took care that she should be often in his sight. He went to operas and theatres where he knew he should see her; and, in spite of his old keen appreciation of any good performance, neither actress nor singer had power to draw his attention from the face he studied. Occasionally he would accept invitations to balls and parties, and watch her when she little imagined he was near.

But though he saw many changes in that countenance, saw it light up into a brilliancy that had no real warmth or sweetness, and pale into a hungry longing for escape from existence, he looked in vain for the moral fall and spiritual declension he so feared.

"She is still pure and unsullied in word, thought, and deed." And the man's strong heart, which bled for her pain, gave a great throb of infinite joy and triumph that he could still love and honor and adore her.

Tom Archer had that native cleanliness of soul from which he could no more have loved an unchaste woman than he could have worshipped an impure God. Had Christie stained mind and body with sin and shame, his love for her would have died, though he died with it. Even had she loved him as he loved her, and had offered to sacrifice her soul for his sake, to cast herself away for his gratification, she would merely have destroyed her power over him, and made him a free man. She could use no surer means of slaying his deep devotion than by showing a willingness to grant that for which he would never solicit. He might have gone on sorrowfully adoring the woman he had believed her to be; but, as for herself, she would have been to him as one dead and buried. Such men cannot love like beasts of the field; and the woman who falls to that level falls too far for them to follow her. To them literally God is love, and love is God. It is their religion, their aspiration, their hope of heaven here and hereafter. Tom's love took a new lease of life with every look at the pure, sweet face he scrutinized with such terrible keenness; for it seemed to him, at times, that of a shining angel, drawing him to a nobler, higher manhood,—towards that heaven which is our home.

In their chance-meetings she tried him sorely by her evident need of him, and longing for his help.

"We never see you now, Tom," she would say, with that wistful look in her eyes. "When you promised to be my brother, I thought I should have you to turn to at every moment."

And Tom would be faint and sick as he answered hurriedly, that he had been too much engrossed in business for visiting of any kind. Christie would look at him sadly and wearily, as though she were too well accustomed to disappointments to be surprised ; and Tom would go away in such an immeasurable rage and disgust at his brother, that he did not dare to see him for days after.

Week by week, in her painful solving of the problem of life, Tom grew to have a larger and larger share in Christie's thoughts. Seeing around her bad faith of every kind, — husbands deceiving their wives, wives slyly and quietly outwitting their husbands, — she naturally turned with almost passionate ardor even to the remembrance of the person in whom her belief was founded as upon a rock. In her doubt of all things, Reginald's trust in Tom strengthened her confidence not a little ; for she fully appreciated her husband's intellectual acuteness and candor.

" I fancy Diogenes has followers even at this day in his search for an honest man, and that they meet with the same want of success," Christie said bitterly one day when some flagrant occurrence was being commented upon.

" Not always," returned Reginald with airy sweetness. " For myself, I may say that there I have the advantage of Diogenes. I have never made myself ridiculous with lantern in a market-place ; but I have seen what he sought in vain ; which goes to prove that the true philosophy of life is to sit still and let things come to you, instead of fatiguing yourself by running after them, and missing them at last."

Reginald liked the sound of his own rich, finely-modulated tones, in which he certainly showed his taste ; and, being always at leisure, was extremely fond of giving out his opinions at any time to a good listener.

" Yes, I think I have a talent for scepticism equal even to that of Montaigne ; and I hold *que sais-je* to be the wisest motto ever adopted : but, with all my doubting, I have never been able to doubt Tom."

" You are right," said Christie. " I had forgotten him when I spoke ; and I beg his pardon sincerely."

Then she looked at the man before her, and wondered afresh how, from the same father and mother, could have been created two beings so unlike as himself and his brother, — one of the mysteries which has perplexed wiser, older heads than hers.

Thus it was, that, though parted from her, Tom still maintained so deep and warm a place in her innermost nature. Unconscious of his limitless devotion to her, she still thought of him and wearied for him through long desolate hours, when he little imagined that she recollected his existence. That last private conversation they had had before her marriage, when he had striven to warn and protect her ; when he had demanded, that, looking at persons

and things with enlightened eyes, she should one day
do him tardy justice, — how it came back to her now!
and how she fulfilled his requirement from the depths
of her crushed heart! Weighing all things in the
balance, and finding so many wanting, it was small
wonder that her soul clung almost convulsively to
the only being in whom they had found certain security and rest. Ah! Tom was not forgotten, as he
sometimes tortured himself by thinking, as the blank
days in which he neither saw nor heard of her went
wearily on.

Being a man of general culture and of strong
taste for the beautiful, he was naturally fond of all
things artistic, but especially of pictures. He carried the same perception and clear original judgment
into this matter as into his business. He knew a
good picture from a bad one, let the surroundings of
either be what they might : and Reginald never felt
perfectly satisfied with his art-purchases until Tom
had given his nod of approbation ; then he felt prepared to face critics, professional or amateur.

Tom liked to hang round old print-shops, and thus
pick up bargains in books and engravings which made
his brother's mouth water. Thus it was, that a
week or two after that evening in Reginald's house,
when the sorrowful, upward, appealing look of the
woman he loved was haunting him day and night,

he chanced upon a little old line-engraving, which became from that moment a treasure he would have purchased at any price. It was merely a pale, tintless head, so young and innocent as to seem almost that of a child; but the raised eyes had the tearful, pleading tenderness which has touched the whole world's heart in the face of the Cenci, or rather the foreshadowing of that divine sorrow which is on the brow of the Mater Dolorosa. The likeness to Christie, not only in expression as he had seen her upon that evening, but in actual feature, was very strong.

Taking it in his hand, he went up to the queer old creature who kept the shop, who had lived among his collection until he parted from each article almost as from a friend.

"What do you ask for this?" Tom inquired.

The old man glanced up pleasantly to see what was in his hand; for he and Tom were on the best terms. Having seen it, he pushed his spectacles up on his forehead, and looked curiously at his questioner.

"So you found out that for yourself! I have showed it to a good many gentlemen; but they didn't seem to see much in it," he said dryly. "I am glad you are to have it, though I shall miss it myself."

And he named a comparatively large price for the small picture, which Tom paid without a word.

"Put it into this frame," said Tom, selecting the least noticeable one he could find.

And the old man did so.

Then Tom took it with him to his private counting-room, and hung it in the shaded recess, just above the desk where he always sat. There it remained unobserved, except that, occasionally, a man more cultured and quick-sighted than others would happen to be near when the sunlight accidentally fell upon it, and would exclaim, —

"What a beautiful little engraving! What is it?"

"Madonna," Tom would quietly reply; and the questioner would go away, supposing that he had been looking at a representation of the Virgin. Tom held that he spoke the exact truth; for she was to him literally Madonna, "my lady," — the object of his love, his life, and his prayers.

About this time there appeared upon his desk, just below the picture, though with no apparent connection with it, a delicate little glass, from which each morning a fresh blossom shed perfume; just as in other lands they place flowers and burn incense at the shrines of the saints they worship. In the hard, money-getting existence which seemed all that was left to him, that one evidence of his inner life was never allowed to wither, or even to droop.

"My dear fellow, you must be growing gay or sentimental, though you don't look either," laughed one of his fellow-merchants, " with your fresh flower every day."

" Each one to his taste," replied Tom coolly. " You wear your bouquet in your button-hole in your play-hours ; and I keep mine before me during my working ones."

" I imagined that it was the flour, rather than the flower, of existence, that both you and I cultivated most extensively, and that it was literally the bread and butter of life which we strove for," his visitor went on. And the young man flattered himself that he had said rather a neat thing, inasmuch as he had come in to inquire about a shipment of wheat.

Tom smiled, and allowed him to carry away that illusion.

This was the degree of attention excited by the change in Tom's office, — slight to others, but to him every thing. In the long, solitary hours of dreaming, rather than thinking, which came to him so often with the ebb and flow of business, this picture grew to be a companion. The silent face spoke to him as but one living countenance had power to do. The purity and love and faith which dwelt in those eyes were a surety of their existence elsewhere : that the heart of humanity had ever conceived them gave proof that they still lived within that heart. That thing of beauty was to him not merely a joy forever, but a poem, a sermon, a teaching from on high. Life had for him peace, if not happiness, as he sometimes sat at evening and saw the soft sunset light fade away from the face, and remembered the end to all suffering and sorrow; the close of life itself, when, after the long day's faithful toil, comes the sweet, eternal rest on the bosom of our Father and our God. Among the many descriptions of heaven, Job's sentence, spoken so long ago, seems to me still the best, the one to which human nature's needs turn with surest longing, concerning a place "where the wicked cease from troubling, and the weary are at rest." These were the words Tom thought of when he hoped for another life, — for its recompenses, its healing, and its peace.

Reginald had been sorely disappointed at his brother's persistent refusal of all his invitations, and had tried every method to induce him to spend much time at his house: but he found that his effort was useless; that Tom's quiet, invariable "No" meant exactly what it said. He regretted the fact as much as he could regret any thing; but was too practical, even in this matter, to waste his strength in fruitless attempts. Tom's manner showed him so unwaveringly that he was unwelcome, that even his gay composure gave way before the resolute pressure; and

his visits to his brother's office became less frequent.
Still he came occasionally for his own amusement;
and Tom had not yet shaken him off.

Since Reginald's marriage, he had, besides his ques-
tionable pleasures, his large establishment, and increased social duties, to entertain him, and so did not
feel such an absolute need of his brother's wit as
hitherto ; and, since Mrs. Van Arsdale had appeared
upon the scene, she had occupied his time and attention. His pursuit of her had been so open and eager,
that it was the common talk of society ; and people
laughed, admired, or denounced, as their ideas of
right differed. The devotion of such a man allows
but one interpretation ; and such was generally given
it. The rumor had reached Tom, rendering him
savage against his brother ; for he knew only too
well the probability of its truth.

Reginald had been bowing at Mrs. Van Arsdale's
shrine for about two months, and was, perhaps,
rather bored by that lady, and indeed by persons
and things in general, when one day he lounged
into Tom's office, hoping to revive himself by a mental tonic. Entering with his radiant grace and shining good humor, Tom physically sickened at the sight
of him. He felt as though it would be a direct compromise with the Devil to have any thing to do with
him. It seemed surrendering his whole standard of

right even to speak to him ; and, indeed, he scarcely did so, though they had not met for a long while.

Reginald made himself comfortable as usual, and for five minutes sustained the conversation with the merest monosyllabic assistance from his brother.

" Upon my word, old fellow, you are crustier than ever this morning," Reginald exclaimed at last with a laugh. " What's the matter? Is it I, or something else, that is annoying you ? "

The self-enjoyment, the unruffled self-complacency of the tone, broke down Tom's fast-weakening nerves and patience ; and he turned suddenly upon his brother with eyes that flashed an anger and disgust he could not control.

" Why do you come here, Reginald ? You know my opinion of you. I have told it to you before ; and why do you tempt me to tell it to you again more strongly than ever ? "

Reginald looked at Tom very quietly for a moment. He was not at all angry ; in fact, he rather enjoyed the idea of a sharp skirmish. He had what might be called an insatiable appetite for pluck, and a hunger for the gratification of his intellectual curiosity ; and both of these Tom satisfied.

" Ah ! " he said slowly, " the old trouble breaking out, is it? and fresh fuel on the fire ! I supposed as much."

The analytical coolness of the words and manner was beyond endurance.

"Reginald!" Tom cried out, "I know it is idiotic to attempt to appeal to you, or to stop you in your course; but I can't help doing it. Man, when I remember that you are my pure mother's son, I almost doubt the God above us."

"Tom," said the other quietly, "you are too hard on me. This is all the wrong I do, if it be any wrong. You and I are entirely different. But I admit that I have a strong natural appetite for forbidden fruit, while other persons have no constitutional taste for apples."

Tom's face flushed crimson.

"Do you imagine," he asked in that low, concentrated tone to which intense passion always reduced his voice, "that all pure men and women belong to that latter class?"

"By heavens, no!" exclaimed the other, as he saw the blue veins rise like cords across his brother's temples. "It is not water that runs in your veins, my dear fellow, any more than in mine. I am perfectly willing to admit that I am the weak man of us two, and that you are the strong one; that we have about the same passions, and you have the pluck and strength to control them, and I have not. I don't blind myself in this matter, or in any other, if I can help it. I well know that to hold the helm of your nature through every thing is the great test of manhood; and that to allow one's self to be driven by inclination, however swift and fiery, can only be the result of weakness. Why, I will confess to you, that you once so fired my young ambition, that, for a little while, I attempted to emulate you. Good God! I can remember it now." And he gave a great sigh of infinite relief, as though the recollection of the weariness of his effort were too much for him even then.

"However," he wound up, "as I was evidently given no moral nature, I don't see how I can be held responsible for one."

"I observe that we are all given an immoral nature," exclaimed Tom bitterly. "They tell us the kingdom of God is within us; but I am sure the kingdom of the Devil is there also, and that the coming of temptation is merely the striking of the hour for an emotion to pass into act. The fundamental passions are in everybody; and the strongest temptations of humanity come to each and all from within, if not from without. That which is a crime in one can never be a venial offence in another: the line must be laid to all, or to none. The moral law is as inexorable, though as invisible, as the physical one; and you violate either at your peril. The ten

14

commandments were written upon tables of stone,
not upon India-rubber : they may be broken, but
cannot be bent. Reginald Archer, your whole life
is entered against you in Nature's great account-book ;
and the day of settlement will surely come."

The man's clinched hand upon his desk, and the
low, thrilling tone which carried his tide of words
almost involuntarily beyond his lips, were but slight
evidences of the tremendous conviction with which
he spoke. The very air around them seemed to vibrate for a moment, as though stirred by his magnetic
intensity. Even the imperturbable gentleman before
him sat silent, with a grave blankness upon his beautiful face.

" Perhaps you are right," he broke out at last with
a slight laugh, " though you and I have differed as
radically in theory as in practice : at any rate, what
I am I am, and shall be to the end."

Ah ! they little thought how near that end was, or
how swiftly it was coming, as they sat facing each
other,— the one in his righteous wrath, and the other
in his smiling, superb carelessness, and both in the
full vigor and heat of manhood.

Reginald rose to his feet, and gave himself a slight
shake, as though finally throwing off a disagreeable
subject. He moved about the room in a silence his
brother was too heart-sick to break. Presently the

picture above Tom's desk caught his eyes. The afternoon sun was striking straight across it, bringing it out in full relief. He had hitherto been in that room in the morning, when the recess was in shadow, and the picture consequently unnoticeable. It struck his attention for the first time.

"Why, Tom, what an exquisite little thing! But you are always picking up something beautiful," he exclaimed, as much by way of diversion from the previous subject as because he really admired the engraving.

He came and stood by his brother's side to inspect the picture more closely. As he did so, the likeness, and the truth concerning it, flashed upon him.

"Ah!" he said slowly, and a curious smile gathered round his lips. He saw the whole story as clearly as though its minutest details had been told him; and the mocking fiend within him stirred, and tempted him to try his brother's strength, courage, and virtue to the uttermost.

"Tom," he said sweetly, "if you object to my company, why don't you go to see Christie sometimes when I am not at home, which is often enough the case. She is very fond of you, and would be delighted to see you."

Tom glanced up suddenly, and caught his brother's look. He had been sitting at his desk during their talk; but he now rose, and turned upon Reginald with a face which was white with suppressed feeling. For a moment, the two gazed straight into each other's eyes; the dare-devil that was in each seeming to strive to stare the other out of countenance.

Then Tom drew a long breath, and spoke very slowly.

" I do not come," he said, " because I hate you, and love your wife; and you know it as well as I do. And now," he went on, his voice deepening and lowering, " go out of this room, and never come in it, never speak to me again, so long as you live ! I renounce you utterly from this hour ! Yes, I mean exactly what I say," he added, as Reginald gave him a quick, piercing glance of scrutiny.

" Evidently," returned the other, instantly making up his mind to the situation, disagreeable as it was to him. " I am sorry for it, Tom ; but, if you will have it so, so let it be. Good-by," he said pleasantly, and bowed himself out with the blandest elegance, which nothing except his own decapitation could have destroyed.

And then Tom, vibrating in every fibre, sank down with his head upon his desk, and wondered afresh how this creature could be of his own flesh and blood.

Looking up, after a long while, to the sad, sweet

face upon the wall above him, there came over him an awful realization of what that pure, high-toned woman's life must be; and he dimly measured the long torture of her continual association with such a nature by the unendurability of his momentary trial.

"My darling! — my poor, innocent darling!"

The words were in his heart at all times; but they were upon his lips at that moment, with a depth of meaning they had never before possessed.

CHAPTER XXII.

PERHAPS a month had passed since that passionate parting between the brothers. Reginald had spent the time in continuing his open and secret pursuit of Mrs. Van Arsdale. He had attained his bad end, and had not yet wearied of his success. He was not particularly elated at his triumph; still less was he personally flattered by it. He knew that Mrs. Van Arsdale had been too long criminal in all but act to make the single step left her an extremely difficult affair; that she had walked to the very edge of the precipice with too many men for it to require wonderful power to induce her finally to pass over it. He did not blind himself to the fact, that in this, as in all such cases, he owed his success to the woman's own nature, and the training of his predecessors, rather than to his attractions. He had an amused perception of the truth, that men and women fall more by temptation from within than from without.

The affair was growing so apparent and shameless,

that people began to scoff and jeer at Mr. Van Arsdale behind his back, and to wonder why he, who was known to be neither fool nor coward, did not take some means of putting an end to the scandal and shame.

But the truth was, that, of all the community, he was most ignorant of a matter which was skilfully and carefully hidden from him by the persons concerned, and about which others lacked both the courage and impertinence to enlighten him. Away from his home all day, how could he know what went on during his absence? As to his wife's conduct in public when he was by, he had too long and painful an acquaintance with her usual habits and manners to be surprised or startled at their present exhibition. The smiling lie of welcome her face told when he entered his home, her more than accustomed attention to his comfort and pleasure, lulled him deeper in his false security.

But even he was beginning to have his suspicions of the black truth; dreading that this was something more than "Lucretia's necessary flirtation," as he had been in the habit of bitterly denominating his wife's constantly-changing love-affairs, which he had so long been compelled to tolerate. A baffled yet subtile perception of the truth was coming over the man; and those who saw him and his wife and Reginald together saw a strange shadow growing in the husband's face, which boded ill for the ease and enjoyment of the others.

A wretched being was Lawrence Van Arsdale during those days, with an awful dread at his heart which he could neither prove nor disprove. To interfere openly might, perhaps, bring causeless public dishonor upon his name and race; while to allow the present state of things to go on might be to let shame secretly stain his hearth and home forever. He did not spare words to his wife in private: he gave her terrible warning. But the shallow, pleasure-loving woman smiled back at him with such careless, serene gayety, that his doubts seemed for the moment ridiculous. She was so utterly trivial, that she did not realize any pain or disaster the pressure of which was not then upon her. She lacked the sense to recognize her danger, as she needed the conscience and delicacy to understand her degradation, or the intellect to comprehend the man with whom she was dealing.

She had no feeling of having done any thing specially wrong: she had merely followed her natural instinct and impulse; and any slight scruples she had hitherto possessed Reginald's arguments had removed. The truth is, it is possible to reason one's self into any thing one wishes to believe, and to build up a strong case from any point of view. For this cause, the woman or man who deliberates is lost. When they leave conscience, which feels, for intellect, which thinks and devises, the result is really won by their wishes. Let them state the sum to their own satisfaction, and the answer is a necessity. Silly as she was, Mrs. Van Arsdale could have made you a respectable argument on the subject from her standpoint, gained from her own experience and her competent teachers.

"Yes," laughed Reginald long before, when some similar person's self-defence was being commented upon, "the arguments of such women, in the present state of society, rather remind me of the fox, who, having lost his tail, tried to persuade his companions that they would be better without theirs. His testimony can scarcely be taken as impartial, and his reasons might be somewhat biassed by peculiar circumstances."

He was right. Tempted by love of luxury, by their own passions, by worldly and physical gratification in some form, they sell themselves to sin for the payment they covet; and, having irrevocably placed themselves in a position from which they can never recover, they are forced to search diligently for some justification in their own eyes and the eyes of others. They make the most difficult of all attempts, — to have their cake, and eat their cake. They first do wrong, and then try to reason it into being right. Such an effort is like the witches' habit of repeating the Lord's Prayer backward: it raises evil spirits instead of good ones; it calls up the powers of darkness rather than of light. Having lost forever the ability to come up to the standard of others, their one chance is to drag that standard down to their own level. They are compelled to say, " Evil, be thou my good : " they are forced to deify their false god, and to draw as many followers as possible to his impure worship. The world holds women of genius who are prostituting it in this cause as they have previously degraded soul and body. Sinning for their own satisfaction, they have parted with the power of choice, and by necessity are so many attorneys, bound to argue the case in one way, and held by that strongest of all retaining-fees, self-interest. Of such persons, as of all sinful men and women, Christ's long-uttered words remain eternally true: " This is their condemnation, that light has come into the world; but men love darkness rather than light, because their deeds are evil."

Whatever were Lloyd Truxton's manifold weaknesses and falsities, his devotion to Reginald was warm and genuine; and he felt danger in the air for his friend as a faithful dog scents a foe for his master, and foresaw the coming trouble which the other really did not perceive. Reginald had outwitted and outbraved so many men, that he could scarcely realize the possibility of meeting his match, and so lived gayly on in confident security.

But Lloyd went about troubled and depressed, fearing to speak, and be called a fool for his pains, and yet scarcely daring not to give some warning of what seemed so evident to him.

At last, one night, he could restrain himself no longer.

It was very late ; and the two sat by themselves in Reginald's smoking-room,— the only persons awake in that great silent house. They had come in from a ball, where, as usual, Reginald and Mrs. Van Arsdale had been " the observed of all observers." Lawrence Van Arsdale had stood quietly by and watched both ; but it was with a look dawning in his face which haunted Lloyd still, the influence of which was upon him even now as he sat in that cosey room, when the music, beauty, brilliancy of color and light, all the striking effects of the evening, had passed away.

Reginald had come in flushed and excited, and had thrown himself upon a lounge, with his cigar in his hand. Lloyd took an easy-chair near him, and began to smoke also. Between them stood a table, upon which was a shaded reading-lamp, that threw its whole light down upon the extended figure on the couch, revealing in full its magnificent beauty and strength. As Lloyd looked, there suddenly flashed upon his weak brain and imagination, not merely the man he saw, but the man he had seen. Like a revelation, he beheld those two meeting in deadly conflict; and the picture was colored in blood.

He could keep back his words no longer.

"Reginald," he said hesitatingly, "I saw Van Arsdale watching you to-night; and upon my soul, if you had seen his face, it would have made you think that you had better take care."

The man upon the sofa slightly raised himself, and looked at the other with a kind of splendid surprise in his eyes.

What is it in genuine physical courage which commands the enthusiasm and respect of every human being? Is it that the majority of men are born cowards, and are impressed by the rarity of the opposite extreme? or is it that there is something so really noble in the quality which we share with the animals, that we cannot resist its influence? Be this as it may, Lloyd had never had such a boundless admiration for his superior as when he saw Reginald gazing at him with a sort of wonder, pity, and contempt for the being who could imagine him capable of fear.

"My dear fellow," Reginald said at last in his usual soft tones, "I have not yet added personal cowardice to my other attractions, and I have no intention of so doing. If Mr. Van Arsdale wishes to call me to account, I am quite ready at any and all times. I can say for myself, that I have always been willing to pay for my pleasures ; and I like fairness in all things."

He had resumed his easy, full-length position by this time, and was indolently smoking as he indolently talked.

"I know that I am not supposed to have cultivated the moral virtues to any very great extent ; but I have a genuine admiration for justice, and I do not consider that I have violated it in this case. I see no reason why I should deny myself for Lawrence Van Arsdale's sake. I know just what he is, — what his life has been both at home and abroad. If I am the chief of sinners in this community, he has done things in his day which effectually prevent him from being my judge. The difference between us is merely that of quantity, not of quality."

"Perhaps he has never looked at the subject in that light," suggested Lloyd.

"But I have," was Reginald's cool rejoinder, "and I act accordingly ; and, the sooner he learns to take impartial and correct views of himself and others, the better. Why, apart from every thing else," he went on, growing interested in what he was saying, " I leave it to any one whether a man who has voluntarily and delightedly placed himself in the society of women who have deliberately sold themselves for luxury can possibly have any genuine disapproval, disgust, or horror, at sin in itself. Having found such women charming and companionable, why should he be filled with sudden virtuous rage at discovering that his wife merely resembles his chosen friends and associates? Sin has been sweet and luscious enough to him on occasion ; and, now that his position in the affair is slightly altered, what can his moral hysterics mean but wounded pride and injured vanity? Upon my word, I cannot see that it is my duty, as it is certainly not my pleasure, to be over-careful of those sentiments in any one but myself ; " and he laughed pleasantly as he spoke.

" Van Arsdale certainly did not look to-night as though any one were being very considerate of his feelings of any kind," said Lloyd, who could not get that haggard, watching face out of his mind. " He seemed terribly wretched."

" So much the more fool he ! " returned Reginald, " when he has had all these years to make up his mind to what was inevitably before him when he married such a woman, after setting her such an example. I often wonder what men's intellects can be made of to be capable of such self-delusion. If

Van Arsdale is weak-minded and selfish enough to wish to deprive his wife of the sugar-plums he liked so well himself, he ought never to have married, or, at least, should have chosen a woman like Christie; though, really, where he would have found her, I cannot imagine. I am aware that my wife is absurdly wasted on me, and that it is a thousand pities that some of those gentlemen with morbidly susceptible nerves could not have the benefit of such a blessing," he added, as he reflectively watched the blue smoke curl from his cigar.

Lloyd did not flatter himself that Reginald's flow of words was meant especially for him. He was used to that gentleman's habit of making himself comfortable, and then uttering his sentiments for his own satisfaction, as he was now doing. The younger man's part in these conversations was slightly trying, as he was always under the apprehension that he should misconceive Reginald's idea, and show it in his reply. Consequently he now spoke rather hesitatingly as he said, —

" Why, you can't mean, that, if Van Arsdale had been a different man, you would have acted differently about his wife ? "

Reginald took his cigar out of his mouth, and sat straight up on the sofa before he made any reply. There was something so much like honest fire and manly earnestness in his face, and in the way in which he drew up his splendid head and person, that Lloyd gazed at him in surprise, and, it must be confessed, with some nervousness.

"I swear to you," he said, and the whole force of the man seemed to go into the tone, "that if my brother Tom, or any man whom I knew beyond all doubt to be like him, had a wife who was Venus and Juno combined, if she were to play the part of Potiphar's wife to me, I would play that of Joseph; upon my soul I would! and would feel that I was only doing what the man and common justice alike had a right to demand of me. But the occasion has not yet arisen, and does not arise, my dear boy," he added, his voice changing to a fine, faint sneer, as he returned to his recumbent posture and his cigar.

Lloyd sat for a moment mute with astonishment, and then, rather fearing to discuss such an unexpected statement, wisely preserved the same silence a little longer. Then his mind went back to the one thought and dread which had been oppressing him all the evening.

"It is terrible to think how much trouble women make in the world, and how little real goodness and purity there is among them," he said presently, shaking his head with an edifying degree of moral regret.

"My dear fellow," answered Reginald with lazy

sweetness, " don't be more of a fool than you can help. When most men criticise women's virtue and shortcomings, it strongly reminds me of a story I once heard told of a great orator, as happening at an abolition convention a long while ago. A man with negro blood in his veins had arisen, and denounced Gen. Washington as a scoundrel and a thief for owning slaves. 'My friend,' returned the aforesaid orator mildly, ' I would not use those epithets in that connection, if I were you. It isn't graphic. Because, if you call Gen. Washington a scoundrel, what have you left for Franklin Pierce ? ' Just so, my dear boy, if you call women hard names for a single slip or two, what have you left for yourself ? Why, how many have you ever known, not actually upon the streets, who are not, by strict mathematics, far better than you ? "

" Oh, yes ! but women, you know, women ! It's so different, you know ! " Lloyd cried out eagerly, with his usual fine coherence and logic.

" Why, and in what way ? " asked Reginald pleasantly.

" Oh ! you know very well what I mean. I can't explain it to you exactly."

Reginald laughed softly.

" No ; and neither can any one else that I have ever seen. I am afraid, for the future, we have got to give freedom, as well as take it; that liberty, equality, and fraternity are going to become feminine as well as masculine nouns; and that the great text and battle-cry for the next generation will be the old, succinct proverb, that what is sauce for the goose is sauce for the gander. I fear we shall be obliged to have one level of morality; and, as I do not feel prepared to be very good myself, I have calmly concluded to allow them to be very bad."

"Yes," persisted Lloyd; "but when a woman does wrong " —

"It's so much more wrong than when a man does it," cut in Reginald; and his delighted laugh rang out like a bell through the quiet room. "Excuse me: I beg your pardon for laughing at you; but I really must request you again to be as little of a fool as possible. Your ideas of right and wrong seem to be movable feasts of the Church, Lloyd, and to be amusingly influenced by circumstances. You remind me of those of our own countrymen who are models of respectability at home, but whose morality, as soon as they cross the water to France, seems, in Shakspeare's words, to 'suffer a sea-change into something rich and strange.' It certainly is delightful to see the way in which human nature can turn and twist and wind again, and fancy itself rather a fine thing after all.

And his infinite enjoyment of the thought was such, that he threw away the end of his cigar, and, instead of taking a fresh one, fell to the sole occupation of contemplating his idea of humanity.

Lloyd's several attempts at reply and explanation had fallen so short of success, that he scarcely felt equal to another effort in the same direction, and so did not immediately break the silence.

Presently he took out his watch.

" Four o'clock," he announced as he looked at it.

" Is it so late, or rather so early ? " said Reginald, rising. " I think I shall go to bed. Of course, there is a room ready for you, Lloyd, if you want it."

" No, I think I had rather go home, as Ellen will be wondering where I am."

" Very well," answered the other, and went with him down to the front-door to fasten it behind him.

As they stood silent upon the steps, in the still night-air, looking up at the quiet stars in the winter skies, Lloyd was again strangely tempted to repeat his words of warning; but he literally had not the courage to do so.

" Good-night! " he said instead, and went his way with a depression of heart which certainly was not a selfish emotion.

Then Reginald passed up his broad stairway to his bedroom, untroubled by fear, care, shame, or sorrow.

He had merely followed the instincts and teachings
of a perfect physical organization and an acute understanding ; and these had logically brought him to
the religion of self-love and the philosophy of a good
dinner.   This creed satisfying his soulless nature, he
lived up to its limits, undisturbed by doubt or dread.

CHAPTER XXIII.

MRS. LESTER had the fortune, good or bad, to live in a house whose rear commanded a near view of the back of the residence of the Van Arsdales. In the early glory of the friendship between the ladies, this proximity was the cause of constant intercourse. They were continually paying each other little visits to fill up their idle moments; and, if they wished, could telegraph intelligence from their nearest windows.

This state of things went on very pleasantly for a few weeks; but by that time Mrs. Van Arsdale had become the decided belle of the season, and had small leisure to waste upon any thing belonging to the feminine gender.

Mrs. Lester had striven hard to keep up the intimacy, pursuing her usual policy of attaching herself to some woman who was usually surrounded by men, and trusting to chance and her own skill to secure such stragglers as could not reach the original attraction.

But Mrs. Van Arsdale had her own share of feminine instinct whenever her power and fascinations
were in question. Whatever sense she possessed
had been long and diligently applied to the subject;
and upon this particular ground she was quite able
to cope with Mrs. Lester. She had no idea of ruling
even a slightly divided kingdom, of drawing men
together for another woman to secure, of making
conquests for some one else to enjoy: above all, she
carefully avoided the danger of having some one near
her who would partially paralyze the effect of her
beauty by emphasizing, through contrast, her mental
inferiority.

Consequently, their mutual devotion fell with
alarming rapidity into the sear and yellow leaf, then
quickly died.

When Mrs. Lester called, Mrs. Van Arsdale was
very apt to be " not at home," even though the former lady had, from her post of observation, become
aware that other visitors had been admitted but a
few moments before. The ladies preserved their outward familiarity, and " my deared " each other as
usual, when they met in society; but each understood that there was now no love lost between them.
Mrs. Van Arsdale was so trivial-natured, that even
anger and dislike were with her only passing spite-
fulness: and she forgot her enmities and enemies as

soon as the latter were out of her sight; they, like all other considerations, being swallowed up in her self-indulgence and enjoyment of the present pleasure.

But Mrs. Lester hoarded her wrath and disappointment, to be faithfully repaid to their cause at the earliest opportunity. She awaited her chance, confident that occasion would arise upon which she could strike a telling blow. Justice requires one to admit, that, in the mean time, she did not neglect any minor advantage towards the same end, but did Mrs. Van Arsdale all the harm she could in a small way; pursuing her policy of injuring each person whom she had failed to utilize for her own purposes.

It must be confessed that Mrs. Van Arsdale played into her opponent's hand with terrible recklessness; and, for once in her life, Mrs. Lester found her talent for misrepresentation and slander an almost unnecessary weapon in her peculiar warfare. It was a case in which truth was stranger than fiction, and facts more damning than falsehoods could be made.

When Reginald's pursuit of Mrs. Van Arsdale became open, and all society was talking of the *liaison*, Mrs. Lester felt that her wished-for chance had arrived. From her windows she could not only watch the house, but, unless the curtains were carefully closed, could perceive much that went on inside; thereby learning far more of the doings of

Lawrence Van Arsdale's household at all times than
that unfortunate gentleman dreamed of knowing at
any period. As the intrigue went on, she followed
the portion of it which she could witness, gleefully
and greedily; forming a chain of dark evidence and
inference so strong, that the case would probably
have held even in a court of law. She sat at her
post of lookout, like Sister Anne in her watch-tower,
for hours together. Behind some one of her windows she was almost sure to be seated during a large
portion of the day, waiting for that which chance
might bring to her sight. It showed her Reginald
entering the house at all hours; and it displayed to
her many of his actions while in it. She gloated
over her surveillance of the guilty pair, and revelled
in the loathsome work which gratified every passion
of her nature. She kept most of her knowledge to
herself, accumulating evidence, that it might fall
with more crushing weight at the appropriate time.
However, from her emanated most of the rumors
with which society was rife; though she took care
that the reports should never be traced to their original source.

At last she had collected such proofs as left small
doubt of their sin; as almost forced conviction on the
most sceptical mind. Feeling now quite sure of her
ground, she resolved to act; to bring matters to that

climax for the sight of which her soul thirsted. She belonged to that class of women with which the anonymous letter — that certain refuge of cowardly malice — must surely have originated ; and it was with this weapon that she instinctively resolved to fight.

The task before her was in every way congenial with her tastes and abilities. She had to state a case, and put the corroborating testimony in such a form as to compel belief in those whom she addressed. She had to make evident that of which there could be no positive certainty; to lead up so closely to final facts, that they were a simple necessity. Her hard, practical shrewdness exactly fitted her for the undertaking ; and she accomplished it as well as a second-rate criminal lawyer could have done, or rather as his clerk who had long been trained to do dirty work.

She sat at her desk over the draft of the letter, altering, condensing, and rewriting, until she had a short, succinct document, every word of which went straight to the intended mark. She had devoted an afternoon and evening to the task ; but, when she read it over in its final form, she sat back in her chair with a triumphant feeling of conscious merit, and a sense of time well spent. Then she applied herself to making two fair copies in a well-disguised hand ; an undertaking which her previous practice in the art rendered easy.

She was thus engaged when her husband entered. She had wisely taken no one into her confidence, fearing to increase the chances of detection; and, indeed, her husband was the last person she ever honored with a knowledge of her secret sentiments and private projects. But not on this, or any other occasion, was she afraid of that disciplined gentleman displaying any undue curiosity, or pushing his inquiries to an inconvenient length. She went quietly on with her occupation; and when, after a little while, Mr. Lester said in his heavy way, —

"What are you so busy over, Marian?" she answered calmly, —

"I am writing letters."

"You seem to require a great deal of paper to do it," he remarked, by way of a ponderous joke, as he looked at the sheets scattered over her table.

"Yes, I want to make them as interesting as possible," she rejoined coolly. And then she gave her usual cackle of delight over her own thoughts and the pictures they brought up, without the least dread of piquing his curiosity. The well-trained gentleman subsided into his newspaper; and Mrs. Lester went on with her work.

It was soon completed; and, gathering up the loose sheets, she locked them carefully away in her desk, and went to bed a contented woman.

She was up by sunrise the next morning. Going back to her desk, she took from it two papers. Putting them into envelopes, she addressed one to " Mrs. Reginald Archer," and the other to " Mr. Lawrence Van Arsdale ; " directing them to the residence of each. These she placed in her pocket, and, putting on a bonnet and thick veil, went out for an early walk. Reaching the poorer portion of the town, where she was unknown, she dropped her letters into a street-box, and then made her way swiftly home, to appear at the breakfast-table in such unwonted spirits and appetite, that she felt called upon to explain them by expatiating on the benefits of keeping good hours over night.

All day she waited in the same restless excitement for the results of her stroke.

She knew the hour at which the letters would arrive at their destinations ; but, when they would reach the persons for whom they were intended, she could not tell, as a hundred small chances might intervene to delay that event. She sincerely hated nearly every one of the individuals upon whom she hoped to bring ruin ; and the neatness and completeness, the circular character, of her revenge, charmed her. She smiled to find herself humming from the French opera, —

" *Je vois tout, je sais tout*," — and then fairly

hugged herself with pleasure to think how true was the quotation in this instance.

She could not remain within doors, but went out, ostensibly on a shopping-expedition, but really to fill up the time with some sort of motion. But she returned at evening unsatisfied and eager; for all was quiet, and not even a rumor of trouble had yet stirred society.

Her impatience was almost intolerable. Yet there was small need for her to wish to hasten the events of the next few hours; for the catastrophe she had invoked was coming surely and swiftly enough, God knows.

CHAPTER XXIV

ON the morning of that day, Christie sat in her room, quietly reading. For the past month or two, she had lived, as it were, in a thick, black cloud of doubt. Its impalpable influence surrounded her at all times. She breathed it with the air; it mingled with the food she ate; and sleep itself could not dissolve its power. Turn which way she would, dark shadows rose, which she could no more reduce to fixed form than she could overcome them or drive them away. It was the intangibility of that which oppressed her which paralyzed her. She could literally do nothing; for she shrank from bringing open shame upon her husband, and its reflection upon herself, by acting upon what might possibly be a mistaken suspicion.

The woman's delicate pride made it almost like death to think of inviting the world to entertain itself with the spectacle of her grief and dishonor. Above all, conscience held her in her place, though almost every instinct and passion cried out to her to desert it. She sank down into a dull endurance, which was as helpless as it was hopeless of happiness.

Yet she felt that this state of things could not continue, that she could not endure it, and that an end must come by some means; and, while she filled up her days with mechanically - performed duties, she waited with forewarning instinct for the moment and the circumstance which should cause the breaking of the cloud upon her devoted head.

That moment and that circumstance had arrived.

The postman's quick ring was heard; then the servant's leisurely step ascending the stairway.

" What is it, George ? " she asked as he stood at the door.

" A letter for you, ma'am," he answered, and, handing it to her, left the room.

Christie glanced at the large, coarse envelope and unknown handwriting, and concluded that some tradesman's account was within. She opened it carelessly, and found, to her surprise, a page of foolscap covered with the same straggling penmanship. Her next idea was that it was a petition for charity; and, as such, she began to read it.

As she did so, there came a growing whiteness in her face, and a sickening horror at her heart, which made actual death seem very, very near.

She went steadily on to the end, and then laid the

paper down beside her without a sound or a movement. Her fears and doubts had become certainties: that which she had previously suspected she now knew; and not only she, but all the world beside. Her wild longing to die, to escape from the sin and misery and falsity which crushed her on every side, swallowed up all other sensations. Utterly defeated in the battle of life, only let her pass out of existence, and at last be at rest. Broken heart, lost faith, and shattered life,— what was there left for her in the wide world?

To think of her husband was to think of one separated from her by worse than death. His house was no longer her home: every hour she remained near him and under his roof was a stain upon her purity and a disgrace to her; for this clear-sighted, high-hearted woman felt her degradation just as a man would have felt it, and held a complaisant wife to be as sinful and shameful an object as a complaisant husband. She must go, and that instantly.

Yet whither, and to whom, could she turn for protection?

Motherless, fatherless, and almost friendless, in the midst of her wealth and splendor a sense of desperation came over the delicate, gently-nurtured woman, as she realized how alone she was, and how unequal to going out into the world and facing it.

“ Whether we meet, or whether we part, remember my promise to be your faithful brother if you ever need me.” Tom’s words, spoken months before in that house, seemed suddenly to sound in her ears; came back to her with such vivid force, that she could scarcely believe they had not been uttered by a living voice.

She started to her feet.

Yes, she would go to him, — to the one man whom she knew to be absolutely pure, faithful, and honest; who had striven to save her from this very agony, and, failing, had given her his pledge for this very hour of trial. If he deceived her, then indeed all would be lost, and she could at least die.

The whiteness was still upon her face to the very lips, and the large eyes were almost weird in their blank darkness; and, as she moved silently about the room, it was with that strange quietude of motion which we involuntarily use when Death has entered our home, and filled it with his awful presence.

She took up the letter, and laid it upon the dressing-table, where it could not be overlooked. It would sufficiently explain her action to Reginald, if, indeed, he needed any explanation. For a moment, she gazed down at the writing which had wrought this work; and then, God help her! there came into her heart, above its agony and shame and loathing horror, — or rather sprang from them, — some such feeling as that with which a slave must regard his freedom-papers, or those Roman criminals bound to decaying corpses may have looked upon the instrument which severed their chains. Yes, free at last from that bondage to which duty and conscience had held her with their resistible power; separated at last from that sinful life with which hers had seemed irrevocably interlocked.

She put on her bonnet and shawl, and walked to the door of the room.

There she turned, and looked back into the apartment. A strange, solemn quietude fell upon her as she did so; for she realized that it was the symbol of her whole present existence, and that she was parting from it forever. She lingered a moment or two on the threshold, and then came softly back.

Kneeling down at the bedside, she slowly whispered that prayer which Maria had made her repeat upon her wedding-day; that awful appeal, — "Our Father which art in heaven," — which frail human lips may well hesitate to take upon them. In the presence of her God, and weighing the searching meaning of the words as she spoke them, she said, "Forgive us our trespasses as we forgive those who trespass against us."

It was the act of a pure, righteous woman, striving, as for her soul's salvation, to fulfil to the uttermost the law of Christ and the highest law of her
nature; but I hold it to be a deed impossible in a
woman whose love and respect for her husband had
survived until that hour, and had then and there
died a violent death. In the wild forces which would
have maddened and torn asunder such a soul, God
and forgiveness could find little place at that moment, however fully they might regain their holy
supremacy in the long, sad, coming years of struggle
and self-conquest. True and noble as Christie was,
I believe it to have been as much the absence of human love as the presence of divine affection which
rendered her capable of then performing this highest
act of religion and faith, of Christianity and humanity. The story of the past—the manner in which
all devotion to her husband, trust in him, and hope
of better things from him, had been literally mur-
dered out of her—was told by the possibility of that
quiet, simple forgiveness, as nothing else on earth
could have uttered it. The woman's pardon seemed
almost to render pardon from a just and righteous
God impossible. Reginald Archer's moral death-sen-
tence appeared written in that wrathless renuncia-
tion. The woman who had loved him until then
would then have hated him; and he had stricken and

ground the power out of Christie to do either the one or the other. When, at the great judgment-day, Reginald Archer comes to stand at the bar of his Maker to give an account of the deeds done in the body, I hold, that, of all his sins, the most damning will be, that he coolly and systematically made it possible for such a woman to accord him such forgiveness at such a moment.

She rose from her knees, went down the stairway, and out of the house.

Tom Archer was sitting in his private counting-room, where he was always to be found at that hour, so busily engaged at his writing-desk, that he scarcely noticed a knock at the door behind him. It was re-peated before he said carelessly, —

"Come in!"

He recognized his clerk's step, and did not turn round until he heard the man say, —

"Mr. Archer, here is a lady who wishes to see you."

Tom glanced over his shoulder as he quickly rose, and saw a small, graceful figure standing by the door. A veil was over the face; but there was little need to tell him whose was the pretty, delicate form. All the blood in his body seemed to leap to his heart.

"Christie!" he cried out, "Christie!"

There was a light in his face, and an irrepressible

throb of joy in his voice, which must have told her the truth, had not the woman's thoughts been far away from any dream of love and happiness. It had been so very long since he had seen her, and this meeting had come upon him so suddenly, that it shook his self-control further than he knew. He came hurriedly forward to greet her with outstretched hands; but she stood perfectly motionless until the clerk had closed the door upon himself.

Then, just before Tom reached her, she lifted her veil, and, showing her white face, looked at him with her terribly altered eyes.

"My God!" cried the man's shocked voice as he stopped short, "what is it?"

But, even as he spoke, the whole truth flashed upon him.

"Tom, do you remember your promise to be my brother when I needed you? I am here to claim it; for that time has come."

The voice was very low, but held perfectly steady.

Tom came forward, and taking the little hands in one of his, and laying the other upon them, looked quietly down at her with his strong, true eyes. He made no other answer; but surely none was needed.

"Tom, Tom!" the woman's quivering voice cried, "you are all I have in the world now;" and she sank upon her knees before him in an agony of weeping.

Tom caught her up, and placed her upon the lounge just at hand.

With his unutterable wrath against the false husband raging at his heart, and his inexpressible love for the weeping woman fighting for mastery over every iota of his nature, he remembered, even at that moment, that she was another man's wife. He could not give her the calm, soothing, brotherly caresses natural in her tried friend and near relation under such circumstances; and he would give her no other. It would be nothing, or all, as he well knew; and he held back his immeasurable love through its very might.

He did not touch her again, but, when the first nervous violence of her sobbing had spent itself, bent over her, and spoke with the exquisite gentleness and tenderness he would have used to a delicate, sick child whom he was soothing.

"I am going to take you home to Maria," he said.

"Yes," she answered quickly. "I can never go back to him, Tom; never see him again!"

"No," Tom replied quietly, but with a curious hardening around his mouth. "Nor I, either; so help me God!" he mentally added.

And yet how soon they would both break that vow!—how terribly soon!

Tom went out for a moment to send for a carriage,

and, returning, drew Christie's shawl around her, and dropped her veil over her face, before leading her to the vehicle. Over and beyond his tender care and consideration for her, there had come into his manner a delicate, added deference, which put a fine distance between them. Wearing the crown of helplessness and sorrow, she had become to him almost as a queen, and he her humble and loyal servant. Above all, it greatly behooved his honor, that, placed as she was, no shade of reflection should fall upon her through even momentary lack of care on his part.

As they passed through the office, the clerks in it wondered who the lady could be whom Mr. Archer was handing out with such grave courtesy.

"Upon my word, when he chooses, he can be as grand and elegant as his magnificent brother Reginald," said one of them, quite expressing the sentiment of the whole party.

Entering the carriage, Tom and Christie drove in sad silence to the house from which she had gone forth upon her disastrous marriage-day to return in far worse than widowhood.

CHAPTER XXV.

IT was eleven o'clock at night when Lawrence
Van Arsdale entered his home for the first time
since his solitary breakfast; at which Mrs. Van Arsdale was, as usual, much too fatigued by the pleasures of the previous night's ball to assist. The
parlors were dark; and evidently no one was at
home.

"Where is your mistress?" he asked of the servant
who opened the door.

The man, who knew far more of his master's affairs
and position than did that master himself, and who
could have given him some startling information,
glanced furtively up, and then, looking down, answered demurely, —

"She's gone to the opera, sir."

"Whom did she go with?" inquired the gentleman quickly.

"Mr. Archer, sir; he took dinner here," the servant returned with perfectly disciplined voice and
manner.

Mr. Van Arsdale ground something like a bitter oath between his teeth, of which the domestic was decorously oblivious. This household had long since come to such a pass, that the attempt to keep its dissensions from the sight and knowledge of the servants had almost ceased; and many a fierce outbreak between husband and wife upon matters important and unimportant did these apparently passive beings calmly witness.

The gentleman went into his library. The servant turned up the gas; mended the dying fire, which the late spring evenings still rendered pleasant; and left the apartment.

Throwing himself into a chair, Mr. Van Arsdale sat blankly staring into the flame, that leaped and smouldered, and then leaped up again, and burnt with a fierce, eager intensity. The fiery light which flickered over his face found something there akin to itself. The circumstance he had just heard awoke afresh, as Reginald Archer's very name had power to do, his dark distrust of him and of his wife. Now, as always, racked by suspicion, he yet shirked the confirmation of his own instinctive perception, turning with sickening recoil from such a truth until it should be thrust upon him. With hands bound by the dread of, openly blasting his home and name, except upon one last necessity, he remained passive and helpless; but his forced inaction seemed to feed the smothered fire, the dumb anger, within him. His long restraint and almost wilful blindness would surely demand their re-actionary price, were his doubt to become a certainty.

He had been sitting thus perhaps half an hour, when the servant re-entered. Mr. Van Arsdale rose hurriedly, with some idea that his wife had returned.

"I forgot to give you this letter, sir; it came this morning," the man said, handing him just such a coarse envelope as had reached Christie hours before.

Slowly, half mechanically, the gentleman broke the enclosure, and glanced at its contents. Suddenly the sight of his wife's name, and, beside it, that of Reginald Archer, fixed his attention; and he began in earnest to read the paper in his hand.

The change that came over him made the servant, lingering in vague curiosity, shrink before him in terror. If sullen rage had possessed that face, what was in it now? If a thirst for blood and vengeance had been growing there, what words could describe it at this moment? Lawrence Van Arsdale, the small man with the pale, square face, and quiet, steel-gray eyes, had disappeared; and a madman stood in his place, in his immeasurable wrath and power. Then he caught hold of the mantle-piece in his mighty effort to control his faculties, which were slipping away from him; while he opened his parched lips, striving to gain the breath that seemed almost gone from them forever.

But his self-containment, and his habit of acting upon his determination, ruled him even then. After a brief space of time, he walked out of the room, and straight to his wife's chamber.

No trace of his past wavering now, but in its place a mad desire to know the worst, and to face it to the uttermost. Instinct led him to this room in his search for proof of the damning truth or lie. Glancing round the apartment in his undetermined course, he caught sight of a little cabinet, which, it flashed upon him, she always kept locked.

He tried to force it open, but failed. .

The reckless woman, silly even in her sin, had thrown down her keys, among other things, upon a table so near, that he saw them, and took the one he needed.

Within the drawers he found — with a characteristic collection of soiled gloves, faded bouquets, broken fans, and similar womanish relics — a quantity of notes and letters from numberless men, such as would have bowed any honorable man in the dust with shame, even had he known that his wife had stopped short of what is called criminality.

But Lawrence Van Arsdale threw these aside; for they were not what he sought.

At last, in a place by themselves, he came upon some scraps of writing signed "R;" and he knew instinctively that he had reached his object.

Without stating in terms the black truth, the notes implied so clearly the guilty connection between his wife and the writer, that any faint hope or doubt to which he might have clung died instantly.

His hand still held the papers, when there came a sound of the opening front-door, and the soft tones and laughter of a brief, merry parting; then he heard his wife's quick, light footfall upon the stair-way. Little dreaming of what she was hastening to, the lady was gayly singing a fragment from the opera, in imitation of the *prima donna* to whom she had just been listening. In another moment she stood in the doorway, with the very smile with which she had parted from Reginald still upon her lips.

In her brilliant evening-dress and the fulness of her exquisite beauty, with her white bosom, her mar-vellous dark eyes, and glowing hair, she seemed to light up the chamber as she entered it. Never had she looked so like Herodias' daughter as at that mo-ment, radiant and reckless, with deadly elements in conflict so near her.

" Why, Lawrence! is it you? You are home ear-

ly," she said lightly as she came towards him. " I
have been to the opera with Mrs. Conrad," she
added with a ready lie.

He was standing with his back to her ; and, in her
careless self-absorption, she did not for the moment
see what he was doing. Just before she reached
him, he turned and faced her, the papers in his hand.

Then she saw the truth. Fool as she was, she
recognized the meaning of that countenance, and
read the bloody purpose written in it.

" Lawrence," she shrieked, " don't kill me ! "

And, falling on her knees before him, all her gay
splendor vanished : she crouched and grovelled upon
the ground in abject animal terror.

He stepped to the door, and locked it behind her.
At the action, the woman's heart and strength died
within her. Then he came back, and looked down
at her. With his wild rage riotous through his
blood, the traditions of his whole race and country
were still unconsciously controlling him. Without
realizing it, his arm hesitated to raise itself to strike
a woman, let her sin and his suffering be what they
might. Her agony of fear was terrible to witness ;
and the man's keen perception showed him, even
then, that it was nothing else ; that neither sorrow
nor remorse, nor even shame, mingled with it. She
dreaded him, not for the wrong she had done him,
but for the injury he could still do her.

" Don't kill me, Lawrence ! " she moaned again.

" Do you think I would let such a shameful creature live ? " he answered ; and the low, fixed tone terrified her more than the words.

As his sentence, and its inexpressible loathing contempt, struck her, the woman suddenly raised her head, and then sprang to her feet. She had given up all hope of her life ; and with despair came its reckless courage.

" Who and what are you, that you dare to despise me ? " she cried out, her words rushing from her lips like a flood. " You have the strength to murder me, and you will do it ; but you lost the right long ago."

Reginald's teaching had not been in vain ; and she used it with a terrible force, born of her terrible necessity.

" You kill me for that which you taught me to do, — which you set me the example of doing. What sin have I committed that you had not enjoyed, and satiated yourself with, long before I ever saw you ? What law of heaven or earth have I broken which you have not broken again and again ? Man ! we are on a level at last ; we are fitting companions for the first time ; and you ought to embrace me now as the proper wife of your bosom ! " And she flung out her beautiful arms to him in mad mock-

ery, while her dreadful laughter rang through the
room.

She had suddenly sprung upon the tremendous
vantage-ground of truth, and from it defied and
defeated him.

*"And the scribes and Pharisees brought unto him a
woman taken in adultery; and, when they had set her
in the midst, they say unto him, Master, this woman
was taken in adultery, in the very act. Now, Moses, in
the law, commanded that such should be stoned; but
what sayest thou? Jesus stooped down, and with his
finger wrote on the ground, as though he heard them
not. So, when they continued asking him, he lifted up
himself, and said unto them, He that is without sin
among you, let him cast the first stone at her. And
they which heard it, being convicted by their own consciences, went out one by one, beginning at the eldest,
even unto the last."*

The wretched woman had unconsciously used
Christ's own argument; and the miracle it worked
two thousand years ago it wrought again that day.
She had literally taken the stone from his hand,
leaving him powerless and weaponless.

The maddened, outraged man before her looked
at her with savage purpose for a moment; then
wavered, looked again, and again faltered in his res-
olution; and finally, without another word, turned
and left the room.

His wife stood absolutely stunned at the effect of her words and her sudden deliverance.

Lawrence Van Arsdale went straight back to the library. When he reached it, his dreadful purpose was more clearly graven upon his face than ever. Baffled in his vengeance upon the woman who had wronged him, he turned to wreak its concentrated force upon the man who had wrought his shame. The white, fixed face, with its deadly intent, was made more horrible by its contrast with the quietude of his movements. Opening his private secretary, he took out a small revolver, and carefully loaded it; then he put on his hat and went out of the house with as little demonstration as though his errand had been of the simplest business-character.

A quarter of an hour after, he was ringing the bell of Reginald Archer's residence.

"Is Mr Archer in?" he inquired of the servant who answered his summons.

"No, sir," the man replied, noticing that the gentleman stood in the shadow, and kept his hat slouched over his face.

"When will he be at home?"

"I really can't say, sir."

"Where can he probably be found?" the gentleman persisted.

"You may find him at the club," said the servant, suggesting the likeliest place.

" Ah ! " returned Mr. Van Arsdale, and went hastily down the steps.

The servant was right; for, in one of the smaller rooms of the club-house, Reginald sat at that moment in his glory, surrounded by a number of his particular set, who were sure to be collected there when nothing more agreeable occupied their attention. He was in such unusual spirits, that even those accustomed to his brilliancy looked at him in wondering admiration. He was sitting with his back to the door, but facing a great mirror, lounging in his arm-chair with his luxurious grace, and keeping up a strain of witty nonsense which drew peal after peal of laughter from his audience.

It was upon this scene that Lawrence Van Arsdale came.

As he entered, most of those present caught sight of him instantly. They were not nervous men; but, as they saw his face, a dread struck to their hearts, the forewarning of what they felt was to come. Sudden silence fell upon that company. Hearing his own voice sounding alone, Reginald looked up in surprise to learn the cause of the quietude; and then, in the mirror before him, he saw the face and figure advancing behind him.

Lloyd, who was sitting beside him, started up, crying out in terror, —

“ Reginald, I knew he would murder you ! It has come at last ! ”

To do Reginald justice, neither his heart nor his pulse quickened their beat perceptibly : he certainly had not attempted a *rôle* which he could not fill. Rising calmly, he turned and stood before the man he had dishonored, with the same grand manner and unshakable courtesy with which he would have received him in his own house.

For a second the two faced each other, the tall form towering above the smaller one ; yet not a person present doubted which was the stronger at that moment. The infinitude of still rage, the immeasurable agony that set every nerve and muscle, above all, the power which could keep its hand upon the throat of both, and compel them to bide his time, gave a frightful force to that slight, pale man, as he stood there mute and motionless.

As for Reginald, those who saw him then never forgot the impression. He remained stamped upon their memories, like the recollection of some wonderful statue or picture ; some glorious work of art seen once in a lifetime, and longed for ever after.

“ I have come to kill you ! ” Van Arsdale’s low voice broke the stillness.

“ Mr. Van Arsdale,” Reginald replied, bowing gravely, “ if you think I have done you any wrong, I am quite ready to meet you at any time, and give you the satisfaction customary among gentlemen."

"Satisfaction!"   Lawrence Van Arsdale's voice had not risen; but there had come such a terrible thrill through it as would have made almost any man alive, but the one before him, shiver and quail. "Do you imagine I would give you a chance for your life? You have robbed me of that which was infinitely more than my life; and I demand yours as the slightest compensation. No! I shoot you down like any other dangerous beast; and the world ought to thank me for ridding it of you. As I told you, I have come to kill you!"

While speaking, he had stood with his hand apparently pressed upon his heart; but, as he quietly took it away, they saw that it held a pistol.

Reginald made a quick, violent movement to dash up his assailant's arm, and catch the weapon from his grasp; but he was too late. The sound of a pistol-shot rang through the room; and then Reginald Archer threw up his arms with a strange, gasping moan, staggered, and fell heavily forward. A cry of horror broke from those around him as they sprang to catch him, and laid him out upon the floor.

"Dead?" was the question in their terror-stricken eyes.

Not yet; still breathing, but with a bloody spot on his left side, which made those who knew most of such matters lose all hope.

"Run for the nearest doctor! quick, some of you!" exclaimed the man who soonest recovered his senses; and more than one sped away to execute his order.

Lloyd was trying to support Reginald's head, and moaning over him in a half broken-hearted way; when Lawrence Van Arsdale came quietly forward, and gazed steadily down upon the man he had shot.. His face could have grown no paler; but it was a shade calmer, or rather wearier; though this was the only change in it. In their absorption in the dying man, the crowd had, for the moment, almost forgotten Van Arsdale; but now Lloyd suddenly cried out, —

"Seize him! hold him! Don't let him escape!"

The bystanders closed in around him; but no one touched him. They had neither the wish nor the power to lay violent hands upon the man, who, each knew in his secret heart, had but executed swift justice.

An awful smile came into Lawrence Van Arsdale's face.

"You can't prevent it, gentlemen," he said quietly. "I provided a sure way of escape before I came here."

And lifting to his head the revolver, which was still in his hand, he deliberately blew out his brains; falling, a shattered, bleeding, senseless mass, by the side of the man to whom he had just dealt a slower death.

Again that cry of horror broke out from those passive witnesses; and then they stood gazing into each other's eyes, literally paralyzed by the situation.

The room and the house were rapidly crowding with fresh comers; for the rumor of Reginald's condition had spread with lightning-speed. Presently they raised the dead body, and decently composed it upon a sofa. Then, the doctor arriving, they gave their whole attention to the scarcely more living form upon the floor. The circle of white faces bent breathlessly forward as the physician knelt by the prostrate figure and made his hasty examination.

He shook his head slowly and sadly.

"He is still alive; but that is all. The wound is mortal. The ball has gone too near the heart for any hope of his life to remain," he said softly, his voice breaking the stillness which closed over them again when it ceased.

Under the application of stimulants, Reginald gradually returned to consciousness, and faintly perceived his situation and surroundings. His instinct of outward propriety ruled him even then; and his disgust at lying there to be stared at was his first sensation.

Lloyd saw his lips move, and bent down to listen.

"Home!" was the word he heard.

Lloyd looked up at the physician.

"He wants to be moved to his own house," he said. "Is it possible to do it?"

"Yes, I think he can bear it. He has amazing physical strength," the doctor replied, and then gave a movement with his eyebrows which plainly said that it made small matter what they did, as the end was inevitable.

Slowly and carefully they lifted him upon a lounge, and prepared to carry him home. Just as they were leaving the house, Lloyd again saw his lips stir, and again leaned to listen.

As before, but a single word, —

"Tom!"

"Yes!" Lloyd answered eagerly: "I will bring him!"

"Quickly!" the wounded man faintly articulated.

Lloyd openly hesitated to leave him; but Reginald lifted his eyes towards him; and, dim as they now were, they still had power to enforce his will.

Knowing that he left his friend in hands as careful as his own, the younger man hastened away to obey that which seemed a dying command.

CHAPTER XXVI.

TOM ARCHER'S home and its inmates were very quiet that night; but there was little sleep under his roof. Past midnight, and each one had gone to his or her chamber; but even the semblance of repose ceased there.

What might come next, what might be the end of all this, was the dread weighing heavily upon each; and to each the very air seemed thick and dark with shadows of the future.

Tom paced up and down his floor, unable to be still.

Christie was now, as always, his first overruling thought. Their meeting after months of separation, and her proximity at that moment, would alone have stirred his blood to uncontrollable flow and beat; but, beyond this, his boundless indignation against his brother fired his whole nature. Then he thought also of Van Arsdale. An infinite pity for the man would have possessed him, had he not felt an equally measureless amazement and contempt for the being who could lift his face to the light, and passively allow such a state of things to continue.

He was thus walking and thus thinking, when a carriage dashed furiously up to the house ; and there came that violent, imperative ring, which startles us under the most ordinary circumstances as the fore-runner of trouble. He was at the entrance before any servant could possibly reach it; and the opening of the door brought him face to face with Lloyd's aghast countenance.

"Van Arsdale has shot Reginald! He is dying, and he is asking for you!" Lloyd's breathless lips managed to utter before the other man could unclose his.

Lloyd's ashen hue was upon Tom also as he stood speechlessly looking at him. He had unconsciously thrown up his arm in dumb protest against the dreadful fact ; and it remained rigid, as the tide of horror, grief, childish love. that seemed dead and buried, surged within him.

Then a strange, stilling change came over his face, and his arm dropped heavily to his side. It was as though, over all natural feeling and passion, he had solemnly and deliberately said "Amen!" for he knew in every recess of his heart and nature, that, placed in the same terrible strait, he would have done the same terrible deed.

"Come!" said Lloyd: "he may not live to see you!"

Tom steadied himself for a moment; and then his practical readiness came back to him.

"Wait an instant!" he exclaimed, and went hurriedly up stairs towards Christie's room.

He met her rapidly descending. She had heard the arrival, and had even caught the tone of Lloyd's voice; and the expression of her countenance left Tom little to tell.

He put his hand firmly upon her shoulder before he spoke, though her eyes cried out, —

"Don't torture me! tell me instantly!"

"Christie," he said, "Van Arsdale has shot him, and he is dying!"

Except for his grasp, she would probably have fallen, she trembled so violently, as a low cry came from her lips; but her self-restraint stilled the sound almost immediately, and held her shaking frame steady, while she listened for that which she felt would be his next sentence.

"I am going to him," he said.

"So am I," her lips formed almost voicelessly.

"Yes, I came back for you; but every moment is precious." And, taking her arm, they went hastily to the door.

But, mindful of her comfort and safety even then,

Tom caught up his travelling-cloak from the hall-table, and drew it around her as he put her into the carriage.

Then the vehicle, with those three blanched faces within, again drove furiously through the darkness.

What a change had passed over that house! and how strangely unfamiliar her home looked to Christie as she stepped over the threshold she had believed she should never again cross! The door stood open; the gas-light flamed garishly out into the night; the servants moved wildly about, — they, like the whole establishment, fallen to sudden disorganization. The hall seemed filled with men, who had either followed the *cortège* from the club, or had hurried hither from friendship or curiosity. Their eager, agitated talking lowered as they saw Tom enter; but it ceased entirely, and they fell back with grave, pitying deference, as they caught sight of Christie behind him. Not merely a wife, but a terribly-wronged woman; not only going to her husband's death-bed, but such a death-bed! from such a cause! No wonder they made way for her with reverence and sorrowful sympathy.

Tom led her directly to Reginald's room. Within stood five or six men whom he knew to be eminent surgeons, gathered from all parts of the city. They had cleared the apartment of every one else, and were

16*

bending over a figure on the bed. At the sound of footsteps, one of them looked round, and, recognizing Tom, came quickly out to him. As he saw Christie, the same curious alteration came upon him which had passed over those she had met below; and he spoke very gently as he answered the question in their dilating eyes.

"He is alive. The wound would have killed any other man outright; but he has such wonderful strength and vitality, that he may linger for hours. You can come into the room; but you had better keep behind him, as he is evidently conscious at times, and any agitation might be instantly fatal."

They followed him into the chamber, and silently took the places assigned them.

Almost within reach of their touch lay the stately form which even death seemed to struggle in vain to conquer. They could watch the faint rising and falling of the broad breast; they could see the eyelids quiver, and then slowly open; and with what emotion at their hearts they did so!

How far he was sensible they could not tell; for he noticed nothing until Lloyd came and stood at the foot of the bed. Then a purpose gathered in his eyes; and, to the astonishment of those around him, he said quite audibly, —

"Where is he?"

" Here ! " Lloyd replied ; and Tom stepped to the bedside.

The downward gaze met the upward for a little while ; for the elder brother was speechless.

" Your words have come true, Tom," the wounded man's faint voice sounded through the still room ; " yet I don't think you are glad."

" Reg, dear Reg ! " Tom cried out ; and with a great sob he fell down upon his knees beside his brother, his head bowing upon the other's hand with passionate tenderness and grief.

A moment after, the doctor's strong grasp upon his shoulder brought him back to himself and the necessity of the case. He rose hastily, and strove to regain his self-control.

The old, sweet smile came upon the dying lips ; but Reginald Archer was Reginald Archer still, and would be himself until the breath left his body. The smile took a careless, mocking tinge ; and he said, with a gay, defiant tone, which contrasted horribly with the weak voice it used, —

" I am dying like a dog, Tom, but a dog that has had his day ! "

The re-action of his effort overpowered him, and he sank away into exhaustion.

Thus he lay through the long, dark hours of the night, the large blue eyes looking ever far away before him, — it almost seemed, into that eternity to which he was drawing so near. Who shall say what he saw in that solemn night-watch ? what thoughts of past and future came over him ? what awful light and knowledge of both fell upon him ?

No change in the man upon the bed ; no change in those who silently sat around him. The night became gray dawn, and the dawn broad day. The rising sun-beams streamed into that room, glorifying even it with their early splendor ; and still no alteration in either watchers or watched.

Suddenly Reginald made a movement, turned completely over with surprising strength, and looked up at his brother with his old fire and vigor, his accustomed glance and expression. The physician beside him rose hurriedly, and lifted his hand in a warning to the others, which an awful something in Reginald's face, despite its apparent return to life, made fearfully intelligible. They gathered quickly about him, with a contraction at their hearts, which was sharp physical pain. There was no room for fear now, as there was none for hope ; and, no longer dreading to agitate him, Christie stood directly before him. But he did not seem to notice her : she had been little to him at any time, and now she was nothing. His whole attention was fixed upon his brother.

" Tom," he said, speaking as distinctly as he had
ever done, " about that unjust steward : I am not so
sure of his wisdom ; I begin to doubt ; I " —

The voice broke and ceased ; the eyes glazed ; a
shiver went over the powerful frame ; and that which,
but a second before, had been a living, speaking man,
was a corpse.

CHAPTER XXVII.

TWO years have passed since that day, and the world goes on as smoothly and joyfully as though such a tragedy had never darkened it.

To those who witnessed the bloody scene, its influence at first pervaded all existence; but most of them became accustomed to the sensation, and gradually threw it off, betaking themselves with relief and renewed vigor to their own projects and pleasures. Reginald Archer and Lawrence Van Arsdale soon lay in almost forgotten graves, awaiting the great final judgment which must come to all.

In Lloyd's weak brain and shallow nature there always remained a certain allegiance to his friend and leader; and, bad and feeble as he was, he rose above stronger men in that he was capable of faithfully loving and remembering the dead. Maria, too, still thought tenderly and sadly of the brother of her childhood. But except for these, and Christie and Tom,—the wife he had outraged, and the brother to whom he had been a life-long sorrow and disgrace,—

Reginald's name would scarcely find a place in the memories of his fellow-beings.

People wearied of feeling and saying, "What a shocking affair it was!" and, after dwelling morbidly upon the subject, turned eagerly from it. It first horrified, and then bored them; and, finally, the individual who enabled them to speak of it with ease and comfort, in fact, to derive some amusement from it, was secretly welcomed as a benefactor. The moral of his story, the sermon his course preached, became less oppressive and personal when its point was removed and its edge turned by a sarcasm.

Again Reginald's set was assembled at the club, and his name had been casually mentioned.

"He did not run a very edifying career, perhaps; but he certainly enjoyed himself extremely," said one of the persons present.

The speaker was a quick-witted, irreproachably fine gentleman, whose morals and manners were Reginald's own; who had fawned upon him and utilized him while living, and who naturally gave him a kick now that he was dead.

"Somehow, it always seemed to me impossible for that man to die; but, as soon as the doctor said the heart was touched, I knew the game was up," reflectively remarked another quondam acquaintance.

"Yes; for it was possible that a pistol-ball should

touch his heart, though we should have found it hard to believe any thing else had done so," said the man who had first spoken. " There is, at least, one satisfaction about this affair; and that is, it settles two points about which we must otherwise have remained in doubt. One is, that Reginald Archer had a heart; and the other, that Lawrence Van Arsdale had a brain."

A laugh, at first rather suppressed, but gradually breaking out freely, rose from the company; and the gentleman was regarded gratefully as having exorcised a ghost from among them, and put a neat, repeatable witticism in its place.

Truly Reginald Archer had neither lived nor died in vain. He had furnished a *bon-mot* to one of his friends, and a laugh to the rest. He would have asked nothing better from them; and he gave all he would have desired. To the end, a certain justice pervaded the man and his career; for he got in this instance just what he would have given.

The guilty woman who had cost him his life went to her own place. She openly adopted the existence for which she was naturally fitted. She chose a rich lover, and lives in more luxury than ever before. Her jewels are finer, her dresses more elegant and becoming; and I am bound to confess, that her satisfaction in life seems to be in equally increased proportion. She has lost her position in one class of society; but she has gained a wider sway, and a larger, stronger influence, over another portion of it. Her former female friends, of course, ignore her existence; but she finds the bad men and lost women, to whose company she is restricted, quite as entertaining and congenial associates. Above all, she has gained that freedom of action, that license to gratify every impulse and passion of her nature, which the world grants men at their birth, but which a woman can only gain by breaking every social tie. No outward punishment has fallen upon Mrs. Van Arsdale; and I cannot learn that she is troubled by any pang of conscience or remorse. Old age may tell a sadly different tale; but as yet there is no evidence that she has found sin other than a brilliant speculation both as to pleasure and as to profit.

As soon as Reginald was buried, Maria took Christie away to a quiet country-house, far from the associations, if not the recollections, of the past. There the stillness, the peace, the fair face of Nature, seemed to hush, if not to heal, the woman's storm-tossed being. It was scarcely grief she felt; for the true, parting death-pang had come long before, when she discovered that the man she adored had never existed. But, apart from natural pity for his dreadful end, the nervous shock had stunned her; and time alone could wear away its effect.

The ineffable calm of the summer-days lulled her to a deeper, more needful rest than sleep; the cool, fresh brightness of the early morning stilled the bound of those feverish pulses, while it faintly woke to renewed life the youth that was in both heart and blood. The forests put on their autumn glory, and the trees took their radiant, changeful tints; and still the two lingered in their peaceful retreat, where Tom did not permit them to be disturbed even by himself. Christie's natural, generous sympathy in those around her began to revive; her interest in their cares came back; and the burden of her own sadness seemed lifted from her heart as she took that of others upon it. She occupied herself again in small, daily duties; and the benefit was hourly visible. Striving to forget recent events, their effect gradually faded away; and her whole married life seemed falling from her like a garment. In many little ways she reminded Maria of the Christie of old, — the innocent, emotional child who had originally come to their house.

The short, dark winter-days brought them back to the city, and saw Christie once more an inmate of Tom's house. No thought that she would ever leave it crossed the mind of any one; for it was her only refuge, and she rested in it as a weary bird in its nest.

Those few persons who gained access to her, and who had greatly wondered what change they would see, found a composed woman, whose lovely face still wore its sweet smile, but whose countenance had a strange capacity for breaking into sudden horror at the least shock, even that of a sharp sound. It is the signet invariably stamped upon those who have ever felt the whole groundwork of their lives sink under them.

But even this faded in its intensity as the days and weeks began to bring with them a certain re-awakening sense of happiness, which she felt with faint surprise, though without comprehending its cause.

And Tom?

It was curious how early his business-engagements now permitted him to leave his office; how entirely that press of work, which had been the alleged reason of his spending long, solitary hours in his counting-room, had passed away. He was always at the service of Christie and Maria: a clerk could invariably fulfil his duties, if he were needed to walk or ride, or attend them in any way. All the woman-like tenderness and thoughtfulness of the strong man found vent at last; and the charm of contrast gave exquisite beauty to his care. For him, no fairest summer-days had ever held the glorious brightness and warmth that these chill, dark winter-hours contained.

It became evident in his appearance.

" Tom, you are growing young again," his friends would say as they saw the vigor and health that were bounding through every vein, that spoke out in every glance and movement. And the man flushed as he thought in how much deeper sense were their words true than they imagined.

With Tom Archer's unbending conscience went his clear, practical sense, preventing his being either sentimental or morbid. At the call of duty, he had sacrificed every desire and passion. When to do otherwise would have been sin, he had put the woman he loved utterly out of his life, — as far as possible, even, out of his thoughts. Now he felt himself perfectly free to take her into the innermost recesses of his being, if he could woo her thither. Having the opportunity, he held that he had now also the right, to use every iota of his strength of mind and body to make her love him. He worked towards this end ceaselessly. He provided pleasure for her every hour; he made himself the light and sunshine of her existence; and, of his own exquisite thrill of happiness in so doing, who shall tell, who shall tell?

Like a flower gaining color and opening its petals under the sun, so Christie bloomed into vitality, beauty, and joy, under the warm rays of love; but as yet, like the flower, she did not recognize the source of her renewed life. She grew to lean upon Tom in all things; to think of him constantly; to watch for his coming, and listen for his step: but she had cared so tenderly for him as a brother, that the change did not immediately strike her; and she loved him as a lover, without knowing it.

He did not disturb her delusion. He was very cautious: he did not dare to be otherwise, having so much at stake.

"Shall I ever gain her? will she ever love me as I love her?" he would think as the beautiful dark eyes looked up at him, unconscious of the meaning which he felt must be visible in his own.

The winter passed, the spring went by; and it was summer before he dared to reply to himself. Then a change came over Christie. The calm sweetness of her manner towards him vanished, and a fitful constraint took its place: there were times when she nervously avoided him; when her eyes drooped, and the rich blood flushed to her very brow at his glance, even at the sound of his voice.

And now Tom Archer resolved to put that question, which he prayed God he might not be madly deceiving himself in thinking had been answered before it was asked.

Christie's business-affairs, which Reginald had al-

lowed to go at loose ends in the hands of a careless
lawyer, had naturally fallen to Tom's care ; and much
time and trouble they cost him. The size of the
estate, and its condition, occasioned many consulta-
tions and arguments in his office between the
lawyer and himself. At these Christie almost always
assisted, at least by her presence ; for Tom would
take no action without her intelligent assent, as
well as her signature to authorize it.

Thus it happened that he and she were alone
in that private office one summer afternoon. The
business-matters had been arranged, the lawyer had
departed, and the two were left together. Christie
was talking a little nervously upon any and all subjects, as was her habit now ; for she instinctively
avoided a silence when no third person was present.
They were both standing by his desk ; and her eye
happened to rest upon the engraving above it.

"What a lovely, sad face that is!" she exclaimed.
"You have never told me whose it is," she continued; "though, the first time I saw it, you said you
would do so one day."

Tom looked quickly at her, with a manner which
agitated her strangely.

"Christie," he said slowly, after a moment, in
which the man steadied himself for the great final
effort of his life, "when others have asked me that

question, I have always said it was the Madonna. I tell you that it is the woman I love, I reverence, I adore." And the low, concentrated voice sank to a whisper.

Pain, doubt, and amazement flashed up in the great dark eyes, which shone from the pale face turned towards him.

" Christie ! " he cried, coming close to her, with all his long-hoarded love and passion breaking beyond his control, " don't you see the likeness? My darling, my darling ! don't you see that it is yourself ? "

The beautiful eyes faltered and drooped ; the splendid color rushed over her face ; the sweet, smiling lips quivered ; and her head would have sunk upon her hands, but that it rested elsewhere. For at last — ah ! at last — Tom Archer held in his strong arms, and close to his throbbing heart, the woman he had loved so passionately, so purely, so faithfully, and so long.

" Tom," she whispered softly, when his kisses upon lips and cheeks and hands at last allowed her to speak, still almost incredulous of her own happiness, " is it really so ? "

" My darling, it has always been so."

And then he told her the story of his love and pain and longing, from the moment he had first welcomed her to his home until this hour which compensated for all.

Tom had waited so long for the prize of his life,

that she could not ask him to wait longer. So one of those beautiful summer mornings witnessed a very quiet bridal; saw them go away to ramble in green fields, to roam over pleasant hills, there to forget the world, and to share, after their weary trial, the peace and joy of a perfect love.

Since then, their existence has been the pure home-life for which God and Nature intended good women; for the great world has small attraction for these two, who have tasted its sweet, and known its bitter. Maria and Arnold still occupy their loved and honored places in Tom's household; and it would not be easy to discover two persons more genuinely happy than they.

In the words of the nursery-rhymes with which this story begins, Maria still "stays at home." The holy fireside element being like " the kingdom of God within " her, its blessing must rest wherever she abides ; and she remains in these later, as in earlier days, the good angel of Tom's home. Essential to those she loves, could such a woman ask any thing further in life ?

Arnold is still " the little pig that got none," — none of the bread and butter of material success. Yet what can a man gain from earth or heaven beyond perfect peace and happiness? To his unselfish heart it is sufficient joy to watch hour by hour the bliss of the being he loves far better than himself.

The honeymoon had long passed, when Tom came home early one evening, as was still his wont, to find his wife dressing for dinner. He leaned against the mirror before which she stood, and watched her putting the finishing touches to her toilet. The innocent, loving eyes that looked at him were so childlike, that they brought a smile of tender amusement into his own.

"Christie, do you know how absurdly young you are growing?" he asked with a laugh as he kissed the sweet mouth.

His real thought had been, that she had already entered that kingdom of heaven, whose inhabitants must become as little children, and remain so forever.

She echoed his laugh softly, taking his words in their lightest sense.

"Still young enough to like pretty things," she answered gayly as she took out the bright cross Tom had given her so long before, and fastened it upon her bosom.

"And there has not been a moment in my darling's life when she could not have worn my talisman," he said gently and slowly as he touched the jewels.

"Christie," he exclaimed a little wistfully a moment after, his searching gaze going down into the pure depths of the eyes that had no shadow of thought or memory to conceal, "are you really happy?"

For his answer, such a radiance, such an adoring love, shone in her face, that words seemed useless. But she spoke them, nevertheless, clinging close to his breast, her voice thrilling with its passionate intensity.

"Tom," she said, "I used to spend my life wishing to die; to go away to some region where I could be good and happy; to attain the rest and joy of heaven. But Tom, darling Tom! that is all passed now; for I feel as though heaven had truly come down to me."